●

On the Threshold

●

DUŠAN MITANA

On the Threshold

SHORT STORIES

•

TRANSLATED BY
MAGDALENA MULLEK

LONDON NEW YORK CALCUTTA

The Slovak List
SERIES EDITOR: Julia Sherwood

LITERÁRNE
INFORMAČNÉ
CENTRUM

This book has received a subsidy from
SLOLIA Committee, the Centre for
Information on Literature in
Bratislava, Slovakia

u.
slovak
arts
council

Supported using public funding by the
Slovak Arts Council

Seagull Books, 2024

First published in Slovak as:
'Horúce popoludnie', 'V električke', 'Jastrab', 'Vianočná cesta', 'Psie dni'
in *Psie dni* (1970)

'Poľahčujúce okolnosti', 'Prievan a tí druhí', 'V neznámom jazyku',
'Začínajúci evanjelista' in *Slovenský poker* (1993)

'Zásnuby', 'Bomba 73', 'Nožom a sekerou' in *Krst ohňom* (2001)

'Ihla', 'Zem je guľatá', 'Prechádzka zimnou krajinou', 'Nočné správy',
'Na prahu' in *Nočné správy* (1976)

First published in English translation by Seagull Books, 2024

ISBN   978 1 8030 9 412 0

British Library Cataloguing-in-Publication Data
A catalogue record for this book is available from the British Library

Typeset by Seagull Books, Calcutta, India
Printed and bound by WordsWorth India, New Delhi, India

Motto

Thirty spokes connect at the hub of a wheel.
The empty spaces between them make the wheel.
A potter forms clay into the shape of a vessel.
The empty space inside is the vessel.
Openings get cut in walls for windows and doors.
The empty space inside is the dwelling.

—Lao Tzu

CONTENTS

•

A Hot Afternoon

A heat wave, the likes of which even the old couldn't remember, had been going on for three days. There was a proliferation of heat strokes, dizzy spells and heat-induced blood pressure drops, leading to unconsciousness. People sought water, but more than that, they sought shade. Shade, shade, shade! The sun was beating down on their heads, and the general level of irritation was rising.

I left the swimming pool around three. Granted, one could hardly call the mass masturbation by any old puddle 'swimming'. The water in the pool was warm, dirty and smelt foul; swimming was out of the question since there was no room to spread one's arms or legs. Hundreds of sweaty bodies with unhealthy, droopy, red skin that looked as though it had been broiled were crowded on the yellow burnt grass around the pool. Only a few people had a nice brown tan; the sun had taken most of us by surprise. Before going out I drank my fill of water from the fire hydrant; it was nice and cold.

I walked through the desolate town, here and there running into some poor sod who for some reason or another hadn't got off the filthy streets; heat billowed up to people's knees over the melting asphalt pavements, it radiated from the cobblestones, the concrete, the walls of buildings, and the gleaming metal of cars and trams. Those of us who were dragging by the walls which provided scant shade, who were having chance encounters when most people had left the streets, felt like members of a sect, united by our common misery; we smiled at each other with sympathy.

I didn't know where to go. People who can take afternoon naps are lucky, I thought, it's easy for them to wait for nightfall. Perhaps I could find a not-too-crowded coffee shop with working fans. At least I could still enjoy a cigarette. I pulled out my pack of Marice; it was empty. As luck would have it, I spotted a pub.

I walked up the stone steps from the street to the pub's outdoor seating area covered in white pebbles; they sparkled in the sun. In the shade of old chestnut trees, the tables were packed. Each table was laden with beer; everyone had at least two glasses in front of him.

As I stepped into the pub, stench joined the heat. All the tables inside were taken as well. Everyone was drinking beer. As if there were an outbreak of beer fever. They must have given up, I thought as I looked at the sleepy, dull faces of the men who were apathetically filling themselves with the stupefying liquid. It must have been their substitute for tranquilizers. I stood at the end of the long line at the bar. It moved pretty well, because a man in a wet white smock did nothing but pour beer, while a woman next to him took the money. I wasn't thirsty, and I had zero desire for beer. It would put me to sleep, dull my senses and make me sweat more. I just wanted to buy cigarettes quickly and get out.

My turn came, but before I had a chance to say which cigarettes I wanted, a beer with foam spilling over the sides appeared in front of me.

'Unfiltered Marice,' I said.

'Marice and beer,' the bartender said to the cashier, and with an automatic movement he pushed another beer in front of the next person in line.

'No, not the beer,' I said.

The bartender looked up, taken aback, offended, and his eyes shot a hostile question at me: What do you think you're doing?

'Just the Marice,' I said in a timid voice.

'Marice and beer,' the bartender reiterated, unwavering.

The woman handed me the cigarettes. I paid with a ten-crown bill. I handed it to her, but the bartender yanked it out of her hand and took over. He spent a moment rifling through change. I got the impression that he shorted me. I counted, and sure enough, I was missing three crowns.

'A hundred per cent markup,' I said.

'What are you talking about? Marice and beer, that's seven crowns,' said the bartender.

'But I don't want the beer.'

Irritated rumbling and an occasional swearword came from behind. I was holding up the line. Obstructing smooth operation. The bartender had a triumphant smile as he pointed a finger at me, and in a voice loud enough for everyone to hear, he pronounced his accusation: 'It's him, he doesn't want beer.'

For a moment, the whole pub seemed paralysed by the affront. It's him, it's him, he doesn't want beer, he doesn't want beer—the words carried from one table to the next, and the spark jumped all the way outside. They all came out of their stupor, and reawakened they watched my every move. I was at a loss, so I decided to have a cigarette to stall for time. Before taking off the wrapper, I noticed the label—filtered. They were Marice all right, but I smoked unfiltered. I handed back the unopened box.

'These are filtered, but I asked for unfiltered.'

The bartender turned red, and he was so angry that his voice cracked. 'Damn it,' he swore, 'we don't have unfiltered.'

I looked around in bewilderment, as if to ask for help. But all around were threatening, hostile faces.

Giving up, I waved it off and pulled out a cigarette. I bit off the filter and spat it out onto the dirty, greasy floor covered in dust, crushed cigarette butts and beer spittle. Then I struck a match. As I was bringing it up to the cigarette, the bartender roared so loud that my arm jolted from fright, and the match went out.

'God damn it!' the bartender yelled, 'don't you spit around here. You think you're in a barn, or at home, or something? There's no spitting around here, God damn it!'

Things were getting serious. I must leave while I still can, I thought, and without another word I turned around and walked towards the door. Halfway there the bartender's voice caught up with me. 'What about the beer? Listen up you, stop pissing me off!'

Without looking back, I said, 'I don't want it.'

'But you paid for it,' the bartender bellowed, and there was a threat in his voice, now completely unveiled.

'So what?'

'Ooh,' he groaned. 'Listen up you, stop pissing me off!'

By then I was almost at the door. A quick exit! But a tall, fat man stepped in front of me, and his 200-pound body blocked the entire doorway.

'Didn't you hear, buddy? You've got a beer over there.'

I gave him a seething look, but like a stubborn ram he just calmly reiterated, 'The beer.'

I was drenched in sweat, and not just from the heat. They're about to jump me—an absurd thought ran through my head—I scurried back to the bar and with an apologetic gesture I said, 'Actually, yes, Marice and beer.'

I put on an embarrassed, self-critical smile, to indicate to the bartender that he was right. I succumbed just in the nick of time; by admitting my guilt I evaded capital punishment. The jury took into consideration the mitigating circumstances—unprecedented heat, possible heat stroke, and associated absentmindedness. The bartender even gave me a benevolent smile, as if to say: 'Don't worry about it, it happens, but that's why I'm here, to know what you need, and I forgive you.' With a nod I thanked him for his forgiveness. I picked up the beer, and ashamed, humiliated, I made my way past a row of sidelong glances to the window. I wanted to go outside, but I gave up on it; it looked like they were guarding the door. The 200-pound man was still standing there.

I placed the beer on the windowsill and very visibly turned my back to the room. I knew they were watching me to make sure that I wasn't going to pull a fast one on them and pour the beer out the window. Indeed, it had been a mistake to stand next to an open window; it reinforced their suspicions. Escape was out of the question; by the time I could have squeezed through the low opening, they would have pulled me back in. Besides which, I wouldn't have got far; they were guarding the outdoors as well— two men were leaning against the railing by the exit.

In order to placate them, I tried to down the beer in one shot; I feigned thirst, and although it felt as though I was pouring liquid into an overflowing vessel, I managed to empty the glass without taking it off my lips. I could feel the bitter liquid pushing up from my stomach into my throat, yet I was thinking about having another; perhaps it would smooth things over with them.

Their unyielding looks full of suspicion were becoming harder and harder to bear. It was as though I had walked into a den of conspirators without knowing the password. I lit another cigarette, though this time I didn't bite off the filter. I couldn't just stand around. I decided to try to leave as if nothing had happened.

I headed for the door. The 200-pound man with the expression of a ram was leaning on the doorframe in a leisurely manner, a beer in hand. Without a word, and with apparent disinterest, his watery gaze slid down me. I got in line at the bar. I was hungry and thirsty.

My turn came, but before I had a chance to order salami, there was a beer with foam spilling over the side in front of me.

'A quarter pound of dry salami and two rolls,' I said.

'A quarter pound of dry salami, two rolls, and a beer,' the bartender said to the cashier, and with an automatic movement he pushed another beer in front of the next person in line. He gave me a questioning look, but I nodded, in hopes of redeeming myself.

I carried everything to my old spot by the window. I ate slowly, chasing the food with beer. Nausea was setting in. I racked my brain for what to do, but I saw no way out. I glanced out the window. The two men were still leaning against the railing at the exit from the garden. A man was walking up the steps. He looked familiar.

When he came in, I recognized him as an old acquaintance from my university days. We had been roommates for a year. He studied medicine. I recognized him despite the fact that he looked very different; he had lost a lot of weight. He was no longer the boy with a red, chubby face. He had lost weight and looked very respectable. Perhaps he was a decent doctor. Yes, he fit ordinary people's expectations of a doctor—they needed him to fit their expectations; it was the only way they could entrust themselves to him. Neither fat nor thin, clean-shaven, clean nails, respectable average, guaranteed reliability.

I was quite relieved. I had never been so glad to see an acquaintance before. Hopefully, he'd remember me. I stared at him until he looked around nervously—he couldn't take my gaze at the back of his neck any more. His eyes landed on me briefly, then they touched another face; it was clear that he was searching for the source of the rear attack. And then. Then he came back to me, and the sight of his face, which showed signs of recognition, made me feel happy to be alive.

He stepped out of the line and walked up to me.

'Hey man, I haven't seen you in years.' He gave me a good-natured slap on the shoulder. 'Say, how long has it been?'

'Five years, I think.'

'You're right. Five years. That's ages. Where do you work?'

'At a magazine.'

'That's right.' He slapped his forehead. 'Every once in a while I read your stuff. So what are you doing here?'

'How about you?' I said quickly, too quickly.

'Me? I live nearby. I'm a regular, my friend. But you,' he said, pointing a finger at me, 'I've never seen you here before.'

I wondered whether I should tell him about the strange situation I was in, and confide my concerns to him, but I didn't know how to explain it; there was no way to explain, it didn't make any sense, it was almost comical. Besides which, since I had run into him the whole nightmare had started to dissipate. What luck that he was a regular, if nothing else, he could confirm that he knew me, he could put in a good word for me, I thought, but it made me realize that I hadn't shaken all of my concerns.

'I was just passing by when I ran out of cigarettes,' I said.

'Oh. So we only met thanks to cigarettes and beer.' He laughed.

'Beer? What beer? What is it with you people and beer around here?' His mention of beer threw me for a loop.

'What are you getting upset about? I'll go get the beer,' he snapped.

'No, no, no.'

'Quit babbling. I can see how thirsty you are.' He pointed to the second glass, which I had just emptied with the greatest self-abnegation, and there was no defense against his argument.

He headed towards the bar.

At that moment I decided to tell him everything, no matter how ridiculous it would sound. I couldn't let him find out about the whole incident from the bartender or from one of them; they'd give him biased information, and I'd have a hard time disproving it. I grabbed him by the arm.

He listened to my muddled tale with astonishment. I kept looking at him, trying to figure out from his expression how much importance I should assign to the whole incident. Although I hate being laughed at, I would have gladly been the target of his ridicule. Instead, I got the opposite impression—his astonishment turned to concern, then to alarm, and by the time I finished, there was visible fear on his face. Needless to say, I felt more than anxious.

'You didn't want beer? Whoa,' he said in a low voice, and shook his head in despair.

'Is it bad?' I asked.

He gave me a stern look. His mouth opened three times, but each time he swallowed the words that were bubbling up in his throat. Finally, he said, 'Let me see what I can do. I'll certainly try. But I must be honest; I don't have great hopes. They saw that we know each other, so they probably won't trust me.'

He looked around surreptitiously; fear came over his face once more. They were all staring at us with a motionless gaze.

He skipped the line and went straight to the bartender. The bartender wiped his hands on his wet smock and motioned for the woman to take his place. There was an empty table in the corner by the bar. The bartender pulled my friend to the table, and they sat down. I saw them talking, and I watched their hand gestures to try to get a sense of how the conversation was going. My friend had his back to me, the bartender was facing me. Once in a while he'd lift his head and look me up and down. My friend was trying to persuade him of something, but he must have been unsuccessful, because the bartender kept shaking his head in disagreement. Then the gestures became more abrupt; they must have been arguing. All of a sudden the bartender stood up and waved at someone. Two men got up from a table; I noticed that both of them were wearing the same flannel shirt and their faces looked alike as well. They must have been brothers.

Once they made it to the table where my friend was sitting (by then the bartender was seated again), they sat down across from each other without so much as a word. My friend lifted his head, glanced at each of them in turn, and then shrunk back in his chair. By this point the bartender was the only one talking, my friend just nodded. I knew that his defense had failed. In fact, he had joined the ranks of the accused.

The bartender got up one last time and emphasized something. My friend didn't react. Then the bartender went back to the bar and started to serve beer. The negotiations were over.

The two brothers in flannel shirts got up. One of them touched my friend's shoulder to indicate that he should get up. My friend stood up obediently.

They set off—one brother on each side, my friend in the middle. I didn't know where they were going, but they were not headed for the exit. As they passed by me, my friend lifted his head. With my face, my hands, my whole body I indicated the question—how did it go? On my friend's face there was helplessness, apathy, despair and blame. In fact, mostly blame. It was brief, but it was enough; that look burned an indelible mark of guilt and shame on my forehead for ever. He went back to walking with a hung head and slumped shoulders.

They stopped in front of a green door with cracked paint and an enamelled sign: STORAGE. Underneath it was written in small letters: Staff only. One of the brothers opened the door and went in. The other one shoved my friend who had paused ever so briefly, his whole body went stiff, as if he were getting ready to leap, but the man behind him put his hands on my former friend's shoulders, and his body went limp again. He walked in, the man in the flannel shirt was right behind him. The door closed.

I was hyperventilating. I pulled out a cigarette. I broke two matches before I was able to light it. A few long draughts helped me; I recovered a little.

The implacable stares of the whole pub were on me. I feigned indifference, as if I cared about nothing but smoking and salami, which was starting to take on a healthy green tinge.

The door to the storage room opened again, and the two men in flannel shirts came out. Their dull faces were inscrutable. My friend didn't surface. The brothers went up to the bartender; one of them said a few words. The bartender grimaced and gave him a satisfied nod. He served them beer ahead of the line. They picked up the beers and went back to their table.

I couldn't take the stifling uncertainty any more, so I set out for the storage-room door. By the time they realized what was going on, I was a couple of steps from it. Two men sitting closest to the door jumped up and blocked my way. They were defending the entrance with their bodies. They didn't say a word, but I could tell they were on alert. The bartender darted out from behind the bar and lashed out at me, 'Where do you think you're going?'

'I want to take a look in there,' I said.

'What? How can you take a look in there? Can't you read? STAFF ONLY,' he said, enunciating every syllable.

I could tell it was useless. I didn't stand a chance against all of them. I chose retreat. Shrugging my shoulders I said, 'Then give me a shot of vodka.'

Everyone seemed to exhale.

'Get in line,' the bartender said triumphantly.

I stood at the end of the line, which wound its way to the door. The 200-pound man with the expression of a ram was leaning on the doorframe in a leisurely manner, beer in hand. Then I noticed that his glass was empty. Why doesn't he go get a refill, I wondered. I realized that the line wasn't moving. I glanced at the bar; there was no beer and no bartender. The beer had run out, he went to tap another keg. This is my last chance at escape, I thought. Everyone looked a bit lax; their attention had waned. As if they were missing their elixir. They didn't have beer, and the bartender, who represented the greatest danger for me, was gone. I felt encouraged.

I pretended to be in a stupor, waiting, like the rest of them. It looked as though I had managed to lull them. They had become too sure of themselves. They underestimated me.

In a split second I turned around and took off. The door guard wasn't ready, he stumbled on impact, and I slipped by him. I dashed down the steps and ran down the street.

It was late, the sun's rays had lost some of their intensity, and many more people were outside than before. Most of them were coming home from a swim. I knew that I was safe in a crowd. I stopped running. I looked back. The 200-pound man and several others were standing at the entrance to the pub. They weren't moving. They just stared at me. I waved at them smugly. They didn't react.

I took a look around. I was standing on a small square lined with old linden trees; all the benches in the shade were taken. On the bench closest to me sat an old woman and a little girl. The girl kept climbing up and jumping down. The well-meaning old woman admonished her, 'Quit jumping, because you'll kill yourself and Mummy will be mad.'

Unspeakable joy washed over me.

I headed for the tram stop.

•

On a Tram

I'm ashamed to admit that I had acted under the pressure of cir-
cumstance, and the whole thing happened purely by chance. I'd
much prefer to think it had all been predestined a long time ago,
because inevitability is a great excuse for actions even more cruel
than those I'm about to describe. Then again, the more I think
about it, the greater my uncertainty. Was what happened, in fact,
cruel? Wasn't it a real, genuine, once-in-a-lifetime union, which
could be called an act of love? I can't tell. At any rate, I must stop
treating the whole thing as a subject of analysis; I must let go of
the countless possible interpretations; I must forget, and hope that
my memory will become a refuge, that one day, at a yet-unknown
but already predetermined moment, everything will bubble up to
the surface, and in that moment of clairvoyance, I will touch the
edges of the unknowable.

But who knows, maybe pressure is the only thing to blame,
for it was truly formidable. It carried me, literally, up the steps and
dropped me into the space between the front and the middle
doors of the tram. The impetus was so strong that I neither managed to toss a crown into the small box on the driver's right which

serves as a piggybank, nor did I manage to take the ticket, which I deeply regretted, because I don't like to betray other people's trust. Even if their trust is only born out of necessity. Due to my innate honesty, I desperately tried to send the crown forward via a relay of other hands, but my own right hand which was clutching the coin could not be freed from the tight grip of the crowd. It was pressed up against a man's thigh, while my left was gripping the handrail above my head, warm and moist from many sweaty palms that had gripped it before me. I felt ill, and grimaced in disgust. I don't like things marked by others' touch; it's as if I had to defend myself against the familiarity of strangers.

No tram had come for almost thirty minutes, and it was rush hour, people were getting off work. To make matters worse, it was sweltering, and it was just a matter of time before a storm would come. When all of the tram's accordion doors huffed to a close (a few people who had been hanging on the steps had to be rudely shoved off so that we could move), the air became unbreathable. It felt like we were in a submarine which had used up all of its oxygen supplies, and I could hardly wait for the next stop when at least a few mouthfuls of fresh air could make their way in through the open doors. It was like a brief surfacing. My clothes were soaked in an instant. Sweat streamed from the roots of my hair down my forehead and face, it tickled me around my ears, it flowed down my neck and over my whole body, gluing my shirt and my trousers to my skin. The toes of my right foot were the only part of me touching the vibrating floor, which left me defenceless against the tram's powerful jolts whenever we slowed down, sped up, stopped, or started to move; the only reason I didn't fall down was that there was nowhere to fall. The mass of people leaned back, forward, right and left as a single body, and no one knew which foot was whose. No one could be certain if they were standing on their own feet, or on someone else's.

At first, I found myself opposite an older, foul-smelling man who was probably returning from some type of a job that involved a lot of dust, judging by the small, black wrinkles drawn by rivulets of sweat across the parchment-like skin of his thin, brown face. I kept trying to turn my head to get my nose away from his mouth; the smell of the wine he had consumed was making me nauseous. Once in a while he'd burp. I also figured out that he was a smoker; he was saturated with nicotine that neither the wine, nor the smell of rotten flesh (lunch, or something from the day before?) emanating from a large cavity (in his lower left molar) could mask. Clearly, he was no fan of dental care. Besides two more cavities, his teeth were yellow, and the backs of them were totally black. A crooked tooth stuck out of his mouth put the finishing touch on his colourful character, but he wasn't to blame for that; his parents were. They should have got him braces when he was a child.

At the next stop, the crowd carried me a few feet over, but no matter how hard I tried to get away from the man, I didn't succeed, which isn't to say that he was sticking to me on purpose. It wasn't his fault. It was outside our control.

Finally, at the fourth stop, I was relieved that my counterpart was gone. I couldn't tell if he had got off, or if he had been carried in a different direction; the important thing was that he wasn't in front of me. I was standing in the middle of the aisle, the handrails were out of my reach, and I was surrounded by sweaty, anonymous bodies—I couldn't see anyone's face. My arms hung by my sides. In front of me was the back of some girl (or was it a woman?), who had short, slightly wavy, chestnut hair, from which emanated the pleasant scent of a nice perfume. I couldn't identify the brand. No surprise there, since I don't know any. In any case, it was a welcome respite from the overwhelming stench, and I kept leaning over her hair which was tickling my face. She was wearing a short-sleeved blouse with a round neckline, which revealed her round shoulders and part of her back with sharply protruding vertebrae. Her skin had a brownish tan, and even beads of sweat couldn't hide its smooth suppleness and youth.

I was pushed up to her body, and I could feel her round, firm buttocks against my pelvis. I realized with dismay that I was getting aroused. My flaccid penis had woken up, and I could feel it grow; it started to stretch the fabric of my trousers. I was horrified, embarrassed, and perspiring more than ever. I knew she must have felt it, and not knowing what else to do I mumbled, 'Sorry', but this stupid utterance just doubled my embarrassment. I tried to move, to turn my hip towards her, since I couldn't vanish, but all my efforts were in vain. Then I noticed the girl's body shaking with suppressed laughter. That was the last straw, because if there's one thing I can't stand, it's being ridiculed, and this was outright, cruel, caustic ridicule. I started to hate her. She must have sensed it, but she couldn't contain herself any more, and she burst out laughing. She laughed so hard that her whole body quivered, and it struck me that she had a pleasant voice. I realized how comical the situation really was, I got swept up in her infectious laughter, and a moment later both of us were laughing. Amid the jumble of bodies, the stench, the noise, the cacophony of voices, our laughter freed us, and nothing else existed in that moment but the two of us, our young, quivering bodies. No one paid any attention to us.

We stopped laughing, as if on cue, and even though everything around us was abuzz, I felt a silence hanging in the air, an oppressive silence, a silence before the storm.

In the meantime, my arousal hadn't diminished at all, quite the opposite. By then, however, it was par for the course, our laughter had connected and freed us. It was completely natural, everything was just as it had to be, we had to have met right then and there, just like that, unable to see each other's faces. My hands, which, as I had mentioned earlier, hung by my sides, touched her buttocks, which were tightly hugged by a short skirt. I could feel the fabric between my fingers, but I couldn't see its colour. I started to caress her gently. The palm of my left hand met hers, yes, I must emphasize this—I knew immediately that the hand was hers; I was sure of it even though it could have been anyone's hand in that jumble of bodies—it was one of those instances when truth could only be intuited.

Our hands were completely dry.

In that steam bath, where everyone was soaked to the skin, our completely dry hands touched. My mouth had also dried out from excitement, and I was sure that it was mutual.

She pressed my hand against her thigh, and slowly, steadily, our hands slid lower and lower, until I could feel her soft, supple, youthful skin. Then I felt her hand on my thigh—higher, higher, I whispered until she caressed my penis through my trousers, tender in its hardness. Her whole body became supple.

Then it happened. There, on that overcrowded tram, embraced by a multitude of other sweaty bodies, in the burning, humid, unbreathable air, I entered the body of an unknown woman who had her back to me. (Yes, she was already a woman.) She opened up, took me in, her hand squeezed my thigh, her fingers dug into my flesh; I felt the spasmodic quivering of her body followed by a lull, a plateau, and finally, relaxation. Her palm was sweaty once more, and I noticed a single, translucent bead of perspiration slowly trickle down from the roots of her hair like a large teardrop.

I managed to zip up my trousers; no one had noticed a thing. I rested my head on her hair, and she leaned her head towards me, gently and submissively; she rubbed her ear against mine as my lips kissed her neck. She tried to turn around, to face me, but we weren't able to look into each other's eyes, which added to the excitement and the tension; I couldn't wait for us to get off the tram and finally take a good look at each other. I had the feeling that even though the outcome could be surprising, neither of us would be disappointed. I paid no attention to my surroundings; I was pleasantly tired, calm and self-confident. Perhaps this waning of attention was to blame for everything that followed.

When the tram stopped with a jolt and people started to push towards the exits, when they tore us apart and carried each of us to a different door, I caught a glimpse of her profile. She tried desperately to resist the mass which was pushing her out; she tried to turn her head and remember me, as if she had suspected the imminent banal ending. She disappeared from my view, but I remained calm, after all, we'd surely meet outside. As I was about to get off, as I was on the last step, new passengers surged in, pushing me back inside, and despite my loud protests, 'I'm getting off, for God's sake, let me off', no one paid any attention. I wasn't the only one who didn't make it out. The tram began to move, leaving behind the woman, whose face I never saw, at the stop. I caught a glimpse of her profile, but that wasn't enough to be able to recognize her later amid the multitude of other women with similar hair, a similarly tan, supple, youthful skin. She had no distinctive features.

The Hawk

1

Peter had it all planned. Although it bothered him that he hadn't found his uncle's shotgun despite searching the whole house, he could manage without it. All in all, a handgun would have been best, but that was out of the question. Uncle Ján wasn't likely to have a gun, and even if he had one, he would certainly keep it well hidden, like all the rest of the things that could remind him of his father and the events from a year ago. It was as though they were hoping to keep away a phantom memory simply by changing his surroundings and erecting a wall of silence about his parents.

He was only fourteen but he knew he could handle a handgun. As a twelve-year-old, he had amazed his father with his good aim when they practiced shooting in their garden at a target attached to a wall with overgrown vines which looked like a living green barrier during the summer. And at the shooting range, where his father used to take him on beautiful summer mornings, many people complimented him when he shot at the elliptical plates that flew out from underground and were called clay pigeons. (He could never figure out why they were called pigeons, since they didn't look like birds at all.) His father was proud of him and he often jokingly introduced his son to his colleagues, the detectives (they called themselves criminologists, but to him they were detectives), as a future Olympic champion in shooting, and although Peter much preferred playing soccer, he didn't want to spoil his father's fun.

No matter, he'd make it work without a handgun. He would have two hours. After several days of observation, he had concluded that on average Aunt Viera took two hours to do her shopping, even though the store was nearby. She always lingered on for a bit of gossip, which Uncle liked to tease her about, even though—as he liked to say—he didn't fault her for it because it was natural for a woman, and the daily grocery run was her only respite from the ennui of village life. Aunt Viera didn't work, and otherwise she was always home, since Uncle, who was a photographer in a nearby city, made enough money so that his wife— as he liked to say—didn't need to exert herself and age prematurely. People envied her, they said she was pampered, but Peter knew that they were stupid and had no clue about the strange, vague tension that reigned in their spacious new home, the distinguishing feature of which was that all the walls were covered in photographs of Aunt Viera; in one dress, another, a third, in all the dresses she owned, in the kitchen, the living room, the garden, Aunt Viera was everywhere; he knew they had no idea about the sad expression on her face which Peter had glimpsed a few times when she was alone and thought that no one was watching.

'I'm going to the store, Peter,' Aunt Viera's voice came from the veranda. 'Go see your friends, if you like.'

He was sitting on a couch in the attic, browsing through old issues of *Start*. The attic was his favourite place. Whenever he couldn't bear the tension any more, the lethal secret that hung in the air, he would find refuge there. And that happened often, especially since the night he had walked into their bedroom and saw Uncle lying on the bed propped up on his elbow, staring at the sleeping Aunt Viera who was smiling in her dream: yes, that was what had stuck in his mind—he saw his uncle's back (he didn't move a muscle, like a snake that's hypnotizing its prey) and his aunt smiling the same way she did later on when he said to her with fear and anxiety, 'Don't fall asleep, Uncle watches you.' She just smiled, as if it were completely normal, as if it were proof of Uncle's love. That was the first time he had felt the indescribable fear for his aunt's life, and since then he kept trying to tear away from it, and rushed upstairs, to the attic, until they both jokingly called him the Great Hermit, but he could sense that their smiles were feigned and covered concern. He was annoyed by their constant covert observation. Their attempts to make sure he was always with his friends were absurd. They watched his every reaction, they anxiously probed whether and how he differed from other children, and they had no idea that their actions, apparent distrust and suspicions were practically forcing him to spite them. He couldn't forget Uncle Ján's words, which he had once overheard, 'He shouldn't be left alone, who knows what's going through his head, he might burn the house down.' In the attic, he felt good. Perhaps it was because the attic walls had been spared the photos of Aunt Viera, perhaps that was why it had become his island of salvation in that mysterious, perilous house. The room belonged to his cousin Ivan, who was away on military service. Peter had only a vague recollection of Ivan, they had last seen each other five years ago, but he had the feeling that they'd get along. Surely, they'd get along—he'd get along with a boy whose room was decorated to his own taste, and who had written him such a cool letter. He wasn't the first to write, but that was to be expected. It was enough that Ivan immediately replied to the letter that he, Peter, had sent him when he came to spend the summer. Peter wrote that they had put him up in his, that is, Ivan's, room, and that he really liked it. He wrote that based on the room's decor, he could tell that Ivan was a football player, and he too enjoyed playing football. He asked to borrow Ivan's cleats for the summer, and asked permission to cut out Pelé and Eusébio from his *Start* magazines. In his reply Ivan scolded him a little for even asking about something so matter-of-fact. 'I'm glad you like my room,' he wrote, 'and it goes without saying that you can use all of my things as if they were your own.' From then on Peter went around in Ivan's joggers, his yellow jersey with number nine on the back, and wore his football cleats. He pinned his Slovan team pin to the jersey, and despite the fact that the clothes were a bit large for him, he was pleased.

He listened for the sound of the door closing, but instead he heard Aunt Viera's voice.

'Peter, would you please help me with a zipper?'

Reluctantly he closed the magazine. 'Coming.'

The zipper seemed endless. He tried to pull it up as quickly as possible, to get away from the sight of his aunt's naked back, her bronze shiny naked back, evenly tanned, without a white line left by a bra; she always sunbathed naked, completely naked; he tried to get away from the sight that made him blush. He was afraid he'd lose control and bite her back. The zipper got stuck. His hands began to shake; he felt his palms get wet with a disgusting, slimy sweat. He kept tugging on the zipper. 'Slow down, be careful or you'll break it,' his aunt said, laughing. She reached her hand towards her back, and their fingers touched. He yanked his hand away as if it had been burned. Then he saw it. On her neck and above her left shoulder blade. The small reddish bruises brought tears to his eyes. He pictured Uncle Ján's thick, greasy lips, he pictured his thin, long hands with their permanently moist fingers touching the most intimate contours of Aunt's body, and he gritted his teeth with hatred. I'll kill him. He panicked; he thought he had said it out loud. Aunt Viera pulled up the zipper. He knew what was coming—she'd send him outside, but she'd word it as though he had wanted to go out but forgot.

'Did you forget about the final today? What time's the game?' she asked casually.

'It's not today. It's tomorrow,' he said patiently.

'Oh, so you have practice today.'

'No. We don't.' He didn't manage to hide his irritation.

'I'm sorry. I thought it was today,' she said in a hurt tone.

'We have the day off today, so we don't overtrain,' he said with a smile, attempting to erase the bad impression, but it didn't seem to be enough, so he added: 'I'm going fishing this evening, you're welcome to come with me.'

'OK, if you'll have me.' She smiled and stood on tiptoe to kiss his forehead. The brief moment when their faces met filled him with anxiety. He got a good look at her green irises; their colour seemed faded (it must have been much sharper once, he thought), and this greyness intensified the sadness of her eyes, she couldn't hide it the way she did with her face. It always confused him. He couldn't tell whether she suspected something, or whether she just felt sorry for him. Many times he had wanted to tell her everything, but when he finally plucked up the courage, he couldn't muster more than, 'Uncle is bad.' The expression on her face discouraged him—her surprise could not have been feigned. No, she doesn't suspect a thing, he reassured himself. She has no idea, and I can't tell her what's going on, because the only thing it'll accomplish is that she'll pity me. She'll chalk it up to my eccentricity, as they call it politely. After all, maybe it isn't true, maybe I'm just imagining things, maybe it really is just a product of my eccentricity.

He knew they thought him an eccentric, and they were worried that he was starting to go round the bend. He was also well aware that his godparents, with whom he had been living since his parents' death, had sent him here to convalesce. Some peace and quiet, fresh air and a change of surroundings should take his mind off things. (Besides, Viera has a lot of time on her hands, she's always home, they have a large house, a lot of money, unlike them poor folks.) Indeed, Aunt Viera took good care of him. Such good care that it made him feel uncomfortable. Every three days he had to weigh himself; he had already put on eleven pounds. He felt like an athlete in training. Regular meals, a daily bath, a morning game of table tennis (when the weather was nice and not windy, they played outside in an area that had been paved for it, and on rainy or windy days they played on the veranda; his aunt and uncle were both excellent players; at first, they were giving him a fifteen-point lead per set, but he improved quickly and now he rarely lost against their handicap, the matches were balanced, they couldn't afford to underestimate him, he had already beaten them both several times), Aunt Viera's massages (he loved those moments—he would lay on the couch, and Aunt Viera would run her soft, warm fingers over his bony body in circular movements; you're putting on weight, she'd say with a pleased laugh as she stood over him, her hair, her bouncy, long, black hair falling into her face), early evening fishing, practice sessions, matches, victories. Before coming here he had been worried about the strangers he'd have to talk to—that was what worried him most of all—conversations—what was there to talk about, especially for him who didn't say more than five words all day. But he was surprised, quite pleasantly at that. He surprised himself with how well he could carry on conversations, how well he was able to answer questions. Aunt Viera often said, 'And they wrote you're a dolt, that you never say a word. They don't know you at all.' He realized that he felt almost as good with Aunt Viera as he had with his father when they used to listen to night-time broadcasts from world hockey championships—which had been the pinnacle of bliss for him. Late at night they'd lie in bed, the green eye of the radio shining in the darkness, the volume turned down so they wouldn't wake up Mother who had to get up early; he'd lie next to his father's large, strong body, his head leaning on his father's muscular arm, he'd tug on the thick, dark hair on his father's chest, he'd feel his father's muscles hard as rock, all in silence; the only sounds that carried through the well-heated room were the announcer's excited voice and his father's even breathing. And during intermission, his father would whisper exciting stories from his detective work into his ear, and he'd hang on his father's every word, and when their team would score, they'd forget it was the middle of the night and that Mother was asleep, and yell 'GOAL, GOAL', and hug and kiss, and that pleasantly familiar smell of tobacco would waft from his father's mouth, and Peter would say, 'Breathe on me, I feel like I'm smoking when you breathe on me', and his father would laugh, 'Enough, or you'll get TB', Mother would wake up and come over, half-asleep and angry, and they'd hug her, 'We're winning, we're winning', and she would grumble, but end up smiling, and then she couldn't hold back any more and burst out laughing, 'Oh, you fools', and she'd lie down next to them, and all three of them would lay there, with Peter in the middle, and Mother would soon fall asleep again.

At first, Peter had liked Uncle Ján. He was always in his dark room, developing photos, lots of photos, and Peter particularly liked how he enlarged photos of Aunt Viera and plastered the whole house with them. He and his aunt would laugh about his uncle's obsession to colour the photographs. Uncle would place a large photo of Aunt Viera on the floor, get down on his knees, and paint it. He wouldn't stop until everything was coloured, exactly capturing every detail of Aunt Viera's dress. He had a coloured photograph for each dress. Aunt laughed at him, saying he had lost his mind and turned into a kitsch-maker in his old age, nevertheless, it must have made her feel good, even though it was somewhat ridiculous. But Uncle Ján was a respected individual; he made a lot of money, and many newspapers published photos with the credit: 'Photo by Ján Biely.' Therefore, this idiosyncrasy could not diminish the admiration and envy of the people, and not just for him but also for Aunt Viera, because of his boundless love for her. Other than photography, he devoted most of his time to a hawk he had brought home when it was very young; he took care of as if it were his own son. ('You didn't even take such good care of Ivan,' Aunt said, laughing, back when Peter wanted to tell her everything but only managed to get as far as—'Uncle is bad'— and Aunt Viera responded with, 'You must not speak like that about anyone, especially not about your uncle,' and then she added with a dreamy smile: 'Could a person who takes such good care of a hawk be bad? No Peter's not bad, he's just a big child.')

Uncle had brought a huge cage for the hawk, which took up almost a quarter of the veranda, he fed it and talked to it, until it was so tame that people wondered how did he manage to do that with a bird of prey? 'The trick is not to feed it raw meat,' Uncle would say, even a predator will get used to comfort. And it was true. The hawk was as tame as a pigeon. The door to its cage was always open, it flew all over the house, in and out of every room, through every open door; it also flew outside, it sat on the roof with the pigeons, and it became so playful that it enjoyed hide-and-seek. Often it would hide in the bedroom, sit on the chande-lier, the mirror, the armoire or under the beds. Aunt and Uncle were delighted, and they laughed at Peter, who always double-checked that he had closed the door to the attic. Don't be such a scaredy-cat, they'd say, it's just a pigeon. He didn't know how to respond, he just nodded with a forced smile, but he couldn't get rid of his distrust (or was it fear?). Naturally, the hawk liked Uncle best, and although it was polite to everyone, it would neither sit on nor eat out of anyone else's hand.

'You have such long legs. I can barely reach you any more,' Aunt said laughing as she kissed Peter's forehead. 'Just like your father,' she added, but then she blushed and bit her lower lip.

'I'm going to read for a while, and when you get back, we'll play table tennis, OK?' he said in a hurry to help her out of the awkward situation. She gratefully grasped at the offered straw, 'And then we'll go fishing.' After a moment of silence, she added, 'There's lemonade and ice cream in the fridge. And have some ham, too.'

'I do nothing but eat.'

'We don't want you saying you went hungry at our house.' She ruffled his short hair and headed for the door.

He watched her, knowing full well that she was battling the impulse to try to get him to go outside, well aware that she was afraid to leave him in the house by himself. She paused briefly at the door, but didn't turn back to look at him; instead, she darted out, as if she were running away from herself. She'll be on edge, she may come home quicker than usual, I must hurry.

He watched her through the glassed-in veranda as she walked through the courtyard to the black wooden gate with her youthful stride, swaying her hips (she was fifteen years younger than Uncle); Chico, which was not a fitting name for a beautifully-built German shepherd, bounced behind her, licked her face by the gate, and then slowly made his way back. She turned around and waved to Peter, as if she knew that he was watching her. Then she disappeared behind the gate.

He wondered whether she had asked him to help her with the zipper because she knew that it was torture for him to look at her naked body. Hopefully that wasn't the case. He didn't want to and couldn't allow himself to believe that she was taunting him on purpose. No! She couldn't have known that the grey, round, dry stains on his sheets were the result of nights filled with anguish from crazy erotic dreams about her. No. She couldn't have known his dreams. What bothered him most was whether she had noticed the undeniable signs of his manhood, which he should have been proud of, but instead were a source of unspeakable shame and torment for him. At first, Aunt Viera used to make his bed, but after one morning, after the first thus marked morning, he started to make his own bed. When he pictured Aunt Viera carrying the sheets to the balcony (each night everything smelt of sunshine and crisp, clean mountain air), when he imagined her face, her sarcastic, yes, definitely sarcastic smile, he shuddered. Since the day it happened to him for the first time, he couldn't sleep. He was afraid to fall asleep, not knowing when those tormenting images would emerge from the darkness. Nights were hell. Sometimes he got the impression that Aunt suspected something, but he'd immediately reject the idea. She couldn't have suspected something and at the same time been so cruel. He was offended and humiliated by the fact that she considered him a child. She'd lie on a lounger in the middle of the garden, stark naked, protected from the gaze of strangers by a tall hedge, and play with Peter's hair. His head would rest on her lap, and he'd read crime fiction to her. Without a second thought, she'd call him into the bathroom and ask him to scrub her back. He was livid when he realized that he was just a substitute for Uncle Ján; he was livid when he imagined Uncle doing with her the things he had dreamt about. After that morning with stains on his sheets, he decided to not go into the garden again when she was sunbathing or wash her back again. But he didn't go through with it. He told himself that such a sudden change would arouse suspicion. He also had to admit that he wasn't willing to give up on such small pleasures. Everything went on as before, but his hatred for Uncle grew. While his aunt could do no wrong, his uncle was to blame for everything. His desire for revenge swelled, and when he discovered that Uncle was secretly feeding the hawk raw meat, it turned into an obsession.

He felt the urge to use the bathroom. 'Nervousness before a crime?' he thought, but he had to take care of it. Although he usually enjoyed going, particularly because of the trip, at the moment it was inconvenient, an unnecessary delay. He liked that he could ride his bike to the bathroom. The house faced a big, long garden, at the end of which was an outhouse. Naturally there was a bathroom in the house, but Peter preferred the outdoor one that Uncle had built so people wouldn't have to run from the garden all the way to the house; everything was made for comfort there. He hopped onto Ivan's bike and pedalled along the garden path. He liked it there, and always spent some time there. He put in a mirror, plastered the wooden walls with cut-outs from sports magazines, and brought in at least twenty beaten-up adventure paperbacks that had been strewn around the attic. Often, he sat there for hours, the door wide open, enjoying the fresh air, sitting and reading. In lieu of toilet paper, he used old train schedules. It was a lot cheaper and the paper was of a better quality. While using the schedules, he memorized almost all of the train departures and arrivals in the country. They might come in handy. He either read or did crossword puzzles. He'd leave the most important squares, the ones that contained the hidden message, blank. He wasn't interested in solving the puzzle. The answer was usually quite banal. 'A mystery should not be revealed. It simply is. We should be left guessing,' his father used to say. Peter would laugh, but it's your job to solve mysteries, and he didn't understand when his father would answer, 'Maybe that's why.' He did puzzles for the pleasure of doing them. The same was true for listening to his father's exciting stories; what he liked most was the manner in which his father told them, the magnificent rapture that would spread across his face once he got going; and although Peter knew that his father was inventing most of it, it didn't bother him; he didn't want to spoil his father's enjoyment of storytelling, the imagination, the playfulness; his favourite part was when his father would get so entangled in the story that he'd forget what was invented and what had really happened. They'd laugh and laugh when his father would stop, and say, 'There you have it, I'm lying once again. It all happened differently, I just can't remember how.' The next day, his father would bring home the case file, and when they'd read it, it would all sound boring, and Peter would say, 'Those files are all wrong, you guys got taken, it couldn't have happened like that, you were right.'

One disadvantage of the outhouse was that it was right by the fence where a neighbour was always hanging around; even now he heard her footsteps from behind, and wasn't sure if she was watching him through one of the many cracks. Naturally, it made him uncomfortable, so he whistled, coughed, rustled paper, did anything he could to cover the unpleasant noises that accompanied the emptying of one's bowels. There was a time when he couldn't imagine that a girl he'd be in love with would also need to go to the bathroom, but he had got over that.

This time he didn't linger. He jumped onto the bike and quickly pedalled towards the house. As he rode, he plucked a few gooseberries and some currants. He leaned the blue bike against the wall; something was making him nervous. Then he realized he had forgotten to urinate. He unbuttoned his trousers and relieved himself as he walked through the courtyard. The hens, which had been pecking at the grains strewn on the ground, got frightened and scattered, and they pecked at the fresh drops with mistrust. He entered the house and ran up the creaking steps to the attic where he had left Ivan's backpack filled with rocks. He had carefully selected them by the river; they had to be just right, not too large or too heavy, just right for his hand, but not too small, so as to fulfil their purpose. The backpack was heavy, the rocks scraped against one another, he went down the steps slowly, holding on to the wooden railing. (One of the first things he had checked when he inspected the house was whether the railing hadn't been sabotaged. He knew that cunning criminals used such dirty tricks.)

The pigeons were sitting on the roof. He breathed a sigh of relief when he counted them and they were all there. That was his biggest fear—that one would be missing. In his mind he asked forgiveness of the nine pigeons that would die in vain, but it had to be done—they all looked alike, it was impossible to identify the right one. They looked majestic against the backdrop of the blue sky, sunlight made their feathers sparkle, they were calm, their heads held high, they cooed as their white crops quivered. The pigeons looked fed, but in reality they were hungry, because even though he had told Aunt Viera that he had fed them, he hadn't; he was afraid they wouldn't fly down when he needed them to. He whistled the familiar signal. It got their attention. When the first handful of grain hit the ground, they rose almost in unison, their wings rustled and stirred up the hot air. Each of them tried to grab as much as it could; they were famished. Little by little he moved towards the woodshed. On the wall of the woodshed hung a crucified rabbit skin, his aunt had slaughtered a rabbit that morning; the sun was beating down on it, it was there waiting for a Gypsy they called Skinner. A narrow trail of grain that followed him was disappearing into the insatiable beaks.

Once all the pigeons were in the woodshed, he poured two handfuls in front of them to keep them busy and latched the wooden gate. It didn't faze them, they had no idea that Peter was capable of such vengefulness. He threw down more grain. He had them all in his sight, just where he wanted them. They were fighting over the grain in a small space, and that was the idea—to kill as many as possible with the first strike; rocks would make that more difficult. A heavy, wide coal shovel was propped against the wall two steps from him. He grabbed it, and lifted it slowly, carefully, so as not to disturb them with its shadow. He put all of his strength into the blow, all of his suppressed hatred for his uncle. It was as though a bomb had been dropped into the huddle of the small feathery bodies. He didn't have time to count how many he had got; he took another swing and another. Out of the clump of blood, flesh, and feathers rose three pigeons; confused, heedless, they flew around the woodshed, running into the wooden walls with hollow thuds, looking for an exit to no avail. In the narrow, slanted strips of sunlight that streamed in through the gaps between the planks, swirled dust and tiny feathers. Six were dead, one was still moving. Peter took a swing, but he had to close his eyes on impact. He had a plastic bag at the bottom of the backpack; he couldn't get the backpack bloody. Cringing, he picked up the bloody flesh by the warm crimson-coloured feet; he could feel the hard, keratinous scales between his fingers. Seven of them filled less than half the bag. He glanced at his watch. Only twenty minutes had passed since Aunt Viera left. He had time. There were three to go, then sweeping so there wouldn't be a feather left, and covering the blood stains with sand. He had even picked out a deserted place by the river where he'd take them. Everything was going according to plan. The pigeons had simply flown away—he smiled at the thought of Uncle Ján's enraged face. He looked at the three remaining pigeons. They were sitting on the cross beams, trembling. It was unbelievable how much they trembled. One of them had a broken wing, that one would be easy. He lifted the first stone. As the stones hit the wooden walls, they made an infernal racket. He didn't care. Thinking about Uncle Ján filled him with enough callousness. Finally, the last pigeon was dead.

Someone was banging on the door of the woodshed. He recognized Uncle Ján's voice and thought with indifference: 'It didn't work out exactly as planned, he came home early today, he must have suspected something.'

'Open up or I'll break down the door,' Uncle roared, and Peter smiled at the thought of Uncle Ján's weak body ramming into the door.

'Go ahead,' he said, and came up to the door.

Through a narrow gap he saw his uncle, deranged from anger, running at the door. When his right shoulder was almost touching the door, Peter swung it open, and then he laughed as his uncle was picking himself up off the ground, as he was righting the knocked over rabbit cages, as he clumsily chased the frightened rabbits that were running around the woodshed. He kept on laughing even when Uncle Ján's face, contorted with hatred, was coming up to him.

2

He felt no remorse. With fierce stubbornness he refused to answer their questions. Aunt Viera, who was defending him, found herself in a very difficult position. She had to temper Uncle Ján's outbursts; he had completely lost control and was choking from anger. A torrent of words poured out of his thin throat, he flailed his long, toothpick arms. Peter watched the wild dance of his Adam's apple, he would have bet anything that it was about to jump out of his skin. His aunt really had it tough. And Peter couldn't help her. He was silent, and her oft-repeated pleas to at least attempt to explain, for heaven's sake, to apologize to Uncle Ján, all of her pleas went unanswered. There was nothing to explain, it was inexplicable.

Naturally, Uncle Ján brought up his prior transgressions. 'This has gone too far,' he said. 'I could forgive you for hiding all the dresses, I could even forgive you for killing the hawk. But this, this is unforgivable. To kill ten pigeons in cold blood, with no remorse, no—it's impossible for someone to have so much depravity, evil, and hatred. What have they done to you, for God's sakes, what have those poor birds done to you? No. This has gone too far.'

'Don't lose your train of thought,' Peter said, 'but you don't need to shout.' Uncle gulped several times, but then he recovered. 'I understand that your parents' death was very hard on you, it was horrific, we were shaken by it too,' he said in a quieter voice, 'but there are limits. No. Either you're sick and need treatment, or you're so evil that you need juvenile detention. All compassion ends here. It's not the first time you've done something like this, is it? Do you remember how you kids used to burn pigeons? I'm sure you do, and yes, I do know about that, so be still.' So they had written them about that, too, Peter thought, filled with hatred for his godparents. Something like that really did happen, but he didn't like to think about it. He desperately tried to suppress the memory of the flailing pigeons, covered in gasoline, and burning like living, flying torches. 'No, this is it. Tomorrow you're going home, I'm starting to feel afraid of you,' Uncle Ján said.

But Peter wasn't listening any more. He turned around, walked towards the stairs, and when he was almost at the attic, he heard his uncle's hoarse, tired voice, 'He gets it from his father, he was also as stubborn as a mule, but at least he didn't kill pigeons.'

In the attic room, he sat on the sofa for a while, but then he shot up and started to take off Ivan's yellow football jersey. The sun had set, the room was getting dark, but he didn't turn on the lights. He was afraid that if the room was lit he wouldn't be able to leave it. The darkness, which was obscuring the familiar, the intimately familiar objects, made leaving much easier. He took off Ivan's joggers; the cleats were the hardest to leave behind. He enjoyed playing in them. Although they were two sizes too large, he had already scored fifteen goals wearing them, and even before the next day's final match it was clear that no one could touch his top striker ranking. What he regretted most was that he wouldn't get to play tomorrow. He hesitated, wondering whether he was betraying his friends, but the thought of his uncle brought back his resolve.

He pulled the dark suit he had worn to his parents' funeral out of the armoire, put on his light-blue Swedish dress-shirt and his worn-out dress-shoes. He felt like he was in a cage. There was no comparison between this and the freedom he felt in the joggers, yellow jersey and cleats. The Slovan team pin, he remembered, and took it off the jersey. He pulled down his dust-covered suitcase from the armoire, and tossed in his shirts, shorts, socks, sweater, jeans and tennis shoes. He felt sad as he closed it. He took one last look around the room.

Naturally they didn't want to let him go at night on the long trip that was ahead of him. But in light of his wilfulness, they had to back down. 'Fine. Let him go, who knows what he'll do if we don't,' said Uncle. Peter ignored him, but the words made him smile. He knew that his uncle wanted nothing more than to get rid of him as quickly as possible, so that he could be alone with Aunt Viera, without anyone else around, without any obstacles in his web of plans. He had always reminded Peter of a spider. Spindly arms, spindly legs, a spindly neck with a big, bald head dangling at the end of it—a huge old spider. Aunt Viera was just a tiny naive fly that was supposed to get caught in his web. But then there was Peter, the bumblebee, and while he may not have been able to incapacitate the spider, he could shred his web. He had already done so on several occasions.

The first time he hid the dresses. All the dresses Aunt Viera wore in those painted photographs. He stuffed them into three paper bags left over from cement and hid them in the attic with all the junk covered in dust that hadn't been disturbed in at least five years. The windows were always open, his aunt often spent as much as half the day shopping, and it never occurred to her to close them, the idea that there might be thieves never crossed her mind. All he had to do was mess things up a little, create the impression of someone being in a hurry, and everyone bought it; that's how unexpected it was.

He didn't want them to walk him to the bus stop. They thought it was just a whim of a stubborn teenager and ignored it. Both of them got dressed, and Uncle picked up the suitcase. Peter started to shake all over, he screamed, and he even stomped his foot like some hysterical goat that always made him laugh at the cinema. They didn't know what to do; he had never acted out like that before. He was also surprised by how far he got carried away by anger, but he couldn't help himself. I've had enough of them, he thought. He could see rage well up in his uncle again, he could see how hard he was working to control it; as if he wanted it to be over, as if he were afraid. Yes, he's afraid of me, Peter thought with satisfaction. He's afraid of me even though he knows I can't hurt him, even though he knows he could refute any argument I could make and use it against me. He knows it, and yet he's afraid of me, because if I decided to tell all, I might be able to instil a seed of doubt in Aunt Viera's mind, and she might start seeing Uncle through different eyes.

'Would you let me walk with you if I went alone?' his aunt asked quietly, and he thought he could hear tears in her voice.

'Yes.'

Uncle Ján put down the suitcase.

'Have it your way,' he said. 'I see that you don't like me, though I have no idea what I've done to you. But it doesn't matter. I'm not going to force myself on you. I know that you don't want to explain anything. I'm not angry with you. Some day we'll make up.'

As Peter listened to him, he started to doubt his suspicions, the same way he had many times before. What if I'm wrong? He can't possibly be faking it so well. But then he recalled the incident when he was standing in the courtyard, and through the glassed-in veranda he saw Uncle Ján secretly feeding the hawk raw meat. Aunt Viera was at the store, Peter was supposed to be at practice, the house was empty, except for Uncle Ján who was sitting at the door to the cage, and with a contented smile he watched the hawk ravenously tear at the chunks of raw meat.

Peter didn't even shake his hand. He pretended not to see it. Uncle sighed and shrugged his shoulders, his thin arm drooped to his thigh.

They walked through the quiet dark courtyard. Uncle Ján stood on the steps in front of the veranda; the lit end of his cigarette glowed in the darkness. Aunt Viera carried Peter's suitcase; it was embarrassing, but she wouldn't let him take it. Ivan's blue bike was propped against the wall.

'I forgot to put away the bike,' Peter said. Aunt Viera laughed and caressed his head. 'You never took me fishing, for as much you kept promising.'

'The fishing rods are in the woodshed. If you remember, let the worms out of the jar.'

'They may already be dead.'

'You think they suffocated?'

'I don't know. Maybe not. Who knows how they breathe since they live underground.'

Chico was jumping up to their shoulders, playing. 'Shake, Chico' she said when they were at the gate. Chico stood on his hind legs and placed his large paw in Peter's hand. 'Hi, you big bear.' Peter shook his paw. Chico licked his face. In turn Peter scratched him behind his ears. The gate creaked. He didn't look back. They were silent all the way to the bridge. The wood resounded with each step and the bubbling brook reminded him of fishing.

'Tomorrow's the final. Did you know they made you a cake?' He didn't respond; he was upset that she brought it up. The whole village knows about the cake, he thought sorely.

'Should we go back? Where will you go at this hour of the night?'

He was still silent, but his aunt went on.

'Uncle didn't mean it. He was just very upset. You know how much he loved those pigeons.' Yes, one of them in particular, he thought, indignant. After the death of the hawk, Uncle started to play with one of the pigeons. It was always with him, and although all of them were tame, only that one would sit on Uncle's shoulder, only that one would eat out of Uncle's hand.

Out of his hand only. Slowly, imperceptibly, it was turning into a hawk.

'Protect your eyes,' he said in anguish.

'What?' she asked, confused. 'Should we go back?'

'No,' he said, irate.

They walked out onto the main road. They didn't meet anyone the whole way to the bus stop. No one was waiting there either. Aunt Viera set down the suitcase.

'Would you tell me why you killed the hawk?' she asked in a soft voice. 'Don't worry, I won't tell anyone.'

She's back at it. He clenched his teeth. He couldn't let her find out that when Uncle discovered the dresses in the attic, when she started to wear them again, he had to kill the hawk.

'You won't tell anyone about the pigeons?' he asked in a pleading tone.

'You silly. Why should I tell anyone? You killed them to spite your uncle. But you're wrong. Uncle loves you, you guys just don't get along.'

'I didn't want to kill all of them. Just one.'

'One? Why?' she asked. 'You weren't jealous, were you?'

He was so offended he stopped in his tracks and he burst out in anger, 'Uncle wants to kill you.' His own words frightened him.

Aunt Viera's eyes got big, but not out of fear, out of pity. She wasn't scared. She felt sorry for him. 'You poor dear,' she said kindly.

The bus was coming.

'I put some oranges and ham in your suitcase. Eat them on the train,' she said, but she didn't hug him, as if she were shrinking from his malice.

3

Dear Ivan!

You may be surprised to get my letter, but so be it.
Perhaps everything I'm about to write is only in my head,
but I have to let you know . . .

After he sent Ivan a letter describing his suspicions, he calmed
down a bit. Still, he spoke to no one, had no appetite, and lost all
the pounds he had put on at Aunt Viera's. He didn't even notice
the incessant questions from his godparents: 'Why did you do it?
Why did you kill the hawk? Why the pigeons? Why? Why? Why?
. . . ' Because.

He hardly went out; since it was summer vacation, even the
few boys from his street were out of town, and although he didn't
consider them friends, they did help him pass the time. He awaited
the beginning of the school year like salvation. The only bright
moment in the dark end of his summer was Ivan's reply. Ivan considered him a peer, he wrote seriously, didn't make fun of anything, and although he wrote that things might not be quite as
bad as Peter thought they were, he definitely felt that something
was off, and he was going to try to get time off as soon as possible
to go home and check on things. That calmed Peter down a lot,
and as time went by, his fear for Aunt Viera dissipated, and when
the grey stains stopped appearing on his sheets, when Aunt Viera
was no longer the subject of his dreams, his mood started to
improve as well. He concluded that he had really been awful and
ungrateful to his godparents, and he decided to try to change. As
a result, the news they gave him one night struck him like lightning. In an instant he despised them, even though he knew it was
unjustified. They said, albeit awkwardly, and with many pauses,
that he was more than they could handle, that he must not have

enjoyed staying with them, that he probably needed a change of scenery, and so on and so forth, until it finally came out. At the beginning of the school year he'd be going to an institution. They didn't say what kind, but he knew—they thought he was crazy. He despised them for it, didn't say a word, but after some time, he told himself, it's OK, I'll be better off there, and later still he came around to thinking that they might be right. Perhaps he really was sick. He thought about his summer vacation again, and now, after some time had passed, he came to the realization that he had made it all up, he concluded that it wasn't his uncle that was evil, it was he, Peter. Now that Aunt Viera was no longer the subject of his tormented dreams he went so far as to admit that he had made it all up on account of jealousy. The whole thing seemed ridiculous. For no reason, out of ignorance, he had assumed that Uncle Ján had the intention to kill, only because he secretly fed the hawk raw meat and watched Aunt Viera at night. Peter had to laugh at his own irrational thinking, but the thought of the hawk attacking Aunt Viera's face, the hawk ferociously sinking its beak into her sad eyes, that thought still made him sweat and tremble.

He couldn't wait for the summer to end. He was looking forward to the institution. Yes, I'm evil, but I blame others so that I don't have to admit it to myself, he thought. I need to get treated for my malice. He wrote a letter in which he thanked both of them for a wonderful summer, and he apologized to his uncle for the dresses, the hawk, the pigeons, for everything. They replied immediately, it was clear that his letter had made them very happy. They forgave him for everything.

Two days before he was to leave for the institution, when everything had been settled, a letter from Ivan arrived, which wrecked his serenity. Ivan was letting him know that he was finally able to take time off and was planning to go home. But first he'd come see Peter so they could go over the whole thing slowly and in detail one more time. The prospect of the meeting frightened Peter. He couldn't meet with him now that he had figured out he had made it all up. Ivan was the only person who treated him as an equal, no, he'll hate me too, he panicked as he recalled saying goodbye to Aunt Viera, the way she recoiled from him and didn't even hug him. When he thought about Ivan's room, which had been his room, Ivan's cleats, joggers, yellow jersey, fishing rods, bike—no, he couldn't meet with him.

He decided to run away. In the evening he packed his things into a backpack and went to bed in his clothes. He waited a long time for all the lights to go out in the flat, so long that he fell asleep. In the morning, his godparents woke him up. They were quite distraught, so much so that they didn't even notice he had slept in his clothes. He got worried that Ivan was already there.

Instead, they told him that Aunt Viera had passed away. They were very careful and considerate; they knew how much he loved her and how worried he had been about her. The first words out of his mouth were: 'Her eyes?'

He waited for their answer with baited breath. 'What about her eyes? What are you talking about?' they asked, perplexed. 'Her eyes! Did something peck her eyes out?' They gave each other a meaningful look, and in a quiet, sad voice his godmother said: 'You poor dear!'

'I take that as a no. Right? Yes or no?' he shouted.

'Hey, calm down, Peter dear, calm down.' His godmother hugged him.

He jerked away from her.

'Will you answer my question?'

'No,' his godfather yelled. 'Nothing pecked her eyes out. And stop acting out. I don't know what's got into you again. I swear it's high time for you to go,' he yelled, but Peter wasn't listening to him any more.

Then it's a no, he breathed a sigh of relief. I had been wrong this whole time.

'Chico got rabies and bit her,' his godmother said. 'Luckily, he didn't bite Uncle Ján. Luckily, Ján managed to kill him,' she added.

Chico. I forgot about him—Peter thought, and he felt weak as a sudden warm wave flooded him with a desperate sense of guilt.

•

A Christmas Journey

The bus was cold and empty. I was the only passenger. The surly driver handed me a ticket without saying a word. I sympathized with him; I too could have imagined more pleasant ways of spending Christmas Eve.

The doors closed with a hiss. We took off. It was two in the afternoon; everyone was somewhere warm, getting ready for the arrival of Santa Claus. Although I was shivering while riding on a run-down bus through the snow-covered countryside, I too was on my way to Christmas revelry. I had a three-hour journey ahead of me. Despite the fact that I was freezing, I didn't want to ask the driver to turn the heat on just for me; it probably didn't work anyway. The windows were covered in frost; I had no view. Good thing it had occurred to me to buy a bottle of Jelínek borovička at the bus station. I pulled it out of the side pocket of my coat and took a good swig. It made me hiccup, but the warmth that spread through my insides was well worth it. I didn't know whether I should offer some to the driver; I don't like to impose. Maybe he doesn't drink, I thought as I put away the bottle.

The jostling of the poorly cushioned seats and the monotonous rumbling of the engine soon dulled my senses. Unfortunately, it didn't put me to sleep. Thus I had nothing to do but think, again (how many times had I done so already?), about the matter concerning why I was sitting there, making my way to an unfamiliar mountain hotel instead of sipping champagne all day in my comfortable, well-heated flat, looking forward to Christmas Eve dinner at the intimately familiar hotel across the street.

The more I thought about the whole thing, the clearer it became that I had fallen victim to a prank. That was a given. I just didn't know what the prank was and who was behind it. It would be really bad if the hotel were closed. I got worried that I was going to show up in the middle of the night, in the mountains, in bitter cold, suitcase in hand, in front of a dark, closed hotel.

I got up and walked down the aisle towards the driver. The engine got louder, we were going uphill. I yelled into the driver's ear, 'Excuse me, is the hotel open?' He didn't so much as turn his head. Silently, he stuck a cigarette in his mouth and waited for me to give him a light. He smoked and paid no attention to me. I repeated my question.

It seemed as though he didn't hear me the second time either; he just smoked and drove. After about three drags, he turned towards me sharply and shouted, 'Stop yelling in my ear, I'm not deaf.' A moment later, he added, more quietly, but with an evil grin, 'You'll see.' I let go of his backrest and sat down in the empty service seat next to him. 'That's a service seat. Get out,' the driver said. I got up, there was no point arguing with him. So, the hotel is closed, I thought as I walked to the back to get my suitcase.

I decided to get off the bus. It was 2.30; perhaps I could still catch a return bus and make the 5.10 train. I felt relieved. The thought of ending this stupid journey in my own flat, the thought of a Christmas Eve dinner in my hotel was more than liberating.

'Stop, please. I'd like to get off,' I said, standing by the door with my suitcase. Once more he didn't answer. 'Stop, damn it,' I shouted. Without turning his head he calmly replied, 'This isn't a bus stop. There'll be one in twenty minutes.' Then he pointed to the sign: *No talking to the driver while the bus is in motion.* I set down my suitcase. There was nothing I could do but wait the twenty minutes. I took a seat near the door. I pulled out a neatly folded telegram the postman had brought me that morning from my wallet. I read it again, even though I already had it memorized:

I AGREE TO YOUR PROPOSAL STOP I WILL WAIT
FOR YOU TONIGHT AT 7PM STOP HOTEL BOBOTY
ROOM 108 STOP

There was no signature, same as with the other letters. I stared at it as if I were hoping that patience would help me uncover the secret behind the words, if there was such a secret. The only thing I knew for certain was that Hotel Boboty was real. I had confirmed it at the Čedok travel agency, moreover, it was listed as the final stop of this bus.

The funny thing was that the telegram was not addressed to me, but it must have been sent by someone who knew me quite well, someone familiar with my lazy disposition and my rule: If I don't have to stand, I'll sit, if I don't have to sit, I'll lie down. The enticement was clever; its author knew that the only thing that would make me overcome my innate laziness would be the suggestion of a secret, a mystery, in short, curiosity. He had guessed correctly. The fact that I was sitting there was clear proof of it.

I took another swig of borovička. A wave of love for my neighbour washed over me, and I offered some to the driver; it was understandable that he couldn't be expected to be thrilled to be driving some moron to a mountain hotel on Christmas Eve. The fact that I was the only passenger made me feel all the more guilty. The driver glanced at me and growled, 'I don't drink at work.' Up yours, I thought, annoyed by his hateful obstinacy. I was standing behind him, and through the glass cleared by the windshield wipers I could see the road; a narrow, icy hairpin turn with steep rocky cliffs on both sides.

I hadn't yet put away the bottle when the bus stopped. I looked at my watch; twenty minutes had passed.

'There. This is the bus stop. Get out,' the driver said and turned off the engine. I didn't like his tone. By then I had enough borovička in me to consider it a provocation. And I hate being provoked. Besides, having made it this far, it would have been ridiculous to go back. I'd end up with a complex from the unfinished business.

'You know what? I changed my mind. I'm going all the way to the end.'

I saw his fist turn white as he gripped the metal handrail.

'I said, get out,' he hissed.

'Nonsense,' I said calmly and stretched out comfortably on the seat. 'You'd like that, wouldn't you?'

'You don't happen to live here, do you?' I motioned outside with my head. We must have been in a small mountain village.

'And what if I do?'

'You'd like that, park the bus and crawl into a warm bed, wouldn't you? I have a ticket to the last stop.'

His fat, red face darkened. He took a step towards me. I got ready to jump. He was a good ninety pounds heavier than me, but I had the advantage of being at least fifteen years younger.

'So you won't get out? You, you imbecile!' he shouted.

He shouldn't have said that. I've read that even hunchbacks don't like having their hump thrown in their face.

'Damn it. Shut up. It's your doggone duty to take me where I want to go. I bought a ticket, and you're getting paid.'

The man looked on the verge of a heart attack. He stopped breathing, his eyes were popping out of their sockets, but he got through it.

'Fine,' he said. 'As you like. But you'll regret it,' he said with another evil smirk.

The first thing that went through my head was that the hotel was closed. That was going to be his revenge. He was going to refuse to take me back. The smart thing would have been to get out, but I couldn't back down. Worst case, I'd spend the night in some staff dormitory. If there was any staff there. Or a dormitory. Never mind. Things would work out somehow.

The engine sputtered and died. There was still a chance that the old rust bucket would break down. But soon that chance vanished too, because the engine started on the third attempt. I was left with nothing but idle thoughts.

The telegram was addressed to Stano Malý, but I was the only one living in his flat. We knew each other from college; a year ago he had let me stay with him in his two-bedroom flat, but two months later he left for a two-year study abroad in France, and the flat became mine for the duration. I didn't know where exactly he was, because he hadn't managed to write yet; he knew that it would take me two years to muster an answer.

The first letter arrived two months ago, on 13 October. It was addressed to Stano, but I opened it without any scruples; we had agreed that I would take care of his mail. It was a confused letter, none of it made any sense. Someone was reproaching him for something, accusing him of acting like a lout in 'that matter'. I had no idea what matter was being referenced, nor did I care. At the time, I was reading Freud's *The Interpretation of Dreams*, and I remember sticking the letter into the book. Then I promptly forgot about it. I didn't think about it again until the next letter showed up two weeks later. It had the same handwriting, and the same unreadable postmark. It also had the same stamp. Someone who didn't sign this letter either was responding to Stano's letter. He said that he had received the reply to his first letter, which was more than he had expected from such a lout, but that he couldn't agree with his justification, that his arguments were laughable, and he should know better. If in his next letter Stano didn't suggest a course of action in 'the matter', he (the letter used the masculine form) would carry out all of the suggested measures, and Stano would regret it. I quickly searched for Freud's *The Interpretation of Dreams*, and baffled, I pulled the envelope with the first letter out of the book. It was there, all of it, undisturbed, just as I had left it. I spent two days in bed with a fever. I ended up so confused that I had to keep convincing myself that I hadn't replied to the letter. Neither I, nor anyone else. The unknown writer was responding to a non-existent reply. After a lot of thinking I reached the only possible conclusion—someone who knew my penchant for mysticism was playing a prank on me. I filed the second letter next to the first one, and started to read positivists instead of mystics. Which was why everything was clear and made sense to me when the next letter arrived. In the third letter, the anonymous moron wrote that he wasn't satisfied with Stano's second reply either, that he had had enough of his loutish excuses, and that if Stano didn't make a specific suggestion regarding 'the matter' in his third letter, he, the writer, would pay him a visit. I just smiled. The anonymous writer had gone too far this time; clearly he didn't know when to stop. While the second letter still had an element of surprise in it, the third removed all suspense from the situation. He shouldn't have assumed that a person with a penchant for mysticism would automatically be stupid. I put the third letter next to the other two in *The Interpretation of Dreams*, which were there, of course, undisturbed. I expected one of my crazy friends to show up soon, beaming about his prank.

Then the telegram came:

I AGREE TO YOUR PROPOSAL STOP I WILL WAIT FOR YOU TONIGHT AT 7PM STOP HOTEL BOBOTY ROOM 108 STOP

The fact that I was on my way to Hotel Boboty proved that the writer had pulled off the prank after all. Of course he did, since he had chosen such a curious idiot as his mark. The closer we got to the hotel, the more my opinion of myself sunk. I didn't know what prank was going to be played on me, but I knew that I had been taken in, hook, line and sinker. I'd have to turn the whole thing into a joke; I'd claim to have got a sudden urge to go skiing over the holidays. I had neither skis nor other ski equipment with me, and to be honest, I had never skied in my life, but you have to start somewhere.

The cold made me shudder; it was old Jelínek's turn again. The bottle was half-empty; evidently, it wasn't bottomless. I was hoping it would last all the way to the hotel. It would be best to arrive wasted.

I lurched forward, the bus slammed on the brakes. The door opened, and a man in a green coat with a black briefcase under his arm got in. The driver handed him a ticket without saying a word, and we went on. The man took a seat about halfway down the bus. I was sitting in the back again, so with the driver in front, humanity had all of the key positions filled.

My guilt dissipated with the arrival of another passenger. The driver no longer existed just for me, my crime was less serious. I felt a certain affinity for the new passenger, and I would have been happy to initiate a casual interaction with him. The bottle could be an avenue, but I didn't know how to bring it up politely; he could have been easily offended. Or a non-drinker. Or working.

Thankfully, he allayed my fears, because he got up, and holding onto the backrests, he made his way towards me. I saw that he was tall and thin, the coat hung on him in an unappealing fashion. His chest was caved in like a kicked-in drum. His face was thin, yellow and drawn. Only his nose was a pretty red colour, with purple capillaries woven throughout. He certainly didn't look like Santa, even though he could have had a few presents in that black pigskin briefcase. I pegged him to be a maths teacher who got hammered on a regular basis and had two stomach ulcers. My theory was that in his briefcase he had plastic explosives for misbehaving children.

'I smell borovička,' he said without beating around the bush.

'You know your stuff,' I said, and handed him the bottle.

As he tilted the bottle into himself, it looked like he was trying to swallow it. For a while there were bubbling sounds, then he pulled it out of his throat and shook it sadly, as if trying squeeze out a few more drops. It was no use. He had sucked it dry.

'I could tell that you were a boozer,' I flattered him, 'but you could have left me a drop.'

He nudged me over to the window and sat down next to me.

'My stomach really hurts,' he said apologetically.

I was pleased. I was right about the ulcers as well.

'How many ulcers do you have?' I asked.

'Two. The third one burst. I'm a maths teacher.' He offered me his hand.

'And you have plastic explosives in your briefcase,' I said.

'Don't tell anyone,' he whispered.

I liked him. I forgave him for the borovička. Then he started talking.

'One time, my brother and I went picking blackthorn. We were really hungry. You know what I mean? We ate our fill. We ended up really bloated. And terribly constipated. But that's nothing. Another time I was with a woman. She took off her clothes. She had a nice figure, but something about her was bothering me. It took me a long time to figure it out. Finally I realized that she had no nipples. You know what I mean? She had nice breasts, but no nipples. But that's nothing. A long time ago, I used to write poetry. But I had to stop because I nearly lost my sight. It was like walking on an unfamiliar road in the dark with headlights shining at you. They blind you completely. I had to quit, or I'd have gone blind. I could get no further. I just kept walking into the headlights. But the thing to do would have been to get into the headlights, into the source of the light. Or rather, into the darkness of the headlights. And then to turn them my way. And light my path. But I didn't make it. My eyes still hurt like crazy. You know what I mean? But that's nothing. My brother had a motorcycle accident. He cracked open his head. You know what I mean? His skull split apart at the seams. Where they come together. He had surgery and recovered. He just has to wear a bandana all the time. He feels that if he didn't have it on, his head would come apart. You know what I mean? But that's nothing. One time, I had a dream in which a woman was following me. A naked, fat woman. She followed me down the streets, everywhere I went. That in itself wouldn't be so bad. But her body was like steak tartare. You know what I mean? It was made of ground beef. Red. It quivered, it barely held together. I woke up wondering where she had the egg. You know what I mean? Steak Tartar is always served with a raw egg. And I couldn't remember.'

Then, as suddenly as it had started, his disjointed monologue delivered in a monotone filled with pain, was over. He exhaled heavily, and wiped his sweaty brow. His face was twitching. He looked at his watch. 'I'll be getting off soon,' he said. 'Perhaps I bothered you, I don't know, perhaps the things I said scared you a bit, but don't worry about it, I know you think I'm crazy. You do, don't you? But that's nothing, I don't hold it against you, but I'm really not crazy, just ask anyone, I teach maths, here, in the next village, just ask, my name is Fedor Sitniansky, yes, Fedor Sitniansky, the maths teacher, you can even ask the driver, Jožko here, he drives me there and back every day, but I don't hold it against you, on the contrary, I'm very glad you listened, I just needed to talk, because I felt really ill, you know what I mean, I have stomach ulcers, and it got bad, I had to be talking to someone, or even to no one at all, I just had to keep talking so as not to throw up.'

The bus stopped. He got up quickly and shook my hand with a light squeeze. 'Merry Christmas,' he said. His hand was hot and sweaty. His yellowed face was twitching in pain, the cramps must not have ceased yet.

'Bye Jožko,' he said to the driver as he was getting off the bus. 'Say hello to your wife.'

The door closed with a hiss. We moved. Once again, I was the only passenger. I looked back, but by then the teacher was just a small black dot on a white background. Soon it disappeared too.

I was shivering from the cold, but there was no more borovička. I didn't want to think about anything. I had a half hour more to go. I pulled up the collar on my coat and started counting to one hundred. At eighty-four, the driver's voice interrupted me: 'You know him?'

I looked at him, surprised.

'Me? Why?'

'He said bye to you.'

'To me? He said bye to you.'

'Listen. Stop pulling my leg. I've never seen him in my life. I've been driving this route for ten years and I've never seen that man.'

For a moment a complete vacuum formed in my head. I had just about had it with that stupid journey. The man in the green coat was the last thing I needed. As if I had nothing else to think about. As if I needed him to barge into my thoughts with his crazy talk and his Grim Reaper face. As if he had nothing else to do on Christmas Eve but to ride an unfamiliar bus on unfamiliar roads. Who was he? Where did he come from and where was he going? I was starting to despise him because I knew nothing about him, and yet I couldn't stop thinking about him. Just like about death.

I was terribly exhausted. And it was all my own fault. A warm shower, a warm meal, a warm bed—that was all I wanted. Meanwhile, what likely awaited me was a closed hotel. And mountain frost on Christmas Eve. Dear God, let the hotel be open—I started to talk to God, as I always did in dire situations. Just like Kierkegaard had said. I don't care what happens, let a thousand of my friends be there, let them all laugh at me until my dying day, just let the hotel be open.

I looked at my watch. We should be there in five minutes. It was getting dark. Once more I was poring over all the possibilities, all the surprises someone could have in store for me. I envied Stano. He could have been sitting down to a Christmas Eve dinner in Paris. I was hoping that everything would work out in the end. The hotel would be open, and the whole subterfuge with the letters would turn out to be Jana's doing. I think that possibility was what had got me into this mess. Two years earlier, we had been engaged, about to be married. Luckily we changed our minds about five hours before our fate was sealed. Had we gone through with it, I'm sure the possibility of Jana wanting to see me would not have lured me out of a warm bed that day. I hadn't seen her since then, but that didn't mean I didn't think about her from time to time. Particularly on such noble holidays like Christmas.

And Easter, and Sunday, Saturday, Friday, Thursday . . . Yes, the possibility that it could be Jana was quite realistic. It fit with her hobby of concocting unclear, convoluted, suspenseful and hopeless situations. She knew Stano, and she must have known that he was away and I was living in his flat. Dear God, let it be Jana in an open hotel.

'Last stop. Get out.' The driver's voice, which was surprisingly loud in the quiet bus, wrested me out of my prayer. I hadn't even noticed that we had stopped. I would have loved to buy a return ticket, but I got up and with a sigh I pulled down my fine cowhide suitcase from the overhead storage.

'So. You happy?' the driver said. Maliciously.

'Are you?'

He cackled.

'The hotel's closed, isn't it?' I said.

'Look for yourself.'

I had no desire to do so. I set down my suitcase and pulled out a packet of Marice from my coat. I offered one to the driver.

'I smoke Starts,' he said, and made a show of putting a cigarette in his mouth. One of his own.

'It's not my fault you had to work today.' I offered him a light.

'You've got that all wrong. I didn't have to. I volunteered for it.'

'Then why were you so irritable?'

'That's none of your business,' he burst out. 'Anyway. Get out already. We're here.'

I grabbed my suitcase and got off the bus. Frozen snow creaked under my feet and icy wind stung my face. An invisible greyness swallowed me; it seemed to be pouring from above. My watch showed five o'clock, it was a white wintery darkness. I couldn't see five steps ahead. The driver's door slammed. Creaking steps.

'Come on, what are you waiting for?' He grabbed my arm.

'I can't see a thing.'

'You have to get used to it.' He laughed. 'Let's have a tea with rum, my treat.'

'How? The hotel's open?'

'Of course. I'm spending the night here too. I don't go back until tomorrow morning.'

'Another joker. That's just my luck.'

'Oh, loosen up.'

'Why did you torment me the whole way? All those vague responses and that evil grin.'

'Maybe I enjoyed keeping you in suspense.'

'You know what?' I stopped and freed my arm. 'Up yours.'

'Likewise.'

'Merry Christmas.'

'To you as well. If you don't mind, we could have dinner together. Or are you meeting someone else?'

'I'd love to know that myself.'

We reached the lit area in front of the entrance. I saw that it was no mountain chalet calling itself a hotel. It was an honest-to-goodness hotel—star and all. I felt relieved.

'I hope they have heating and hot water,' I said to the driver, who has stomping his feet on the metal grate to get the snow off his shoes.

'Don't you worry, as long as you have enough money.'

We walked in through large glass doors. The reception area was empty, except for a large, fat dog lying under a low table; it looked like a calf. A lazy household calf. It lifted its head, looked us over in a friendly way and wagged its tail. The driver scratched the dog's head; they must have been old friends. Then he said hello to the woman behind the reception desk.

'I brought Santa,' he said, pointing at me. 'I'm going to the kitchen.'

He left.

I stared at the receptionist, and I couldn't figure out how such a young woman could be so fat. Then again, who knows whether she was young. She could have been twenty just as easily as forty. I thought that if I had stuck a knife in her, a layer of pork lard would be left on it. I couldn't believe I had come up with such a stupid idea, but I couldn't help myself. She grated on my nerves. Her bored expression was particularly irritating. Her whole appearance exuded boredom and laziness. She reminded me of the calf-dog under the table.

'Do you have a reservation?' she asked in a soporific tone.

'No, I didn't think I'd needed one. I don't expect you have many guests on Christmas Eve.'

I noticed that slot 108 was empty. There was no key; the letter writer must have been upstairs in the room.

'We have fifty guests. Mostly Germans. They came to ski. It's really boring here.' She yawned.

I didn't ask who was staying in Room 108; let it be a surprise. I wouldn't go there until 7, as the telegram instructed.

'Your ID, please.'

I placed it in her fat hand that had long fingernails with a thick layer of nail polish. She batted her artificial black eyelashes and started to write down my information. The air smelt of powder; a light dust kept falling off her face.

'Unfortunately, all single rooms are occupied. You'll have a double to yourself. I hope you'll enjoy your stay,' she recited in a practiced professional tone.

'I hope so, too.'

'Room 203,' she said, handing me a key. 'Second floor. The lift is out of service.'

'It must be lazy.'

'Would you like to dine alone or with everyone else? We're having a group dinner.'

'I prefer to eat alone.'

'As you wish,' she said, and picked up a book.

She started to read with the same bored expression on her face. I noticed the title. It was a mystery—Ellery Queen. That irritated me. She had no right to be bored while reading a mystery. She. Perhaps she knows it by heart, I thought. We'll see if she's really bored or just putting it on.

'Are you reading Queen?' I asked matter-of-factly, and she gave a dispassionate nod.

'Dreadfully boring, don't you think?'

She nodded again. Then she yawned.

'The first one's a bit better than the second one, wouldn't you agree?'

'I just started *Cat of Many Tails*,' she said, and her tone made it clear that she found our conversation boring and exhausting.

'Take a guess who the killer is.' I smiled.

'No, no. I don't know yet. And I don't like guessing.'

'Should I tell you?'

'For heaven's sakes, don't be so boorish,' she said, and finally there was some other emotion in her voice. Fear. I decided then and there to reveal the secret; I couldn't think of a more cruel revenge.'

'Mrs Cazalis did the killing,' I whispered loudly, with unconcealed pleasure, and I delighted in seeing her face turn yellow with anger. She breathed in fits, premortal sweat popped up on her forehead, as if my words had taken away her raison d'etre, as if I were making an attempt on her life.

'You . . . you . . . scoundrel,' she yelled, and saliva sputtered from her mouth.

'So. Not bored any more?' I picked up my suitcase and headed for the stairwell.

I didn't look back.

I paused on the first floor. Room number 108 faced the stairs. The only sound coming from behind the door was the radio, which was playing 'Christmas Is Coming'. A narrow band of light emanated from under the door. I overcame my desire to knock and walked on. The stairs, like the hallways, had a thick carpet; it muffled every step. Silence reigned in the hotel, a Christmas silence, and I thought I could smell pine needles.

I unlocked the door to my room which opened onto a small entryway with a sink, a mirror and a coat rack. A door with opaque glass led from the entryway into the bedroom, which had two beds against a wall, an armoire, a shag carpet, a small coffee table, two upholstered chairs, a phone and a radio. Above the bed hung paintings that were skilful imitations of Bazovský. Vacuous motifs, vacuous atmosphere. The radiator was on, the room was pleasant, warm and clean, but the thing that interested me most was the bathroom. I was really looking forward to a bathtub full of hot, clear, greenish mountain water. Of course, my anticipation was in vain. Although the door from the entryway led to a narrow, tall space, there was nothing but a shower in it. It looked like a private gas chamber. And there was another door, the shower was shared with the inhabitants of the next room, if there were any. I tried the door, it was locked, and there was silence.

'Fuck, there went my bath,' I said aloud, and it made me feel better.

I took off my coat and shoes, and unpacked my suitcase. Then I sneezed, which made me remember the tea. I called down to the reception desk and ordered an awful lot of awfully hot tea and a bottle of rum. Aspirin I had. I felt the urge to urinate, which I considered the first sign of a cold. The room didn't come with a toilet, so I relieved myself in the sink, just as I had done a long time ago in the short story 'Monotony'. The receptionist's voice sounded much more pleasant over the telephone, so I apologized to her for the mystery novel. 'Don't worry about it,' she said. 'I'm just a receptionist.' It irritated me that she didn't sound the least bit offended. She had regained her stupid superiority.

'Had I known that I was getting a room without a private bath,' I said, 'you would have seen what a barbarian I am.' 'As you wish,' she said. 'Tea and rum. That's all.'

'One more thing. Could you tell me where the toilet is?'

'First door by the stairs,' she said. I wanted to thank her and hang up, but another question popped into my head. 'Did anyone ask about me?' 'No.' I hung up.

It was 5.40 p.m.

I spread out the letters and the telegram on the coffee table. Room 108 at 7 p.m. I had an hour and fifteen minutes. I wondered what Stano would say about the way I dealt with his mail. He'd have a good laugh when he found out. I lit a cigarette.

There was a knock on the door. The receptionist walked in with a tray.

'Thank you,' I said. 'Is the staff already partaking in the festivities?'

'How long will you be staying?'

'I thought I had ordered hot tea.'

'It was hot,' she said, sounding offended.

'Oh. It cooled down on the way. I forgot that the lift isn't working.'

'Is there anything else I can do for you?'

'Not right now. After I shower.'

'I'll be on my way then.' She turned around and walked out, undulating her large bottom.

I drank the tepid tea; at least the rum warmed me up. I took off my clothes and climbed into the gas chamber.

A hot shower made me drowsy. It was a 6.15. I lay down on the bed to rest a bit.

I hadn't expected the trip to wear me out so much.

When I woke up, it was 7.05. I threw on my clothes, splashed some water on my face, and stepped into the hallway. I put on my tie on the way to the first floor. For a moment I paused in front of Room 108. I lit a cigarette. My hands were sweating. A narrow band of light emanated from under the door. All I heard was the monotonous sound of a running shower. I took a good puff and walked in, full of resolve. The door was unlocked, and creaked as I opened it. I expected to be greeted by laughter, but there was silence. The entryway was dark, but there was a light on inside the room. It was a room with two beds, just like mine. The pictures above the beds were the same too. One of the beds had been used, the other was untouched. The ashtray on the coffee table had a narrow stream of smoke snaking up from an unfinished cigarette; the column of ashes was intact. A glossy magazine lay open on the bed. The radio was off.

The person must be in the shower, I thought. It was 7.10. I didn't know whether to open the door and peek into the shower or wait. But for whom? What if it's some stranger who has nothing to do with this stupid joke? He'd be quite surprised if I barged into his shower. I wasn't in the mood for a Christmas Eve scandal. I wasn't about to give that much satisfaction to that fat, bored receptionist.

I decided to wait outside while the person finished showering, quietly walking out of the room and closing the door behind me. Then I froze. In the dim light shining from the bedroom into the dark entryway through the opaque glass, I noticed a rivulet of blood flowing from under the door.

Without thinking I opened the door.

Under the running shower, on the floor that sloped towards the centre of the brown-tiled room, sat a naked man with a gash on his forehead, his back leaning against the wall, his head slumped on his chest. Water beat onto his forehead, washing away the fresh blood. It must have been a hard and unexpected blow, because knowing Stano Malý, a single blow would not have taken him out. There was no sign of a struggle. I looked at my watch. It was 7.13 p.m. I was thirteen minutes late.

It looked like the opening of a mystery novel. But I had no desire to take on the role of a detective that someone had set me up for. The letters, the telegram, Paris, Hotel Boboty, the bus, the driver, the man in the green coat, the receptionist, Stano with a cracked skull. It didn't make sense, and yet I had the feeling they were all connected. The facts were there, but there was no apparent explanation.

I turned off the shower. The sudden silence magnified the unreality of this bloody and very real situation.

I left the room and walked down the silent hallways covered in thick crimson carpet towards the reception desk; not even my own steps could be heard. The bored receptionist was slurping her Christmas Eve sauerkraut soup. Through the large glass doors I could see into the dining room. Guests dressed in their holiday best were sitting around a table for the Christmas Eve dinner. Someone was praying out loud in German. The dog that looked like a calf was snoring in the entryway. The driver was sitting at the table and talking with the maths teacher Fedor Sitniansky, who had to keep talking so as not to throw up. Fedor must have just got here, because he was still wearing his green coat. Both of them waved at me. The receptionist put down her spoon and gave me a questioning look.

'It won't be as boring around here as you thought,' I said.

•

Dog Days

It was the dog days. I can't think of a more fitting name. I had run across it in a French dictionary. It said—*canicule*—dog days (period of great heat).

I didn't feel like going to the public pool, instead I decided to find a secluded spot by the river. I was walking to the bus stop when a man who was about thirty bumped into me, mumbled an apology, and hurried on. I don't even know why I turned around and didn't just continue on my way. His facial expression must have caught my eye, because it didn't fit that listless afternoon when everyone was glad not to have to move; yes, even the fact that he was in a hurry may have been the source of my spontaneous interest. His face was red and sweaty, his lips were clenched and angry, yet he was out of breath, therefore, his mouth should have been open—the contrast made it look as though he had forgotten to breathe normally on account of his anger. As it was, I turned around and followed him for a few steps. Had I known what I'd be getting myself into, I would have most certainly gone on my way, and I wouldn't be in the middle of trying to figure out the reasons behind the death of a stranger. I find myself in an unfortunate situation. I know that I won't uncover anything; I know that everything will remain in the realm of theories, and I'll only be left with guesses. Yet it'll take me a long time to forget about the whole thing. The worst part is that by coincidence or by the hand of fate, I am the only disinterested person who knows that the death of the old man is connected with the episode, or more accurately, the incident, I had got myself entangled in when I turned around to follow the thirty-year-old man who had bumped into me. He knows the whole secret; I only know a part of it. I stand on the threshold of a secret in full awareness of the fact that I will never cross that threshold, which is quite irritating. I know that the secret will remain hidden, because one man is dead, and the other has a vested interest in evading clarification. Moreover, I'm convinced that he's gone, and I'll never see him again.

The man who had bumped into me and whom I followed caught up with an older man who was walking alone and reminded me of my old history professor. The old man looked surprised, and quite frightened, as I observed. It was clear they knew each other. The old man extended his right hand, but the other man seemed not to notice, which made me feel sorry for the old man who made a clumsy attempt at covering it up by scratching his head. I was about fifty feet from them, and there wasn't a soul on the entire street (a narrow street tucked in between old houses). The younger man was angry, and the older one tried to calm him down. It looked as though the younger man was asking the old man for something, but the old man either didn't have it or didn't want to hand it over. He kept shrugging his shoulders and shaking his head; it looked more like an apology than a refusal. Out of nowhere the younger man slapped him. The old man put up no resistance, he neither resisted nor defended himself; he didn't even lift his hand to rub his cheek. It looked like he had been expecting the slap and that it was fully deserved. When the younger man slapped him again, I started running towards them.

I can't remember my exact words, all I know is that I placed myself between the two of them, and to my great surprise, the old man was much more alarmed by my intervention than his adversary. He begged me not to interfere, saying that it was their business; he begged me to leave them alone. Throughout my intervention the younger man stood aside with his hands in his pockets and a smug smile; I couldn't tell whether his smugness was in response to me or to the old man's visible fear.

I must admit that my pride was somewhat wounded, and I felt like they had made a fool of me, so I left without another word, angry at the old fart who had spurned my help. A little later, on the bus that was taking me to the river, I felt guilty about my pride, but I still couldn't shrug off my anger.

I found a secluded spot where the river flowed freely. Sharp rocks protruded from the water and empty oil barrels littered the shore. I took off my clothes and got in the water. I couldn't plunge into the cool waves, because I would have most certainly torn my belly on a hidden rock. With the soles of my feet I felt around for a path that would lead me to a safe depth. The rocks were slick and treacherous; one wrong step and my foot would land in a narrow opening and break, making a cracking sound which would be dulled by the water; above the surface no one would be any the wiser; they'd only find out once the foot emerged; bloody meat pierced by shards of bone.

I swam to the middle of the river, where I felt a strong, irresistible current, and I let it carry me. I would have loved to be carried, farther and farther, I would have loved to become one with this force of nature, I would have loved to give in to the river and flow into the sea, but I felt a sudden urge to smoke a cigarette. I started to swim towards the left bank, cutting the surface of the water with powerful strokes, struggling against the strong current which didn't want to release me from its clutches.

By the time I stepped ashore, I was out of breath. My arms, my legs, my whole body shook from the effort. I broke into a run on the riverbank. The hot pavement warmed the soles of my feet; soon they were dry. My body also dried off quickly in the heavy, dense, burning air. The exhaustion was gone, and I was enjoying the shore and the fresh breeze, which had been conjured out of the burning shroud by my moving body.

I found some flat rocks, got naked, and lay down on the hot surface. It scorched my skin; I jumped up, scooped up some water in my hands, and baptized those mute faces, which came to life as the water touched them and they hissed in irritation. Then I lay back down, and with unspeakable delight I smoked three cigarettes in a row with my eyes closed, the cold water lapping at my feet. I felt the taut skin all over my body, but especially on my face; as if it had shrunk, dried out; it was constricting my expanding muscles.

I don't know when I fell asleep. What woke me up was the crashing of waves breaking on rocks. The spray of cool water made me shudder. A big barge with a tricolour flag flapping in the wind was sailing upstream. The crew was looking at me with binoculars. I waved my fist at them in outrage, but they misinterpreted my gesture and waved back. Soon the surface of the water calmed down again. I brought my head to the level of the water, and I saw an infinite plane glistening in the sun and merging with

the blue sky off in the distance. The horizon disappeared; everything was blending with everything else. Unbridled. The water
flowed calmly and evenly, and it never occurred to it to turn back
towards its source. My head was burning, blood rushing against
my skull. My throat was parched. I rolled onto my belly and stuck
my head into the water. It felt as though the water was evaporating
as it made contact with my hot skin. Then I drank. I took in long
draughts; the water had no taste.

When I tore my lips away from the water, I spotted a dog not
far from shore, flailing as if it were drowning. I wasn't sure if dogs
could swim; this one must not have learnt yet. I thought about
jumping in and pulling it out, but then I saw a long branch. I held
it out to the dog, and the dog was smart enough to grab it with
its teeth and let itself be pulled ashore. It was a small dog and by
my estimate young as well, practically a pup. Its wet fur was
matted and bristled. Its whole body trembled, I didn't know
whether from fear or the cold. It must have been one of those
dogs condemned by merciful owners, who didn't have the heart
to kill their mute friend; they just dragged it far away from its
home in hopes that it wouldn't find its way back. I set it down on
the hot stones so it would dry off and warm up. It occurred to me
that the dog probably didn't belong to anyone and I could keep it.
After all, I did save its life. I seized upon this thought, smiled at
the dog, petted it, and spoke to it in an unfamiliar language. I was
thrilled I'd finally have a dog, like all of my neighbours. I'll
befriend it, train it according to some dog-training manual, we'll
be inseparable. I won't demean it with guard duty; it'll sleep on
my bed. I felt so happy that I lay down on my back again and
placed the dog on my chest. It balled up trustingly and warmed
itself in the blazing sun. Once it was dry, it livened up. I got worried
that the dog would bite off my little animal—shrunk, resting,

huddled in the black thicket between my legs. But it went the other direction. It fidgeted, crawled up my chest, and settled down on my shoulder. I felt its snout on my neck, its breath, its wet, rough tongue. Then I panicked, thinking it could bite into my carotid artery. My whole body stiffened with fear, shivers ran down my spine. I wanted to grab the dog and take it off my shoulder, but as I made the sharp movement, I poked it in the eye. The dog growled in pain, and in the midst of the commotion, it bit my finger. My brain was clouded with rage. So that's how you're going to be. That's how you repay me for saving you. My human impulses took over—I demanded gratitude and when I didn't get it, I growled back at the dog, gnashed my teeth, and bit it in the neck. The dog defended itself and bit my cheek. I repaid it in kind. For a while we kept biting each other. I felt fur and ear cartilage between my teeth. Then I snatched the dog and hurled it into the water. My injured cheek was bleeding. I was spitting fur, picking up rocks, and throwing them at the dog that was flailing in the water. The fourth rock finished it off. The water turned pink. The dog stopped flailing, it was far away, and I thought I saw it sinking.

Disgusted, I got dressed. I hope it didn't have rabies, I thought, and I decided to go have the wound treated, just to be on the safe side.

When I came out from behind the bushes that had been protecting me from potential curious glances, I saw a man. His back was turned to me. He had just thrown a white rope over a thick tree branch. The ends of the rope swung freely, and as the sunlight that was making its way between the leaves hit them, they glistened at irregular intervals; it was clear that the rope was brand new. The man was old and frail, and already from behind he seemed familiar. As soon as he turned around, I recognized him; he was looking around helplessly, as if searching for someone to assist him. Before I could hide, he waved at me. Reluctantly I stepped out from behind the bushes. He was taken aback because he, too, recognized me. Without losing his composure he greeted me politely.

'We keep running into each other today,' I said, smiling.

'I apologize for refusing your help earlier,' he said, 'I hope you weren't offended.'

'No, not at all.'

'Still, I must thank you, even if it is after the fact. I was too agitated back there.'

'I understand,' I said, 'I don't think you're used to getting slapped out on the street.'

'Please, let's not talk about that any more,' he said. 'I'm sure you understand . . . '

'Of course,' I interrupted. 'Would you like a cigarette?'

'No, thank you. I smoke a pipe,' he said, and pulled out a pipe in a leather case from his pocket. 'I'd like to ask you for a favour . . . ' he started evasively, glancing towards the rope.

'Certainly,' I said, because I knew what it was about. It was obvious that it would be difficult for him to climb the tree and tie the rope on the branch.

'Thank you,' he said, as he watched me climb the tree.

I tied the rope and made a noose without any trouble. The rope seemed a little thin, but I thought better of meddling in his affairs, given my prior experience.

'You're very kind,' he said when he finished smoking.

'It's no trouble at all. I just don't know what you'll step up on,' I said. 'I mean, I could lift you up to the noose, but that could be construed as murder, and I'd rather not get mixed up in that.'

'Oh, heavens, no, I wouldn't want to get you in any trouble.'

He looked around and saw the oil barrels littering the shore.

'They're empty. That'll work,' I said.

Together we brought over a barrel and set it under the noose. It left an oil stain on the old man's white shirt. That completely threw him off. He must have had a strict wife. I tried to calm him down; I didn't want him leaving this world in a state of mental turmoil. I more or less managed. Then he shook my hand and said he was glad to have met me. 'Really, I'm very glad to have met such a kind and helpful person,' he said.

I responded with a set phrase. 'The pleasure is all mine.' Then he asked me to leave. 'I'd like to spare you a sight that may not be too aesthetic.'

Although I had a strong desire to ask him why he was doing it, I didn't want to tarnish his good opinion of me, besides which— granting someone's last wish is the right thing to do.

I went to the river and thoroughly washed my oily hands. When I came back, I concluded that contrary to my expectations the rope had held. He had already turned stiff. He looked good except for the oil stain on his shirt, which was an eyesore.

I left in a hurry. I didn't want anyone to figure out that I had been a witness. I could have offered no clarification, and no one would have been interested in my theories.

My head felt like it was on fire. I had a splitting headache, blood was rushing against my skull.

Mitigating Circumstances

Before I begin, I'd like to emphasize my role in this story so as to avoid unnecessary misunderstandings later on. I am only an observer! An observing narrator, with no influence whatsoever on the events. Observation brings me a certain—shall we say—aesthetic pleasure. It's true that I discuss my observations, so one might say there's also an ethical element at play. There's no point denying it: I'm an undercover ethicist. My intentions are purely humanistic. Humanism is also the motivation for my testimony. Humanism and an irrepressible desire for truth. Yes, I'm interested in truth—as an aesthetic category. I offer this testimony in hopes that it'll carry the weight of mitigating circumstances for the subjects of my observation.

I am the only person who knows how long it took Johan to bring himself to make a decisive move. His long-standing, atavistic dislike for decision-making was to blame. And besides, he loved her. (Despite the fact that, naturally, he hated her.) I know that because I know Johan better than he knew himself; that would be the ever-so-popular objectivity. Yes, he hated her, but he couldn't find the courage to leave her; clearly, she was a woman beyond his capabilities. When he finally realized it, the rest was just a matter of time and opportunity.

It was definitely not a cold-blooded murder. I don't know whether it vindicates Johan, but I'd be willing to testify under oath that in the time between the decision and the act, he experienced some of the most difficult moments of his life. It made him a particularly interesting, hard-to-peg subject; I didn't know whether he was going to go through with it until the last moment. No, it was definitely not a cold-blooded murder.

He had confided his decision to me one day in April, in a drunken stupor. I'm convinced that before he had spoken those words, the thought had not crossed his mind. He said them out of anger, in a fit; it was the alcohol talking. He wasn't in control of his tongue, that small appendage, and so a tiny flame kindled a big fire. When he said it, his own words frightened him; he got pale as wax and a small red spot appeared under his left eye. Indeed, the tongue is a flame, a world of injustice, it stains the whole body and fuels the circle of life from birth, and is itself wrought by hell. I had known him since childhood, and the waxy colour of his face with the tiny flaming stain under his left eye was an unmistakable sign: he was serious.

I said, 'Oh, you'll sleep it off.'

He just looked at me without a word and downed another glass of cognac. I must admit, when I heard his words I felt a certain satisfaction, and he was well aware of it. I know he worked hard to cover up the conflicts that had been wrecking his marriage with Agatha long before that day in April; yes, had he not misspoken in his drunkenness, nothing might have happened. But once it was out, once he had failed to tame his tongue, that restless evil, the tongue full of deadly poison, he had to be true to his word; he couldn't stand the idea that I might think him a coward, that I might disdain him.

A month later he called me at the office, stuttering from anger. He said he had to meet with me that afternoon; he had to talk to me because (supposedly) he was going out of his mind.

Then he repeated his words, but this time he was completely sober [sic]. Once more I said to him, 'Oh, you'll sleep it off.'

He swore at me for a long time. Yes, Johan had a particularly rich vocabulary, unlike mine. I used to envy him. With his saccharine words he had sowed discord between me and Agatha. He had won her with words; he had separated us with the sword that was his mouth. It took me a long time to come to understand that language had been the instrument of his victory, but it was also going to be the instrument of his doom. My weapon was silence.

When he stopped swearing at me five minutes later, he said, 'Are you glad to be glad?'

I shrugged.

'You were right, huh?' He went on.

I yawned.

'You can't imagine what hell it is. You can't imagine what a viper she is.'

'If I'm not mistaken, I said that to you seven years ago.'

'Fine, you warned me. But you don't understand my strange love for her. I'm not capable of leaving her.'

'I thought you said you've made up your mind. Stop making a fool of yourself.'

'You'd like that, wouldn't you? No, my friend, I won't give you that satisfaction.'

'I won't kill her just to spite you.' I said, laughing. 'Cut the drama. Let's go sleep it off.'

It worked every time. He got pale as wax and the crimson mark flared up under his left eye.

'Fine,' he said. 'I'll prove to you that I'm not a coward.'

'What's there to prove, my dear Johan? You want to kill her because you can't bring yourself to leave her. Stop making it sound like you want to kill her to do me a favour.'

'It's awful how much you despise her,' he said a moment later, perplexed. 'And I love you so much, you swine.'

'That's nice, but—sorry. I can't help you. My predilection for the opposite sex must be genetic.'

'You swine, what a genetic swine you are.'

Once more I turned necessity into virtue; for lack of vocabulary, I shrouded myself in the raincoat of silence. It was pouring outside.

At our next meeting he confided in me, drunk, 'It's in the works, you've got something to look forward to.'

'What's in the works?' I asked, confused.

'A little murder, he—he—he.'

I watched him, with apprehension, pity and eyes full of concern. He noticed, took it in, and reacted in a surprisingly sober manner, 'You think it's paranoia—not yet, darling, not yet.'

'When?'

'Soon. On a family vacation.'

'Gun, knife, rope, strangulation?'

'Don't joke around, you may regret it. You'll piss me off and I won't go through with it.'

'What are you talking about?'

'You rabble-rouser, I hate you. If only you knew how much I hate you.'

'Why?'

'Because I love you, you slut.'

'And because I had her before you.'

'Get lost, dear.'

I was starting to believe that something might come of it, although there was always a chance that Johan would change his mind at the last minute; you never know with neurotics. He couldn't hold out much longer though: the fire sparked by the tongue was glowing . . .

Summer came, and Bratislava was as empty as my soul. Johan hadn't been in touch, and I didn't look for him. After all, I'm just an observer, with no influence on events. The fire glowed, and I kindled it with my silence. I was silent in three ways: words, wishes and thoughts.

Near the end of July, my phone rang—it was long distance. I found out that the family vacation had begun. Johan said they had already been there a week, and he asked me to come right away. I didn't hesitate. A good observer should be near his subject; besides, I couldn't refuse to help him because I was his only friend. Indeed, I was the only one still loyal to him, the rest had abandoned him because of Agatha. Or more accurately, he abandoned them—Agatha didn't like sharing him with anyone.

They were vacationing in the High Tatras—novelty had never been Johan's strong suit. I checked in at Hotel Panoráma, having reserved a room in advance. They were staying at the Patria. Johan didn't want Agatha to know about me; he was afraid of 'arousing her suspicion'. We met that night at my hotel bar. Johan looked underslept, stressed, and pale as wax.

'It looks like your vacation isn't agreeing with you,' I said like a total dimwit.

'It's high time for me to go through with it. A few more days, and I'll be fit for the loony bin.'

'You're full of it, my friend, and you don't even know it.'

The hellish rose bloomed under his left eye.

'Tomorrow,' he said. 'I've got it all figured out.'

After a few glasses of cognac, he told me his plan. Simple, effective. They went for a hike in the mountains every day. He had picked a spot, remote and isolated—a rock wall and a deep precipice.

'Do not follow your base desires, but restrain your appetites.' I warned him against falling into the precipice, but he wasn't listening. He said that all he had to do was give Agatha a little push and then call the Mountain Rescue Service and play a loving husband insane with grief. As I said, the plan had promise thanks to its simplicity. The only potential catch in the plan, or even its downfall, would be Johan's resolve. I confided my doubts. Justifiably indignant, he drank himself into a stupor; I had to bring him to my room. It only cost us 1,000 crowns, the receptionist handed me the bill. Johan fell fast asleep. A baby. In my bed.

I wasn't tired, so I decided to go for an evening stroll. After walking around Štrbské Pleso twice, I stopped in front of Hotel Patria, filled with nostalgia. Clearly, I desired Agatha, yes, I desired her. I wanted to make love to her one last time. God be with her, but I still loved her to death, and when I realized that the next day it would all be in the past, I must admit, I felt like crying. But I curbed my base instincts. For twelve minutes, I stood beneath the windows of my dear Agatha's hotel, and then I went back to my strange bed. To Johan. But more about that later . . .

As I walked towards the bed of my beloved Agatha's future murderer, a scream shot out of a window on the sixth floor like a poisoned arrow—it pierced my head, passed through my spine (it missed the heart, which nevertheless skipped a few beats), and left my body through my groin, nailing me to the ground.

'Johan,' Agatha shouted. 'Johan, come back!'

However it happened, she spotted me. God only knows why she had been looking out the window just then. (*Editor's Note*: Such a coincidence would not occur in highbrow literature, but life is fairly crass and doesn't give a damn about rules or the aesthetic canon—which is why it looks the way it does.) She waved her left pinkie at me, and less than five minutes later I was where I wanted to be!

Situation report (9.03 p.m.–11.05 p.m.): on top of Agatha, under Agatha, behind Agatha, under Agatha, but always in her—then, wear and tear.

'Fuck, did I need this?' I raved in the insatiable arms of the nymphomaniac sentenced to death, feeling guilty as I caressed her velvety red pelt.

'You did, you did, it was absolutely necessary.' She wiggled her bum, almost with remorse. 'Hey, I must come clean about something.'

'Dark, dark, dark mountains, many a time did I cross them . . .' Singing hikers passing by the hotel walked into our bare story.

I got frightened! Was I awake or dreaming? Here was Agatha, over there was Johan, and the next day I was going to be an accomplice.

'Agi, I have to come clean about something, too.'

'Shhh.' She pressed her salty pink oyster to my lips. 'After,' she whispered.

'After what?' I mumbled into the shell.

'After, when it's all over!'

'Agi, it's already over, and tomorrow it'll all be done!'

'It's over?' the little fox asked, checked and, disappointed, answered her own question, 'You're right. It's over. Your birdie used to be able to sing 'til dawn.'

'We were younger.'

'You were younger, I haven't changed.'

'Prove it.'

'We'll raise the dead, don't you worry.'

Agatha dispersed my dark thoughts with several contractions of her carmine-black lips—the silent language of her tongue was sweet and meaningful, the way it had been in the fifties of our past life—she made me visible again. Sadly, it only lasted a few seconds. I imagined Agatha and Johan on a hike the next day, and the bird was done for. (I'm no necrophile, and Agatha was de jure dead.) I freed myself from under that load (she must have gained at least fifty pounds), and apologetically, I placed my cold hand on Agatha's breast. 'Agi, my pet, let's be serious.'

'Are you saying . . . that you've been kidding around until now?'

Testing the waters, hopeful, she squeezed my balls.

'Ouch, Agi, cut that out, I'm sore.'

'Soar, soar, you used to soar, but those days are o'er,' the disappointed Agatha improvised, and then she went to the bidet.

That's when it hit me—poor Agi isn't just fat, she's also hard of hearing; that's why Johan wants to kill her, the swine. While she was thin and her hearing was good, he used her without any scruples, but when God punished her for spreading alarming news . . . no, no, killing the hard-of-hearing Agatha, no, I didn't like that one bit. I watched the old, fat, wrinkly and hard-of-hearing Agatha hovering over the bidet, and my soul was torn by a dilemma: Should I warn her? Does she deserve it? Will she consider my sincere warning a betrayal or, alternately, snitching?

'Agi, I have to come clean about something.' I plucked up my courage for the Judas act.

'I know.'

'You know?'

'Dumbass, I've always known. I love you, too.'

I'm afraid we're victims of a huge misunderstanding, I thought, but what I said was: 'Too late. You shouldn't have left me.'

'It's never too late for love. I've got it figured out. We'll start over. I'll come back. To you.'

'Agi, stop babbling, you're going to die tomorrow.'

'Today, tomorrow, the day after tomorrow, yesterday, the day before that . . .' Dear Agatha clearly didn't believe me.

'Damn it, did I need this?'

'You did, it was always you I wanted.'

'Agi, focus, I want to . . .'

'Me too . . .'

'Emigrate?' She threw a towel at me, 'Dumbass,' she said. 'Dry me off, thoroughly. I want to go back, to you.'

'I'm afraid you're repeating yourself. And what about Johan?'

'I'll kill him,' she said. 'I've got a plan . . . '

Agatha's plan was simple yet effective. The next day they'd go hiking. She had picked a spot, remote and isolated—a rock wall and a deep precipice.

'Do not follow your base desires, but restrain your appetites.' I warned her against falling into the precipice, but she wasn't listening. She said she'd give Johan a little push, etc. . . .

I'm sure you can understand how my moral dilemma was becoming monstrous: Whom should I warn? Johan or Agatha? Agatha or Johan? I washed my bird and went back to my hotel.

Johan was sprawled on my bed and pretended to mistake me for Agatha, 'Darling, please be a little kinder to me, I can't help being the way I am . . .'

After a few slaps he confessed gratefully; he was using Agatha to get inside me, because love doesn't choose its victims based on genetics, love is cruel and merciless, it'll burn out a fire, in short, Gomorrah. He took a liking to getting slapped, 'yeth, thweet-heart, yeth, too bad you don't have a whip' . . . Truth be told, I couldn't blame Agatha, what with such a lisping husband! But the thing that upset me most was his self-justification; he even dragged God into it. He was interpreting the next day's murder as an act of self-defence, and at 4 in the morning, he was trying to persuade me: We all act in self-defence, imitating the ancient gesture of our Creator, who cast us out of paradise in self-defence, and then he persecuted us in self-defence, yes, in self-defence he descended from heaven to prevent us from building the tower of Babel; in self-defence he scattered us all over the Earth and confused our languages so we wouldn't understand one another and threaten his despotic rule, 'thweetheart, he ith the one rethponthible for all of the current national unretht, for all the thivil and non-thivil wars, I'm only imitating him, yeth, thweetheart, I mutht kill Agatha in thelf-defenthe, becauthe she realithed that her body ith only a bridge between you and me, we all act in thelf-defenthe, take my word for it, and thtop thulking . . .'

I yanked the telephone cord out of the wall and whipped him for ten minutes in self-defence, cruel and merciless, and I was more or less unhappy, but the happy Johan Gomorrah unhappily squealed in delight, and I was once more up to my ears in a dilemma: To warn or not to warn? And if to warn—then whom? There was a brief glimmer of hope: perhaps prophecies of inevitable events only come to pass if the conditions that make their fulfilment possible remain unchanged, but, if the three of us attempted to come to an agreement . . . I stopped whipping Gomorrah, and plugged the telephone cord where it belonged. Johan anxiously watched my unscrupulous endeavour, and when I asked him for dear Agatha's phone number, he sounded embittered, but he retained his dignity and said almost matter-of-factly: 'I knew you'd betray me . . . you sadist.'

He got dressed and went to do what he had to.

In the doorway, he said in parting, 'I had hoped you were better and smarter. I chose you. You have to immerse yourself up to your ears in the mud of sin in order to be saved and start a new life as a beginning evangelist. Unfortunately, I see that even for the chosen ones the veil is only lifted gradually.'

He left me alone, deep in thought: Couldn't I have sacrificed myself and requited his love? After all, he wasn't asking that much of me. I'm sure he would have been content with whipping. By whipping the despised Johan, I would have been in the role of a masochist; by refusing his masochistic demands, I established myself as a sadist. Do I have the right to judge Johan for his predisposition towards both sexes? Even angels are hermaphrodites. Would my instinctive preference for the opposite sex be an adequate excuse for my complicity in Agatha's death?

I found out at 4 in the afternoon. The phone woke me up. It was the reception desk. 'You have a visitor.' I invited the visitor for a short audience.

'Can you believe it, that asshole tried to kill me.' Agatha's face was smouldering with justifiable anger.

'I warned you.'

'He actually wanted to push me . . . into *my* precipice.'

'How come he didn't?'

'I pushed him first.'

'Thank goodness. Did a red spot appear under his left eye?'

'How do you know?'

'You don't need to feel guilty. His mind was made up. You acted in self-defence.'

I lasted almost two years with her. Johan was right; she's a viper, an unbelievable viper. I'm scared of her. I'm scared I'll end up like my best friend who let his tongue loose, that small appendage, and yet what hellfire it unleashed. That's why I decided to give this testimony, motivated by an irresistible desire for a truthful life. There's nothing to be done; dear, deaf, fat Agatha gained another twenty pounds, and she must pay for her crime. Love and truth must once and for all vanquish lies and hate. But I'd be grateful if you showed her leniency. After all, she acted in self-defence.

●

The Breeze and the Others

1

It happened on a sultry day at the beginning of July. The forty-five-year-old Veronika Studená, employed as the administrative assistant to the director of the Central Institute for Research on the Effective Use of Public Lands in Bratislava, came home from work tired and apathetic, and without thinking about anything in particular, she automatically started to open the envelopes she had picked up from her letterbox on the ground floor. As usual, all of the letters were addressed to her husband, which didn't surprise her, because ever since she married Viktor many years ago, not a single envelope with her name on it had appeared in the post box. Mrs Veronika got married, and from that point on it was as though she ceased to exist.

After taking a shower, she opened all the windows in hopes that a breeze would cool down the stifling hot air a little; she was dizzy from its stillness, and felt like her blood pressure had dropped to its lowest limit. Two shots of cognac later, she felt noticeably better, and so, wearing nothing but a towel made of a delicate fabric that gently caressed her wet shoulders, she walked up to the window, and in a friendly manner, without a trace of exhibitionism or flirtation she waved at the seventy-nine-year-old Zoltán Horváth, just as she did every day; he was sitting on the balcony of his flat across the street, stripped down to the waist, with his head uncovered and completely bald, heroically and with no concern for potential heat stroke exposing his body to the blitz of the sun's rays.

When he noticed Veronika in the window, he moved a primer off his lap, jumped up, and gallantly, with one hand over his heart, he bowed. Mrs Veronika blushed like an innocent schoolgirl when she noticed Mr Zoltán's elegant swim trunks, on this particular day gleaming bright red, the colour of fresh bull's blood.

'That may be pushing it,' Veronika whispered, knowing full well there was no point in shouting, because the street which separated them was always teeming with traffic: the noise made any attempt at verbal contact impossible. In truth, they didn't need to speak; they understood each other without words, they both knew where they stood. A long time ago Veronika had sensed that Mr Zoltán was madly in love with her, and since she was kind-hearted by nature, she unselfishly afforded him this daily glance at her naked body—out of pity, as it were. She knew that besides reading the primer it was his only and possibly his last pleasure in life, of which, according to Viktor Studený, Mrs Veronika's husband, there wasn't much left.

And she always took her husband at his word, but what's more is that she was so devoted to him that during the course of their matrimony (sometimes she felt like they had been married for an eternity) she had never been unfaithful, though this fact introduces an undesirable element of improbability, even unreality, into our real-life story, but what is to be done—that is how it was. She was so devoted to him that when he, having studied the works of prominent futurologists at length, reached the conclusion that bringing children into a world on the brink of an urbanistic, ecological, atmospheric, nutritional, demographic, and a number of other kinds of catastrophes was completely irresponsible, Veronika agreed with him without any hesitation, and what's more—when her husband informed her on their wedding night (after having completed an exhaustive review of a number of expert sexological treatises) that undeniably the best protection against unwanted conception is complete abstinence, Mrs Veronika, with a dose of nostalgia, agreed with his argument— she had to concede that it really was the most effective method.

But ever since May, when she unwittingly stood in front of the window of her fourth-floor flat for the first time and met old Mr Zoltán Horváth's spellbound gaze, something so peculiar was happening to her that it frightened her. She wandered around the flat inexplicably confused, soulless, she kept touching objects which used to be intimately familiar, a part of her everyday life, but which now seemed mysterious, foreign, practically hostile; she wandered around the flat as if searching for something which had never belonged to her, yet she felt as though she had lost it. What am I looking for, what do I seek so urgently and senselessly, she kept asking herself, and in her faithful, loving, obedient soul sprouted a heretical seed of distrust towards her own husband, which grew into an apprehensively formulated question: Is this really it? Does it have to be the way Viktor says? Is life really nothing more than a hyphen between two catastrophes? Are there no alternatives?

Viktor, who was twenty years older than Veronika, very quickly noticed that there was something wrong with his wife, but when he asked her for an explanation, he received no reply.

Veronika was depressed and anxious, she felt that speaking and remaining silent were equally dangerous. She had a vague sense that if she were to confide her doubts to her husband, he'd accuse her of lying, because he was convinced that after having been together for so many years, which at least in his mind had been filled with harmony and mutual understanding, there could be no room for the demon of doubt in Veronika's soul. But silence is not the answer, she kept telling herself. If I don't say something, he'll accuse me of disapproving of our way of life. And he's not one to substantiate his accusations, because he believes that the accusation itself is proof of its own veracity.

Veronika wasn't the only one who had changed since that memorable day in May. From the moment he caught a glimpse of the naked Veronika framed by the rectangle of the window, the seventy-nine-year-old Zoltán Horváth had been undergoing such visible changes that there wasn't a person around who hadn't noticed them.

With each passing day, Mr Zoltán seemed to get a year younger.

The man who used to sit on the balcony had been frail and had had one foot in the grave, but at the end of June, Viktor said to Veronika with barely suppressed anger, 'Have you noticed that dirty old man across the street? He must have got a girlfriend. He's taken up swimming and supposedly he's working out with those exercise springs. What an idiot, the whole street's laughing at him.' Thus spoke Viktor, and then he got back to work, because having been an industrious person since childhood he continued to work now, five years after his retirement, serving on the Civic Committee as a speaker at civil funerals. Each performance earned him forty-six crowns, on top of which he had been issued a Lurex robe. The robe was made of a black-and-silver woven fabric; Viktor loved it so much that he would have slept in it had it not been for his innate respect for government property, honed by years of work as a stock-keeper. Truth be told, it wasn't just the Lurex robe, what had led him down the path of funeral oration was mostly his atheist persuasion. He decided to fight religious obscurantism, because ever since he had an appendectomy ten years earlier, he became a staunch atheist. He had it all figured out—if there was a thing as useless as an appendix, then clearly there was no such thing as absolute God-given purpose, which was supposed to be the proof of our creator's wisdom. The existence of the appendix became his refutation of the existence of God. Finally his soul found peace, though the truth of the matter was that every time before he started to write an official farewell for a departed taxpayer, he secretly said a quick prayer—better safe than sorry.

'Veronika, what do you think of this for an introduction? River waters flow eternally through their riverbeds down to the sea, then they return to land, the mountains, the fields, thus completing their endless cycle. And so it is with life. It begins, it blazes, and it dies out. Constantly, with no end or beginning. Consequently, love too is eternal, and so are death, birth and dying. Our dear friend, who had reached the finish line of his life, was like the May rains, fertilizing our lives with his existence, industriousness and his abilities, and now it is time for us to say goodbye . . . Good, isn't it?' Viktor rubbed his hands together, burning with creative fervour, and continued to write.

Veronika knew that Viktor couldn't have cared less about her opinion, that he only read aloud out of habit and out of a desire to impress her with his wit and originality (he really believed those were his own words, because he had been using them for so long that he had them memorized, and he had forgotten that he used to copy them from an instruction booklet for funeral speakers, and so years of repeating formulaic thoughts evoked in him a blissful feeling of originality, so dear to the hearts of all epigones), she knew his enjoyment would not have been diminished had he been reading it aloud to a pet if they had one, although that was completely out of the question; five years ago, when she confided in him her desire to get a cat or a dog, Viktor flew off the handle, and bellowed, 'Stop spewing nonsense!', but when he noticed the frightened look on her face, he added in a voice full of fatherly empathy, 'Don't you realize it's animal torture?' Back then she still believed him, she thought he was really speaking out of compassion for the poor animals that were wasting away in bleak corners of the city's blocks of flats. Back then, she believed him, but now as she listened to the zeal with which he read the introduction to his eulogy, she was struck by a terrifying thought: No, it's not compassion motivating him not to want a cat or a dog, it's that they're living beings; he doesn't want them because he hates life.

And suddenly, in a moment of dejection-induced clairvoyance it occurred to her that the thing she had been seeking with such urgency was herself, the lost Veronika—she had been searching for herself and for love, a love which could fill the emptiness of the flat and of her desolate soul; and with panic on her face, in a voice trembling with surprise at her own audacity, she said, 'Viktor, do you realize that I'm still alive?'

Viktor raised his head and, for a second, he stared at her in disbelief—as if the armchair had spoken, or the table, or one of the three painted Easter eggs covered in the dust of oblivion in the china cabinet between the porcelain and the crystal. Then he got up from his desk, walked up to her, stroked her hair gently, and said to her in a soothing voice, 'I'm sorry, Veronika. That will change.'

Upon hearing his words Veronika's blue eyes got wide, revealing an unspoken question, which brought Viktor back to his senses. He realized that his answer had a certain inappropriate meaning, or at best was a double entendre, so he quickly added, 'What I was trying to say was . . . that I've been neglecting you lately. You wouldn't believe how much time the deceased can take up. You know, darling, we're both getting up in years. It hasn't occurred to me that everyone wouldn't have the same amount of dignity and composure in dealing with the change. We'll take a beach vacation next year.'

The change, so he thinks that I'm a mentally disturbed woman going through menopause—Veronika's breathing was agitated and indignant, but she wasn't able to stand up to him. Her will was paralysed by Viktor's tone of voice, the protective, caring tone of a father, full of revolting condescension, which left her helpless and humiliated. It would be so much easier to stand up to him if he spoke to me with disdain; if he scorned me, I could hate him for it, she often said to herself, but Viktor didn't afford her even this slight satisfaction. There was never even a hint of disdain in his voice. His long tenure as chief stock-keeper had made him a decent psychologist, and he knew all too well that patience worked much better than disdain to keep people in line. Since the most important part of his job had been refusing requisitions for material which should have been in the storeroom but —for reasons beyond his control—wasn't, he learnt to listen patiently to the cursing of his indignant petitioners, and whenever such a maligner would finish covering him in bile from head to toe, Viktor would nod his head in agreement and smile indulgently, which would embarrass the person so much that instead of hating Viktor, to his own astonishment he'd turn red from shame, stutter apologetically, and leave the premises. He'd realize that Viktor could have dismissed him with arrogance and disdain; he'd realize that he needlessly chewed out a decent man, and the shame over his own brutish behaviour usually resulted in him never returning to bother the stock-keeper. Thus Viktor gained the reputation of being an incompetent but extremely polite person; over time everyone forgot about him, and he was finally able to prepare in peace, with a single-mindedness inherent to those who have an extraordinary amount of self-confidence or an extraordinary number of issues, for a post-retirement career as a funeral orator. Having stuttered since childhood, Viktor brought pockets full of pebbles to work every day, and since no one disturbed him during business hours, he taught himself to speak with pebbles in his mouth like Demosthenes, though not on the seashore but in an empty stockroom, so that when he was retiring, he stunned his colleagues by emerging from the cavernous space like a long-forgotten aquatic creature from the depths of the ocean, but more importantly, he stunned them with his incredible rhetorical prowess aptly demonstrated by his thank-you speech for the gold watch the company gave him to mark the occasion.

The change, so he thinks I'm a hysterical woman in menopause, Veronika reflected, recalling Viktor's words as she smiled at Mr Zoltán, who was standing on the balcony across the street in his elegant swim trunks the colour of fresh bull's blood and blowing her a kiss; the gesture came across as ridiculously old-fashioned, because Mr Zoltán looked like a strapping man in his prime that day, and in the reflective lenses of his dark sunglasses, Veronika could see her own body, the firm, shapely body of a mature forty-five-year-old woman, which made her feel all the more embarrassed when she remembered the day Viktor had indulgently said to her: 'It hasn't occurred to me that everyone wouldn't have the same amount of dignity and composure when dealing with the change . . .' and she replied in a quiet voice full of submissive resignation, 'You're probably right.' Viktor watched her tensely, like a trainer who observes a tamed lion that has been trying to disobey him for years and hesitates before jumping through a flaming hoop, but when he heard her response he laughed with relief, a short, abrupt laugh, like the crack of a whip, and Veronika reiterated, 'I'm sure you're right. I really didn't realize we were quite that ancient.'

So Veronika was standing naked in front of the window, and when Mr Zoltán blew her that ridiculously old-fashioned air kiss, she felt a sudden breeze, which finally stirred up the still, musty air in the flat. A delightful, exciting and heretofore unknown sensation permeated her whole body; she had to hold on to the windowsill, because the sweet tremors radiating from deep within her were so powerful they made her think—if I don't hold onto something, I'll lift off and fly out the window, if only I flap my wings. She cupped her hands over her breasts, which had just recently been drooping and lifeless and which she had regarded as a useless and repugnant burden, but thanks to Mr Zoltán's intoxicated gaze on that memorable day in May, they had turned into succulent fruit that ripened and filled with life-giving sap, and she was overwhelmed by an agonizing desire, if only someone would pluck them, suck out their sweet nectar and give them purpose, because a ripe harvest which doesn't benefit anyone is a sinful waste demanding the punishment of a ruthlessly just pagan deity, or of some other governing body in charge of the effective use of fallow arable land. In a slight daze Veronika realized that in her mind she had been dialectically conflating her own bountiful breasts with the day's state-wide meeting on irrigation use at which she had been the stenographer, and so with a subtle movement of her left hand she waved one last time to old Mr Zoltán Horváth, who had rivulets of perspiration streaming down his bald head, his glowing red face, and his tanned-to-perfection naked chest, and she stepped away from the window. She sank into an armchair languidly. All of a sudden, she felt tired and her eyes filled with tears, but this time they weren't tears of sadness, and just as she started to wonder why am I crying, what am I crying about, the ringing of the doorbell filled the flat. She looked at her watch—a quarter of five. Then she remembered that a TV repairman from Multiservis was supposed to show up that day, so she got up from the armchair and headed for the door, wiping away the shimmering salty drops that were slowly streaming down her face and beyond, forging a riverbed between her blossoming breasts.

She opened the door.

2

From that day on, Veronika never stood naked in front of the window again, but every day she hid behind the closed yellow blinds and looked at the balcony across the street, where old Mr Zoltán Horváth still sat and stared longingly, though in vain, at Mrs Veronika's window. With sadness and gratitude in her kind heart Veronika watched his gradual, relentless decline; ever since he stopped seeing Veronika in the window, he aged by a year each day; and when the summer heat was gone, and time in its eternal cycle imperceptibly brought cold autumn days on the wings of the north wind, he was once again a frail old man of seventy-nine with one foot in the grave, who bore no resemblance to that strapping man in the prime of his life from July.

And the day came, a cold, drizzly, November day, when Veronika placed a hand on her chest with a start; she thought she felt a tiny vein pop right under her heart. With her hand still on her chest she turned towards the china cabinet. She noticed broken pieces of eggshell which were all that was left of one of the delicate painted Easter eggs, and she immediately ran to the window. Old Mr Zoltán Horváth was sitting motionless on his balcony covered with a warm chequered blanket made of Scottish wool with his head thrown back, and his eyes were still turned towards Mrs Veronika's window, but there was no more yearning in his glassy stare, it was vacant. Veronika broke down in tears—she realized that Mr Zoltán Horváth's heart had broken, unassumingly and quietly, like the delicate painted egg.

The next day Veronika interrupted Viktor who was working on the eulogy for Zoltán Horváth, with these words: 'River waters flow eternally through their riverbeds down to the sea, then they return to land, the mountains, the fields, thus completing their endless cycle. And so it is with life. It begins, it blazes, and it dies out. Constantly, with no end or beginning. Consequently, love too is eternal, and so are death, birth and dying. Our dear friend, who had reached the finish line of his life, was like the May rains, fertilizing our lives with his existence, industriousness and his abilities, and now it is time for us to say goodbye.'

'What sort of drivel is this?' Viktor snapped at her, not recognizing his own words from an old obituary, having written dozens more since then.

'You could use it as the opening of Mr Horváth's eulogy,' Veronika suggested.

After a moment's thought Viktor dismissed her idea with a wave of his hand. 'Nonsense. That doesn't fit the old lecher.' He burst into a hearty laugh and added, 'You've really done it this time. Like the May rains, you said, fertilizing our lives with his existence, industriousness and his abilities . . . Oh, Veronika. He didn't even attend the May Day parades, besides which he was an incorrigible skirt-chaser and a habitual drunk. Do you have any idea what he died of? He drank himself to death, supposedly because a woman had left him. He was seventy-nine. Revolting . . . ' Viktor stopped talking for a moment, then he cheerfully slapped his forehead in an unexpected burst of inspiration. 'I've got it, how about this for an introduction?' he asked, all giddy, and as was his habit, he started to write and read aloud the introduction to his eulogy for Zoltán Horváth: 'They say that in ancient times the Greek hero Sisyphus expended a tremendous amount of effort rolling a boulder up a hill. Every time just before he would reach the peak, his foot would slip, and the boulder would tumble back down to the valley. Sisyphus had to start over. Are our efforts similarly wasted on battling alcoholism and its destructive consequences? . . . Well, what do you think? It fits, doesn't it?' Viktor asked, obviously pleased with himself, and his face beamed with the all-too-familiar delight and cheerful zeal which always accompanied his creative efforts. His question was only rhetorical, of course, and he wasn't expecting an answer, which is why Veronika's words caught him off guard and left him speechless: 'While an eagle may occasionally swoop down lower than a chicken, a chicken will never soar in the clouds.' Viktor gave Veronika a long, questioning look, as if trying to decide whether her absurd comment related in any way to his introduction to the eulogy for Zoltán Horváth, but after a moment of deep concentration, he must have concluded that Veronika's words were clearly a non sequitur. However, the combination of her nonsensical words and the gratuitous and unprecedented smile that lit up her face made him shudder with concern for her mental health. He got up from his desk, came up to Veronika, and spoke to her in his caring fatherly tone, tinged not only with benevolence but also a certain degree of trepidation and anxiety, 'What's wrong, my dear? Are you not feeling well? I'm sorry, my darling, I've been neglecting you lately. You wouldn't believe how much time the deceased can take up. You know, darling, we're both getting up in years. It hasn't occurred to me that everyone wouldn't have the same amount of dignity and composure in dealing with the change. We'll take a beach vacation next year. Perhaps I can find someone to substitute for me for a couple of days.'

'Perhaps when you're not around, people will stop dying,' Veronika chimed in with a smile. Is she being sarcastic? Viktor wondered, carefully observing her facial expression. No, he ascertained, there wasn't a hint of sarcasm in her smile. But there is something disturbing there, much more disturbing than sarcasm, damn it, what's all this about?

'What's with the stupid smirk?' Viktor barked abruptly, as if cracking a whip. But this time the lion didn't jump through the flaming hoop. Fear flashed across Viktor's face: Veronika's smile was a picture of self-assured triumph bordering on contempt. Viktor felt like he was suffocating, he loosened his tie with his shaky fingers, and squeaked in a muffled voice, 'Veronika . . . you're right . . . you're right . . . I've been thinking . . . you must be feeling lonely . . . I've decided you can go ahead and buy yourself one of those . . . live dogs . . . or would you prefer a live cat?'

'Thank you, Viktor, you really are unusually kind, but soon . . . Do you know how to write anything besides a eulogy?'

'Such as?'

'A speech on the occasion of the birth of a child.'

'That's not my area of expertise,' Viktor blurted out, and his whole body shuddered with loathing. 'Wait a minute! You're not, you're not telling me . . . '

Veronika nodded. 'I went to see a gynecologist. The test came back positive. I'm going to be a mother, Viktor!'

'Impossible! That would mean that I'd have to be a father. And I've never committed anything so irresponsible!'

'Don't worry, Viktor. You won't be a father,' Veronika reassured him.

Viktor turned pale and for quite some time he gaped straight ahead with blank, unseeing eyes, then he covered his hate-stricken face with his hands and sank heavily into an armchair.

'H-h-how? Y-y-you've b-b-been un-un-unfaithful?' The sudden shock instantly obliterated the results of years of diligent training with pebbles under his tongue in the enormous empty storeroom where he had been preparing for the career of a funeral orator— his stutter was back.

Veronika walked up to him and gently put her hand on his shoulder: 'No, no, Viktor. I've not been unfaithful.' And with a dreamy expression on her face she added, 'I think it was the breeze.'

Viktor jumped up from the armchair, and without so much as a stutter, he slapped her. 'What? The breeze? You bitch, are you telling me that you've been impregnated by the breeze?' Veronika looked at him with compassionate benevolence and nodded in agreement.

'Yes. I'm sure it was the breeze. You know how it is Viktor, it's in the air.'

'What? What's in the air?'

'Life, love, freedom, I don't know what to call it. But it's definitely in the air. You just have to stop being afraid and open the windows.'

'Stop with this nonsense! The air is contaminated with deadly pollutants. Should I read you the statistics? Or are you trying to tell me that live male sperm just float around in the wind? I'm not buying that, you harlot . . . Wait a minute! It was the TV repairman, wasn't it? I've been thinking for some time now that our television breaks suspiciously often . . . '

'Please, Viktor, don't be crass. I understand you're going through the change, but try, if at all possible, to bear this inevitable plight with dignity and composure,' Veronika said and gently stroked Viktor's sweaty bald spot. 'We'll take a beach vacation next year. All three of us . . . '

'Then it was the postman,' Viktor cut her off, fuming.

Veronika shook her head.

'Or one of the men who came to replace our radiator,' Viktor kept guessing.

'You're wasting your time, Viktor. You wouldn't understand. Just go back to writing your eulogy for Mr Horváth . . . When it happened, he was sitting on the balcony and reading a primer. As soon as he noticed me in the window, he jumped up and gallantly, with one hand over his heart, he bowed. He was wearing elegant swim trunks, red as hot bull's blood . . . '

'What? So it was that old lecher from across the street?'

'Come on, Viktor, I told you it was the breeze!'

'Enough already with the breeze!' Viktor shouted, but a moment later he was pleading quietly, 'Veronika, tell me, who was it? Don't you understand how important this is?'

'Actually, Viktor, I really don't. Does it matter—TV repairman, postman, plumber, Mr Zoltán or the breeze?'

'Oh,' Viktor sighed and waved his hand at Veronika's foolishness. 'Of course it matters. It's a question of fundamental worldviews. Idealism or materialism, mind or matter, don't you get it? If it really was the breeze, then you're living proof of the religious doctrine of the Immaculate Conception. It wasn't the breeze, was it?'

Viktor was noticeably suffering, and he awaited Veronika's final verdict with both dread and imploring hope in his eyes.

Veronika felt sorry for the anguished Viktor, so she decided to stain her conscience with a merciful lie.

'All right. It was the TV repairman.'

But after seeing the triumphant smile on Viktor's face (as if to say—I knew it, I knew all along that it was the TV repairman, and you're just an ordinary whore), she added in a cruel and uncompromising tone, 'But the TV repairman was nothing more than the erect penis of the breeze that couldn't stand to watch our dying any more.'

Viktor, deeply offended by Veronika's vulgar language as well as the sudden cruel tone of her voice, stuttered smugly and triumphantly, 'A d-d-dick, and not the breeze!'

And then, feeling grateful and relieved, he stroked his bald spot, sat down at his desk, and went back to writing the eulogy for Mr Zoltán Horváth who was sitting on the balcony across the street, reading a primer, dressed in elegant swim trunks, hot as fresh bull's blood.

In a Strange Tongue

And these signs will accompany those who believe: In my name
they will drive out demons; they will speak in new tongues;
they will pick up snakes with their hands; and when they drink
deadly poison, it will not hurt them at all; they will place their
hands on sick people, and they will get well.

—Mark 16:17–18

1

Once again I've failed; I rub my eyes, on the boundary between
dreams and consciousness, and a gradual assault of sensations
wakes me up. The silence on the retina finds words in the images
emerging from emptiness; the language of details begins. I see the
foot of the bed which is hiding a brown armoire. Movement is
created and maintained by continually changing the viewing
angle. I look at a large square clock hanging on the southern wall
of the dwelling. It ticks loudly and shows 10.20. A naked light bulb
hangs on a long black cord. Its faint light disappears in the flood
of sunshine streaming through a sheer, gathered, dingy white curtain. But the eyes that would approach the curtain at a four-inch
distance would see that the perception of dinginess is illusory—
the curtain itself isn't dirty, although we're unable to grasp its
cleanliness with our language or our intellect. In the bottom left
corner of the windowpane, a bloodstain with fossilized fly wings
is turning black. A healthy resolution crosses my mind: I should
eat something and not smoke on an empty stomach, as I always

do after waking up. But on the heels of it I realize that everyone is aware of my lack of willpower, and I open another pack of cigarettes from my stash. I lie on my back enjoying a cigarette, and watch the swirling smoke. Pestilent flies circle around my head, they tickle my face and hands, they land on the covers, the wall, the curtain; the only place they avoid is the fly-paper hanging from the ceiling like a dead snake yellowing in the sun. They whir like a race bike in the distance, on a flat section of the track; the incessant, grating sound beats against my skull and worsens my depression. Yesterday I got plastered again, and my wife gave me my final ultimatum—either I go to alcohol rehab, or next week she'll file for divorce. I know she means it this time, and I've no idea what I'll do without her.

On my nightstand, under a bottle of beer, there's a flyer with the words:

WARNING: On 28/10/1992, Jesus will return with the clouds! As God promised, over the last 5–6 years he has been revealing to his faithful servants around the world that which has hitherto been a secret. Many prophecies have not been fulfilled because they were calculated by men who overlooked the absolute condition for the return of Christ—the appearance of the Antichrist. He will appear this year before the distancing in . . . a guise.

A biblical examination of the date: biblical schedule of human history: period of the Old Testament (4,000 years)—period of the New Testament—(period of God's mercy for non-Jews: 1,992 years)—Jesus' return on the clouds and distancing (28/10): The end of God's mercy and the beginning of sorrow (7 years). Christ's return to

Earth (1999)—1,000 years of God's Kingdom on Earth—
eternal Kingdom of God in heaven . . . The day of recon-
ciliation will come to pass during the 7-year sorrow,
because the Jews will accept Jesus as their Saviour. If you
dismiss this message, and refuse to accept Jesus as your
one true Saviour, on 29/10/1992 you will begin 7 years
of tribulations, during which most people on Earth will
be brutally killed. Distancing is the only hope. If during
the time of tribulations the mark 666 appears on your
right hand or your forehead, you will go to Hell.
Therefore, prepare for distancing with penance, deep
prayer, and serious study of God's word! Very few people
will be distanced. Only those who love Jesus more than
their own lives will be distanced. After the Resurrection,
Jesus is once again fully God. He doesn't know the date
of his own return yet.

Mission for the Coming Days

The warning didn't frighten me; my conscience is clear—two
years ago, I accepted Jesus as my personal Saviour. At the Pasienky
Stadium. The atmosphere was intense. Like at a death metal concert. Except that in the vending area they weren't selling beer and
metal posters, but Bibles and religious literature. The band on
stage was cosmopolitan; they sang in English and Slovak. Their
playing was confident and poised, but spontaneous. The sound
wasn't as clear as it could have been, but it didn't detract from the
quality of the show. Spirituals and songs about Jesus alternated
with short percussive interjections by the Man of the Day. (He
spoke in English, but I can't remember his nationality any more,
because I attended several such events; they featured perform-
ances by missionaries from all over Europe and from across the

ocean—one had come to turn Slovaks towards God all the way from the other side of the globe.) ANGELS OF JESUS were in full swing in a hyper-fast, but super smooth style. (I taped a few of their songs on my tape recorder.) Missionary Tom was a real front man; when he wasn't singing or shouting, he was headbanging for all he was worth. His assistants and translators, Stano and Jano, were noticeably calmer, but their repertoire didn't lack the obligatory headbanging. Tom was suggestive and insistent as he kept telling us, 'There is only one who can save! The living, resurrected Christ! I am the way, the truth and the life, no one comes to the Father except through me. Jesus! Not religion! Not morals! Not good works! NO, NO, NO! Christ, the son of the living God! He is the way! There is no other path to God, except through Jesus! Not through Moses, Krishna, Buddha, Mohammed or Confucius! Not through a minister, a priest, the pope or the church! Only through Jesus! Will you let him save you?'

I wasn't sure if it was just a rhetorical question, so I kept quiet, but a few affirmative shouts came from the audience, and the invigorated preacher went on, 'Yes, my friend, trust Jesus! Accept him! Believe in him! Reject all else! Only he can save you! Trust Jesus and you will be saved! Will you do it? Do it! Accept him! Now! NOW!'

The ANGELS shot a salvo from the stage: YES, Jesus, YES . . . I was fascinated, and I wasn't the only one. Another thirty or so sinners stepped out of the anonymous crowd; we left our seats and lined up by the stage. I don't know how many of us had succumbed to the suggestive atmosphere or how many of us had answered the call out of curiosity, on a lark, or as a common courtesy (to reward the energy and effort Tom had expended, since he had come from so far away), but the out-of-town missionary was enraptured. He prayed, kept raising his arms to the ceiling, praised God and us, thanked God and us, it was spectacular. Several people broke down in loud sobs, and when Tom placed his hands on us and baptized us in the name of Jesus, six fell onto the floorboards as if he had mowed them down with a Kalashnikov. Tom had enough energy in his hands to run the nuclear power plant in Jaslovské Bohunice. I got a good jolt too, the vibrations in the arena could have rivalled a heavy metal concert. It was dynamite!

Then we had one-on-one sessions with local evangelists. They divvied us up (I don't know based on what criteria), and took us hither and yon—into locker rooms, showers, I ended up under a basketball hoop with 'Brother Imrich'. In a kind, friendly voice he asked me whether I was drunk, or whether I had gone to the stage as a joke. I assured him that I had only had three shots of borovička before coming to the stadium, so inebriation was out of the question; stepping out of the anonymous crowd was an impulsive decision, I still couldn't say why I had done it. 'Looking for a new experience?' he asked with an understanding smile. Taken aback, I nodded. 'I think you hit the nail on the head. Are you a psychologist?' He said he was an electrical engineer, and three years ago he had started the same way—he had four shots of rum to work himself up to it. He won me over; charisma radiated from him as if he were a radio. I confided my troubles to him: alcoholism, nicotine addiction, debauchery, blasphemy . . . I realized that besides murder and theft, I had committed all of the deadly sins. 'We're all sinning all the time,' he reassured me. 'You too?' He admitted to it without any shame: 'A hundred times a day, and I'm not even aware of it.' That piqued my interest, I had not thought about the whole thing from that perspective. 'Can one sinner save another?' I asked. Eventually we agreed that only

Jesus Christ can save, because even the apostles sinned constantly, yet Jesus sent them out to preach the gospel and heal, in short, he gave them full powers. 'Let's begin with the occult,' he said, 'are you committed to the occult?' I adamantly rejected his presumption. 'Have you ever studied secular or oriental philosophy, yoga, astrology, prophecy, parapsychology . . . ?' Damn, I've been in Satan's snare ever since I learned the alphabet, I thought, so the first thing he did was break my ties to the occult with a short prayer in a strange tongue, and at the end he asked Jesus to free me from my addictions to alcohol, cigarettes and pornography . . . for starters that was enough. Then I repeated a prayer after him, 'Lord Jesus, I admit that I've ruined my own life. I see no other option than to put it all to right. Lord Jesus, I thank you for not having to rely on human abilities and my own strength, I thank you for taking my affairs into your hands and paying for my sins—completely and for ever. Don't ever let me forget what you've done for me, and keep strengthening my faith. Amen.'

To my own surprise, *without prompting*, I added, 'I accept you as my personal Saviour.' Still, there was no euphoria: I felt like someone who had hoped that a window to heaven would open in front of him, only to find a locked door to the attic.

Brother Imrich clairvoyantly sensed my disappointment, he smiled and assured me that it was OK, not everyone rejoices or faints, the sensation isn't important, sometimes it can take years! As proof of my sincerity, I handed him my newly opened pack of Spartas (eighteen were left), and he crushed them in his hand with loathing and threw them symbolically into the basketball hoop, under which I started my new life. 'That's it?' I asked. 'That's it, Lord Jesus will do the rest for you.' I pressed him for a more concrete answer, and because of my insistence he prayed once more in a strange tongue, listened intently for a moment, and dismayed, he reluctantly tore out a piece of paper from a small notebook, wrote something on it, handed it to me, and was about to say goodbye. Just then it occurred to me that I could write an article for *Smena* about the whole thing, so I asked Brother Imrich for a short interview. My request caught him off guard; he must not have had instructions for what to do in this kind of a situation.

'Reputable advertising can't be bad for our cause,' I said. 'I'll publish a first-hand account in a print run of 100,000, and I'm sure it'll reach thousands of people who would have otherwise not heard about Jesus.' At first, he was opposed to the idea, saying that everyone had already heard about Jesus, but then again, he said, people have biased information. He took a liking to my idea, though he still had misgivings.

'Of course, I'll let you read it beforehand. I won't publish a word without your consent.'

'What would you like to know?' he asked.

'Speaking in tongues. Most Catholics and Protestants don't know that it's one of the gifts of the Holy Spirit still available to us today.'

'I see you've studied scripture,' he said. 'You're right. They believe that this gift stopped working after the death of the apostles.'

'Endow me with it.'

'What?'

'The gift of tongues. I'd like to speak German.'

'You must be joking.'

'I'm sorry . . . I know that even you don't know what language you're praying in, but there's the rub. How do you expect to persuade me that you're not making it up?'

'I'm not trying to persuade you of anything. Excuse me, but I have to go attend to people who have a serious interest . . . '

'There's no one more interested in this entire arena . . . But, do as you like. I'll write that you confessed in private.'

'Confessed to what?'

'That you don't have the gift of tongues, you're just spewing nonsense, and pretending to be talking to the Holy Spirit.'

'You're crazy. I warn you. Sinning against the Holy Spirit will never be forgiven.'

'Place your hands on me, and baptize me in the Holy Spirit. If I start speaking in tongues, I'll believe you and won't smear it all over the papers.'

Brother Imrich was frightened. He looked around helplessly searching for the organizers; he wanted to have me escorted out of the stadium.

'Jacob also fought for a blessing and he received it,' I said. 'Are you more than God? I'll write that you said—I'm greater than God.'

He realized that he was facing a dangerous lunatic. He concluded that the easiest way to get rid of me was to fulfil my request, but he warned me alibistically, 'Not everyone receives the gift of tongues when baptized in the Holy Spirit, you may be one of the people who don't.'

'We'll see.'

I pulled the tape recorder out of my pocket. 'Begin,' I said. 'And no sloppiness!'

'You're crazy,' Brother Imrich said again.

'You're right,' I said. 'I'm crazy about God.'

'You're possessed by the devil,' said Brother Imrich.

'Quit stalling!'

That was how I got baptized in the Holy Spirit. Brother Imrich placed his hands on me, prayed for the gift of the Holy Spirit, and *against my will* I started to say: 'Vijavijapranavijamanipuramudra-suptavirazalabhaustraparvakarnachakravakramakarahalakona-januzirapidanidrakarmanagavrksagarudachakrazavago . . . '

I didn't expect something like that to happen to me, it scared me. I remembered Nils Runeberg, who had died on 1 March 1912, in Malmö. What if I had committed the gravest of sins? What if I had *really* blasphemed against the Holy Spirit?

I wandered the streets of Bratislava in a stupor, a tropical heat wave was raging, I was parched, I *had to* have at least one beer. As I stood there, beer mug in hand, in a smoke-filled, spit-covered dive, I asked God for forgiveness, and bought a new pack of Spartas—I *had to* smoke. On my way home, I stopped by a book-shop. I couldn't resist temptation and curiosity, so (guilt-ridden) I bought a bag of books: Reinecke's *Astrology*; Nostradamus' *The End of the Millennium*; Osho's *Meditation Techniques, Indian Philosophy, and Christianity*; Abd-ru-shin's *The Grail Message*; Sai Baba; Bataille's *Story of the Eye*; *Prophecies About the End of the World* and the latest issue of *Playboy*.

I was so ashamed that I *had to* get drunk.

The next day, I couldn't remember a thing. I lost the bag of books, my ID, as well as the note from Brother Imrich, thus I never learnt 'God's answer' that Brother Imrich had prayed for and facilitated for me practically against his will.

2

I set aside the 'Warning' and take a swig of beer. The large square clock on the southern wall of the dwelling shows 10.25, it's Saturday, and my wife has gone to the market. I'm tired, hungry and have the taste of a slash-and-burn field in my mouth from the cigarettes I smoked all night, one after another, like in my younger days. And I have the urge to urinate, like an aging guy with prostate issues. I hear the toilet flush—with a bucket of water—the flushing mechanism is broken. I've completely forgotten that my sister-in-law is home; she's renting a room from us. A college student. A sexy chick, enormous temptation. Prostate or no prostate, my bell still rings once in a while, though after twenty years of marriage, it's most likely to ring at someone else's door. And the devil's working overtime: What if you walk into her room, naked? *Apage, satanas,* I'm not an exhibitionist! But whether I like it or not, the idea he put into my head excites me; my cock is standing at attention. Curiosity propels me out of bed, I wonder, how will she react? Will she be appalled, leave the rental in panic, and tell her sister on me? Unanswered questions demand answers; there's no stopping me. The arousal curve is growing exponentially, no, I can't go in there with a loaded gun; it has to look like an accident. I just woke up, ran out of matches, and I had no idea that my sister-in-law was home. I need to calm down! How? Think about something else, that's it! Let's peruse yesterday's mail.

I open an envelope and read: 'You scribbling asshole, you cosmopolitan whore, you traitor of the Slovak people, pack up and join your friends in Prague, or you and your children will end up hanging . . . ' Jingoist love letters have a sedative effect on my cock; the arousal's over, I can go test the waters. I get out of bed, my bell hangs indifferently, swaying from side to side like a sailor on dry land. I walk into the living room. The sexy chick is sitting in an armchair, her long slender legs spread out on the table crack open a window to heaven. She's flipping through a fashion magazine; a cat's sleeping on top of an armoire. When she sees me at the door, she shifts around, annoyed, crossing one leg over the other; her bathrobe barely covers her velvety brown thighs. My mouth's dry, I feign surprise. 'Oh, sorry, I didn't know you're home. I ran out of matches . . .' She looks me up and down with her sleepy feline eyes, focuses on my slacker, which really appreciates the attention; it stands up, proud and smug, just take a good look, I'm not messing around! 'Hi,' the cat says in a sleepy voice. 'Feel free to smoke, I don't mind.' I sit in an armchair opposite her. We sit, we're silent, we swallow saliva. I pick up the cigarettes from the coffee table and offer her one. She accepts. I get up, lean over to give her a light, and what do I see? My bell's dangling haphazardly between my legs with such arrogant indifference as if it weren't mine. We were quiet too long, it got bored. I feel hot, my face is burning with shame, that lazy bum is putting me in an incredibly compromising situation; it's doing whatever it feels like, the jerk. My sister-in-law is disappointed, nigh onto offended. I click the lighter. The chick squeezes the cigarette between her pouty lips, relishes a long drag, and looks at my ignoramus with disdain. Finally! Finally, an image wakes him up, a lightning fast chain of associations: lips, cigarettes, smoking. In a split second it rises menacingly like the barrel of a cannon and takes aim at my sister-in-law, as if trying to defend me, and to atone for its prior failure. The kitten is pleased, she feels a healthy and righteous satisfaction, she asks in a conversational tone, 'Are you writing anything?' Her matter-of-factness raises my adrenaline level —I love counterpoint. 'This short story,' I say, 'and you?' She's enamoured with staring at my red giant, 'I'm working on my thesis.' She gives it an appreciative pat on its exposed noggin.

'What's wrong with him?' She's indignant, and rightfully so. The red giant is becoming a white dwarf, the cannon turns into a machine gun, the machine gun into a shotgun, and the shotgun into a ladies' pistol, small enough for a purse. 'Something must have scared him.' I make an excuse for the traitor, unaware of the fact that its rightful owner's on her way. 'Let's keep talking,' I say, 'maybe it'll join the conversation.' She purses her lips disparagingly, 'Is he a wordsmith too?'

She kneels down, my reputation's on the line, she explains, grabs that pagan of mine in her hand, caresses it gently, rubs it, squeezes it, yanks it, pats it, rolls it, jiggles it, massages it, kneads it, jerks it, pinches it, and shakes it like a shaker. The slacker wakes up again, I'm sprawled out in the armchair like a lord, my eyes are half-closed with delight her tongue is tickling me I feel her lips tighten around the head of my penis ooohhh I spill like the Danube in Gabčíkovo I gape at my wife in the doorway heads of cabbage peek out of her shopping bag my sister-in-law is choking she can't swallow the onslaught fast enough 'When you're finished, I'll call you a cab,' my wife says on her way to the kitchen.

I'm lying in bed, wet and sticky, God, why did I leave her? I wipe myself thoroughly with a handkerchief, and continue writing this short story. Oh, Lord, dictate, and forgive my typos!

3

Yes, dear readers, I accepted Jesus as my personal Saviour, but, as you've just read, it was to my own detriment. What the true proverb says happened to me: the dog returned to its own vomit, and the sow, after washing herself, returned to wallow in the mire!

In vain do I pray regularly and ardently; I am forever overcome by doubt and persecuted by sinful, lewd and blasphemous thoughts, which are the progenitors of deeds. The more I try to chase them away, the harder they pursue me. Are you surprised that I'm ashamed to go see my brethren? In vain are their invitations, in vain are their warnings not to avoid group prayer meetings, because the devil stalks around like a roaring lion looking for its next meal. I only went to see them once; I felt most embarrassed in front of Brother Imrich. He had done everything he could for me, perhaps more than he would have liked, and how did I repay him? I came among them like a stinking goat, reeking like a wine barrel! No, I was neither drunk nor filthy, I had a clean shirt and underwear, my hair was washed and my teeth brushed, my nails were clipped, but what good are clean clothes to a body saturated with alcohol, nicotine and prurient seed, 'Not even a monk's robe can cleanse a dirty soul!' Brother Imrich hissed into my ear. 'Aren't you ashamed to come be among clean people?'

I think the main reason why my attempts at rebirth were unsuccessful was that I had doubts about original sin and the redeeming sacrifice. I couldn't come to terms with the idea that Jesus had to make a blood sacrifice to the Father in order to redeem mankind from original sin through his death and reconcile God with me. Jesus did make the redeeming sacrifice—but to Satan, I insisted, and they accused me of blasphemy.

I couldn't keep writing, I couldn't see the pages, on account of tears. I wept over my wretchedness, wickedness and helplessness, I felt abandoned by God and people (my sister-in-law had moved out and didn't give me her new address), I didn't know what was going to happen the next day, where I was going to be, and who I would stay with when my wife kicked me out into the darkness where only crying and gnashing of teeth could be heard. I was crushed and I knew that I'd never, never, never be able to start a new life . . . After this sentence there was ringing. At the door. I didn't get out of bed; my wife opened the door.

Less than a minute later, my old friend Maťo Malovec from my short story 'Geraniums' was standing at the foot of my bed (I wrote and I cried in bed). We hadn't seen each other for seventeen years. He looked well and he had a bag over his shoulder, the kind in which Socialist repairmen used to carry their tools before the revolution. I surmised he had started his own business.

'Don't cry,' he said. 'I was able to do it.'

'Maťo, is that really you? Where have you been?'

'I've been spreading the gospel on the island of Borneo as a renowned Slovak missionary.'

'I was hoping you could fix our toilet, we've been flushing it with a bucket for three months now.'

He looked at his watch, 'Maybe I'll have time for that, too,' he said.

I sat up on the edge of the bed, 'Welcome home.' I wanted to shake his hand, but he stopped me, 'There's no time for ceremony. I have a return ticket, in an hour I go back to my pagan flock. The harvest is great, but the workers are few.'

'Don't waste your time on me. I'm beyond help.'

'A good shepherd cares about every sheep. And he loves those that have strayed from the flock and are lost in the labyrinth of the world more than the rest.'

'Do you love me, too?'

'I do, and I care about you. Lie down and listen!'

Mat'o acted with unexpected authority; I had to do as he said. I lay down and listened.

'All of your problems stem from the fact that you refuse to accept the dogma about original sin, you doubt the purpose of the redeeming sacrifice, and you can't understand why God inevitably needs our prayers.'

'That's true, I really think . . . '

'Be quiet, or I'll miss my plane! God really is constrained by our prayer life, and he can't do anything for humanity until someone asks him to do it.'

'Aren't you blaspheming? God is all powerful, he's in charge of everything . . . '

'He is all powerful, and he is in charge of the whole Universe, except for this planet. God does not rule Earth, but soon he will, thank God. But for the time being his will is not done on Earth. It is only done in the lives of the people who give themselves over to him and accept Jesus as their personal Saviour.'

'I did accept, and it turned out very badly for me. I sin worse than a heathen.'

'I know, I'll heal you today,' he said and patted his bag with medicine. 'If God did rule everything and force his will on the people, he could immediately establish a thousand-year kingdom.'

'Maybe it would be better if he were a little more strict . . . '

'He has to respect his own laws. He gave us free will and dominion over Earth . . . '

'By way of Adam, I know.'

'No! God didn't say to Adam, I'll have dominion through you. God said, I give you dominion over everything I've created.'

'If I understand it correctly, Adam was in some way the god of this world.'

'Yes, but then came Satan, deceived Adam, and Adam committed high treason. He sold out to Satan, and ever since then, Satan is the god of this world. Satan has dominion!'

'Why doesn't God take over?'

'Because Adam's lease isn't over yet, but it's coming to an end, thank God.'

'Six thousand years?'

'Correct. Until then, legally and justly God can't interfere and remove devil from power . . . '

'Why not?'

'Because he'd be going back on his word, and he's being watched by the inhabitants of the whole universe. God cannot act unjustly, you see, it would create legal chaos, and that would be the end of the world. The devil has legal dominion, he has certain rights, because he owns Adam's lease, and God can't do anything until someone down here asks him to. He can only intercede when Christians ask for his intercession in their prayers.'

'Why only Christians?'

'Because of the redeeming sacrifice that Jesus Christ, the Son of God, had made.'

'To God? I can't help it, but a father who has his own son crucified because he's incapable of forgiving people otherwise . . . '

'Many quibblers get stuck on that one, but theologians are partly to blame as well. They don't know how to explain it well.'

'And you do, Maťo? Forgive me, but you've spent most of your time in nuthouses . . . '

'God revealed the truth to children and fools. To redeem means to buy back. Adam sold humanity to Satan . . .'

'So you're trying to say . . . Jesus made the redeeming sacrifice to Satan?'

'Of course.'

'Thank God. You have no idea how relieved I am.'

'I do. You were searching, lost, but you were on the right track. God loves those who genuinely seek him. Anyone who thinks he knows something knows nothing. Anyone who seeks has understood it all.'

'Does he love me as well?'

'More than you can imagine. Jesus is your best friend. Remember that! With his death he had bought us back from Satan at a slave market. And the price he paid was his own blood. God created us to be greater than angels and all of creation. When Satan saw it, he couldn't stand it, so he rebelled against God rather than serve man.'

'Damn, I suspected as much . . .'

'Ever since then Satan has been trying to destroy man. He envies us terribly, and he's jealous of us. God wants us to be his number one, but he needs our help. We're as important to him as he is to himself. This world would have perished a long time ago if it weren't for us, Christians. That's why we must pray. The more of us there are, and the stronger our prayers, the more space we create for God in his fight against Satan. Terrible things are happening, but if it weren't for us, prayer warriors, it would be much worse.'

'How long will this go on?'

'A few more years. But not even the Son knows the exact day, only the Father. In my opinion, mankind must find itself in a situation with no way out. Only when mankind reaches a point when it admits that it's unable to solve its own problems will it turn to God in despair and accept his help. We must break so as not to be crushed. That's actually what I came to tell you, that's your problem too, isn't it?'

'How'd you know? Do you have a direct line to the Holy Spirit as well?'

'You've got one too, it's just been temporarily cut off . . . First you must break, or you'll be crushed. If you humbly let yourself to be broken, you won't be crushed into dust.'

'What's the difference between breaking and crushing?'

Maťo looked at the clock, and slapped his forehead, 'My God, the plane.'

He opened his repairman's bag.

'There's no time for theorizing,' he said. 'It wouldn't help you anyway, you'd just start looking for a loophole again.'

He pulled out a hammer.

'Now I'll explain the difference between breaking and crushing,' he said and hit the toes of my left foot with all his strength.

'This is crushing,' he said. 'If you can't heal someone with love, you have to do it with pain,' he mumbled apologetically, and hit my right shin with the hammer.

Looking at my broken tibia, I understood: That was breaking.

I regained consciousness at the hospital. My right leg was in a cast, but the left one was better off—it was just the foot. My sister-in-law dressed as a nurse was standing over me, explaining patiently, 'If you devote your energy to base things like sex, alcohol and pornography, you shouldn't be surprised that your ego manifests at the lower sublevels, where the battle between attraction and repulsion breeds pain and suffering, you shouldn't be surprised that your base thoughts and interests create hordes of demonic beings which are hostile towards you. You need to recognize the importance of spiritual growth, and I'm sure you'll start to devote your energy to things and ideas on a higher spiritual level. Now, I'll sweeten it a little.' She ripped off my covers and started to gently massage my helplessly naked willy.

I objected, 'I refuse oral sex without a banana-flavoured condom.' Then I broke down in tears from pain.

'Don't cry,' said Maťo. 'I'm grateful that in your pain and grief I've been charged by the Lord to personally attest to you that he sees you, and your pain makes his heart ache, which is why he's telling you through me, "Get up and walk."'

'Should I pick up my bed too?'

'Try. We'll test the strength of your faith.'

It didn't work. The bed must have been bolted to the hospital floor, and my crushed left foot wasn't cooperating either, not to mention my broken right leg. I burst into tears again.

'Don't cry,' he said. 'I'll heal you.'

I stopped crying as if by miracle. Maťo exuded divine calm, his blessed presence dried up the wellspring of my tears. Immense love radiated from his eyes, and I humbly broke, saying, 'Lord, I thank you for my indescribable wretchedness and deplorability, thanks to it I'm completely dependent on you. The more loathsome are my offenses, the happier is my soul, which turns to you in the greatest shame and deepest submission. The sight of my unworthiness fills me with peace and grace, because I know that through me you yourself want to do all the great things you've called me to do. You know my wickedness and misery much better than I do. I know that you see my wounds and scars, and I patiently await healing. I'm aware of my failings, and I humbly ask for your forgiveness. I want to bear them until the end of my life, if that is your will. I trust that my sins do not offend you, because you know very well that deep inside I don't agree with them and, therefore, I'm not responsible for them. Amen.'

Maťo rubbed his calloused hands together, pleased, 'Finally, you broke and opened your soul to the Holy Spirit. Don't worry. From now on you're in his hands. The aberrant desire for authenticity and originality has definitely left your ego. Congratulations.'

He laid his hands on me, 'You're healed,' he said. 'They'll release you in six months. I can return to Borneo. Yesterday I missed my plane because of your crapper. It's been healed too. So long.'

4

I came home from the hospital six months later; the broken leg got complicated by double pneumonia. Maťo kept his promise; he had healed my body and soul. The compulsory six-month abstinence freed me from my addiction to alcohol and cigarettes. I drink and I smoke, but I don't have to.

When I was finalizing this short story, I played the tape I had made when I was baptized in the Holy Spirit. Language of angels poured from the tape recorder: Vijavijapranavijamanipuramudra-suptavirazalabhaustraparvakarnachakravakra . . .

I got interrupted by a visitor; it was my friend, Dio Sladký. He listened for a while, then asked in surprise, 'Are you learning Sanskrit? It's about time.'

That's how I found out that Brother Imrich had given me the gift of Sanskrit. Dio translated it for me.

Vija—knowledge / vija—knowledge / pranavija—the breath of knowledge / manipura—navel / mudra—seal / supta—sleeping / vira—hero / zalabha—grasshopper / ustra—camel / parva—exit / karna—ear / chakra—circle, wheel / vakra—bent / makara—alligator / hala—plough / kona—angle / janu—knee / zira—head / pida—pain / nidra—sleep / karma—fate / naga—mountain / vrksa— tree / garuda—eagle / chakra—circle / zava—corpse / go—cow

KARMA
Vija vija pranavija
manipura mudra
Supta vira zalabha
ustra parva karna
Chakra vakra makara
hala kona janu zira
pida nidra karma
Naga vrksa garuda
chakra zava
go

Literal translation:

FATE

Knowledge, knowledge, breath of knowledge.

A seal's navel.

The hero sleeps on a grasshopper.

A camel comes out of his ear.

An alligator bent like a wheel.

Plough angle knee head.

Painfully sleeps fate.

On a mountain is a tree, on the tree an eagle.

The corpse in the circle is a

Cow.

Unfortunately, my knowledge of Sanskrit was not a permanent gift of the Holy Spirit; since my baptism I hadn't uttered a word in 'Indian'. But I remain at the ready: if I wake up tomorrow morning and speak Swahili to my wife, I won't be the least bit surprised, and I won't prattle on about a miracle. Miracles don't exist.

Epilogue

I opened another envelope from the pile of unopened mail on the nightstand. It contained my ID which I had lost 3 years ago. Perplexed, I flipped through it, as if I were hoping to find a message, an explanation—who had had it until then, and why did he send it to me? All I found was a scrap of paper with the following: 1 Peter 1:5. It made me think of Brother Imrich. I remembered his prayer in a strange tongue. Out of my memory emerged Brother Imrich's face at the moment when he was handing me the piece of paper from his notebook, grudgingly, indignantly, yes,

Brother Imrich clearly didn't agree with the message. But why? I read it again: 1 Peter 1:5. I found the First Epistle of Peter in the Bible, Chapter one, Verse five: 'for you (who have been chosen), who through faith are shielded by God's power until the coming of the salvation that is ready to be revealed in the last time.'

I shook my head in disbelief: Me? Saved? Lord, aren't you mistaken? Now I understood where Brother Imrich was coming from, it didn't seem right to him either, that's why he was such a reluctant intermediary, he didn't consider me a worthy candidate for salvation, he even had his doubts about God's wisdom and fairness, in fact, Brother Imrich *envied* me, he-he.

The large square clock on the south side of the dwelling showed midnight. The naked light bulb hanging on the long black cord exploded like a supernova. In my head. Blinding light blew apart my skull. The forces and powers of darkness were unleashed, and in their death throes they spewed words of blasphemy through my mouth. A strange hand threw me to the ground; I shivered and yelped like a dying dog.

The door creaked. On the threshold of my cell stood Death in a white robe, flames shooting from the palm of her hand. 'The breakers blew,' she said. She came closer, shined a light on me, and said in disgust, 'Three sheets to the wind. You're at it again?'

I was lying on my back, my painfully erect penis stuck straight up like a spear aimed at the sky. My wife leaned over, her nightgown reached all the way to her feet, a hot tear burned my stomach; wax had dripped from the candle.

'What's wrong with you?' she asked.

'I'm not drunk.'

My hand hugged her ankle, I went up, but I only reached her calf; it stiffened in defence. I caressed her gently, soothingly; it felt as though her hair was standing on end from fear.

'Come,' I whispered. 'Mount me.'

Her calf muscle tensed and relaxed three times, as if the heart of a frightened bird were pulsating in my hand.

'No,' she said.

'Yes,' I said.

'Let go of me.'

'No.'

'I'll set down the candle.'

'You won't run away?'

'Let go of me.'

I felt her calf relax, her skin softened, and her hairs turned into delicate down. Reluctantly I let go of her, I didn't believe she'd stay.

I closed my eyes; I didn't want to watch her leave. Tears burned under my eyelids; I was scared she'd leave for ever.

She squeezed me in her hand. With her legs spread apart, in an athletic squat, she held my cock in her hand, as if she didn't know what to do with it. Finally, she sat down benevolently.

Surprise issued from her throat: Oh, I've forgotten the taste of power. She rose and fell, her head turned towards the sky, slow deep penetrations, deep, deep, all the way to the bottom, oh, oh, oh, her moans aroused me more than the act itself, oh, oh, oohhh, not yet, she cried and left me. For a moment. She moved from a squat to a horizontal position. She lay down between my outstretched legs, squashed me, impaled herself. We embraced as if it were for ever. Our movements synchronized; we found a forgotten rhythm. I thrust from below, and she matched it beautifully from above, sharp and quick, faster and faster, we impaled each other over and over again, ah, ah, ah, not yet, she separated, I want to keep going for a long time, she said, me too, me too. She knelt, propped up her elbows on the ground, do it to me from behind, like a stallion. I mounted the mare, grabbed her breasts, we went from an easy trot to a fast gallop, oh, oh, oohhh, the contractions of her underbelly signalled a triumphant finish, not yet, I said, and left her. Noo, I can't hold it any more, she whimpered, where are you? Here, I'm here, I lay her on her back and entered her from above. Pillow, she sighed. I reached towards the bed, she lifted her bottom, waited for the pillow, good, she said, where are you? Inside you. Inside, in-side, inside you, she squeezed her legs as if she never wanted to let go of me again, more, more, more, oh Jesus, when she invoked Jesus, I knew that the window to Heaven was open, all I needed to do was fly, oh Jesus, Jesus, Jesus, OH, JESUS, I love you, I said, remember that! Yes, yes, yes, YES, we finished together; there was a flood in seventh heaven.

I embraced her, picked her up off the ground, and carried her to my bed.

She fell asleep like a baby.

Her damp, sleeping face told me—you're saved—and I believed. I stopped fighting grace. I realized that God wants me the way I am, because he has better eyes than Brother Imrich. God's eye sees clearly that the curtain isn't dirty, even though we're not able to grasp its cleanliness with our language or our intellect. I felt deeply humbled, awed and astonished. I had been the victim of a miracle, and I survived.

Miracles don't exist. Only the absence of a miracle would be miraculous.

The Beginning Evangelist

Motto

Very truly I tell you, whoever believes in me will do the works
I have been doing, and they will do even greater things than
these, because I am going to the Father.

—John 14:12

Not long ago I got the feeling that I should fast. Even though I
wanted to be energetic and strong, I couldn't ignore that quiet,
gentle voice of the Holy Spirit which was talking to me. I skipped
breakfast, lunch and dinner. I didn't eat the next day either, and
by noon of the third day it became apparent that I should keep
fasting—no reward had come. By the fourth day, I was physically
exhausted but spiritually vibrant; I knew—God was guiding my
steps. By the evening of the fifth day, the time for fasting wasn't
over yet. Why does the Lord want me to fast? I didn't know the
answer. I learned it on the sixth day.

I spoke to the Lord in a prayer, 'Dear Heavenly Father, I'm at
your disposal, make me into a divine guitar, and I'll do everything
you ask, although right now I don't know what you expect of me.
Even so, I am willing, determined and ready to obey you.'

The Lord said to me, 'Go home and till the land under the
pear tree!'

I obeyed the Lord's voice. I got in my car and drove home. A
fire burned between Bratislava and Pernek. It had started on
Saturday morning in multiple places at once. The highway was

engulfed in stinging smoke. The sight of flaming trees in close proximity of the road was terrifying. It wasn't a single blaze, but a series of little fires, small local bonfires—the kind on which my father and I used to roast bacon. People talked about arson, but this year's catastrophic drought also supported the theory of spontaneous combustion.

By the first houses of our village there was a lively bustle. Citizens with half-empty buckets were trying to put out the fire in hopes that the flames wouldn't jump over the wide asphalt strip of the highway.

When I arrived, the door was locked. The key was under the mat, my father was in bed. As usual. With chills. Only the top of his head was sticking out from under the covers, he had a scarf on, the windows were closed, the shades drawn, he was sweating and sleeping. For three years he had refused to talk to me, he couldn't forgive me for taking him to the hospital; back then I was still a heathen.

Calendar of Saints

January: Names that dropped out of the names folder—Drahoslav, Gaspar, Melchior, Balthazar, Malvina, Bohdana.

Household notes—1. nice day, the sun was shining, snow melted, cousin died 4. hard freeze, cousin's funeral was postponed until it warms up, the ground is frozen solid 7. big blizzard, the house is snowed in, God knows who'll come dig us out, Grandpa's losing it again he spent the whole night walking around with a flashlight looking for his money and his sons, where are my sons, he lamented, he wandered around the house, shining a light into every corner and under the beds but I had sons, where are my sons, I remember having two sons, where are my sons? 9. Grandpa wanted to kill me because he thinks I've been stealing the money saved for his sons and I've got no sex appeal and he hasn't been able to sleep with me for thirty years which is terrible because I'm not fulfilling my wifely duties and God must punish me for it because I've made him impotent and that's not right 10. young Žuták hanged himself at the soccer field, from the top bar, I hope there'll be a championship this spring, old Barčák set fire to his house with my old classmate Irenka inside, luckily it was snowing and the garage didn't burn down 11. was my birthday, seventy-five years, no one wrote to me and Grandpa didn't remember either, but we made up anyway, Grandpa isn't a bad person when he's sober he cried and kept apologizing, saying that he's not indifferent to my charms, but he blamed me for wearing trousers all the time so that he can't get it up, because a woman in man's bottoms dampens male desire 12. it finally warmed up and we were able to bury my cousin, Grandpa got drunk at the wake and kept feeling up my cousin's wife, he told her that I've lost all sex appeal because I've felt cold in a skirt for the last thirty years and 13. he wanted to set me on an electric burner as punishment for giving up my womanly wiles, I don't know why God's punishing me so I just hope it doesn't get worse, we're set for firewood and coal, we bought slivovica brandy from Jožo S. 14. picked up medicine can't sleep even though it's warmer and my brother-in-law Imro died after midnight, my sister's so lucky, had he died before midnight, he wouldn't have been eligible for the next day's pension check, on the fourteenth I sent Grandpa to the larder for canned apricots, on the fifteenth our older son came over and Grandpa came back from the larder without the apricots, what was I supposed to bring? apricots! right 16. he came back without the apricots, where was I supposed to go? to the larder! right 17. he came back without the apricots, where's the larder? right there, next to the bathroom, that's when Grandpa got mortally offended, he started to beat me with a pickaxe, why do you keep sending me hither and yon couldn't you have told me straight up that the larder is next to the bathroom, to hell with your apricots and to the hot stove with you to cure you of your arthritis, thank God our son was home, he saved my life and 18. poor Grandpa ended up in the hospital, the weather was nice, the sun came out, whatever will happen to Grandpa?

Grandma's letter, unsent:

My dear sons,

During my last visit at the hospital Grandpa told me that he has three savings accounts, but he can't remember the account numbers. Poor Grandpa has severe dementia, I spoke with the head physician, I gave him a thousand crowns, he prescribed me two oxycodone, good man. He told me that Grandpa has two months left, and done. I didn't know that memory loss was terminal, but I must admit that Grandpa's losing weight, he's disappearing right before my eyes, the poor dear. On the 10th I had the whole house painted, so people wouldn't badmouth us after the funeral and say that our house is smoked up like some Gypsy hole. 14. and 16. I cleaned after the painters, I worked like a dog, then I was laid up for three days, I couldn't move a muscle, but God rewarded my efforts. Among other things, I dusted out the carpet on the stairs to the attic, and I found 15,000 crowns under it, as well as three account numbers, unfortunately, all three accounts require a password . . . As soon as I felt better, I ran to the

hospital to see Grandpa, but he wouldn't reveal the password even on his deathbed, the rascal. Ever since then I've
been visiting him on Wednesdays, Saturdays and Sundays,
you can imagine what it's doing to my health, I'm worried
I'll beat Grandpa to the grave. I bring him vanilla wafers
and canned apricots, trying to please him, but he's silent
as the grave. On March 7, I got lucky, they left me in the
room with him alone, and I told him that if he didn't
reveal the password, I'd disconnect his life support. He
had tubes wrapped all around him, needles stuck in his
veins on his arms and legs, they were torturing him all
over, I felt so sorry for him, the poor dear, but I had to
think about your future, you need more and more money,
so I cried and pleaded with him, Daddy, please, tell me
the password, our kids and grandkids need that money
like salt, and he cried too, but he didn't divulge it. I started
to disconnect him from all those bags of IV fluids, vit-
amins and fresh blood, Daddy, I said to him, my heart's
breaking, but if you don't tell me the password, I'll have
to take you off life support. He started to thank me and
kiss my hands, but just then a cute young tramp barged
into the room and raised an alarm, the bitch. She gave me
quite a scare! I'm done for, I thought, they'll say I tried to
kill him because of the money, and in my old age I'll end
up in prison for aggravated assault, which is more than I
can bare. A moment later the room was full of hospital
staff, and I cried like I was being paid for it, and those good
folks cried right along with me. They said I shouldn't let
it get to me, they understand that I feel sorry for him, but
the law doesn't allow for helping our poor Grandpa by

taking him off life support even though he's suffering needlessly and robbing the state of healthcare funds, can you imagine, he'd even begged them to get it over with and promised them the savings accounts, unfortunately, they couldn't take pity on him, because he didn't know the account numbers. That was when I realized that the poor dear really didn't remember the password, so I let them move him to the psychiatric ward. What a good decision that was! There they didn't torture him with any tubes, they just gave him some good pills, which he liked a lot, I almost envied him how happy and content he was. By April he couldn't remember his own name any more, he confused his doctor with President Masaryk, and he hated the nurse, because he thought she was his late brother, Uncle Karol, who wanted to steal his inheritance, he kept telling the head physician stop pissing me off, Dad, but he liked me, he always caressed me, my dear grand-daughter, how you've grown, he kept groping my breasts, what nice titties you have, what can I say, I laughed and cried at the same time. I had to wash and bathe him because he wasn't able to hold his urine or stool, and the nurses had had enough, and our neighbour Adam, who was his roommate, kept saying that Grandpa wouldn't last a week, and gossip was spreading through the whole vil-lage, I was too embarrassed to even go to the store. On May 7, at 1.30 in the morning, a nurse found him in the window and caught him by the leg, and our neighbour Adam immediately started spreading the rumour that Grandpa tried to commit suicide by jumping out of a seventh-floor window, what an idiot, he didn't understand that Grandpa was just trying to go home. The next day, I called a taxi because all of the ambulances were booked for a month, and I brought him home to die. As we were coming into our village, he started to recognize everything, houses, gardens, he could name trees, that's a pear tree, he said, that's a plum tree, that's an apple tree, over there's our walnut tree, and when we came into our yard, he said, those are our chickens, and then he remembered the password for the accounts. Two of them listed you as beneficiaries, and the third, I still cry when I think about it, would you believe it, the third one listed me, that old vagabond must have loved me, even though he made me suffer his whole life . . .

Calendar of Saints

December: Names that dropped out of the names folder—Nicholas, Lucy, Isaac, Adam and Eve, Stephen the Martyr, John the Evangelist; we don't have a lot of red beets or groats, I don't know what we'll feed those stupid chickens of ours, it's nice and warm and it's snowing, Grandpa's happy at home, ever since I brought him home from the hospital he's been in bed all the time, in the morning he lets out the chickens, unlocks the gate, smokes a cigarette, and goes back to bed, he puts on a sweater, ties my towel around his head, in the evening he closes the chicken coop, locks the gate, smokes a cigarette, ties on the towel, and goes back to bed, he lives like a king, I bring him breakfast, lunch and dinner in bed, he doesn't eat much, he likes lemon tea, vanilla wafers, Marína cookies and canned apricots, what will happen to him if, God forbid, he outlives me . . .

February: Names that dropped out of the names folder—Tatiana, Prokop, Pravoslav, Etela, Victor; it's freezing, then it warms up and there's a thaw, seven people died in February, including Betka, who was fairly young, fifty-six. 12. Šándor, the chimney sweeper, was here, cleaned the chimney 13. I went to the doctor to get Grandpa's sleeping pills, he keeps sleeping and watching television when there are half-naked women in swimsuits doing exercise, then he's mean and sends me away, get out you old hag 17. I washed the curtains, Šándor came by and chopped wood for us, I gave him some borovička, he said he'd come again, his wife ran away to the Czech Republic, he's sixty-five and lives alone . . .

November: Names that dropped out of the names folder—Bohoľub, Bohumír, Mladen, Ernest, Vratko; I haven't written things down for a while, there was no time, Grandpa's been in bed and there was a lot to do around the house, our sons came over twice, but I couldn't manage without Šándor, in March he tilled the garden, in April he cleaned the septic tank, thirteen buckets, Grandpa was jealous, every time, I'm in love, I think it's for ever, Grandpa didn't outlive me, on June 9 at 10.30 in the morning, Šándor was here, cleaning out the attic, Grandpa was clutching a matchbox with a picture of a naked woman, Šándor wanted to go get the doctor to fill out a death certificate, but Grandpa was supposed to get his pension check the next day, I would have lost 3,500 crowns, what's a day here or there, I've read in the papers that in three months retirement pensions would go up because everything has got more expensive, when Grandpa was well he made my life a living hell, and now, when I had to take care of him like a new-born, when we were enjoying the best moments of our lives together, he died just to spite me, why does God keep punishing me, life keeps getting more and more expensive, and our children live in the city, where life is hundred times more expensive, Šándor found a tailor's dummy in the attic and a washtub in the shed, then he cut down the weeds by the ditch, he stayed until nightfall, closed up the chickens and locked the gate, brought in the eggs, at night he tilled a bit under the pear tree, the ground's not frozen yet, but the weather report said that a hard freeze is coming, how will I survive the winter here all alone, I have no idea . . .

So that's why I had to fast for six days! The Lord is infinitely wise and merciful—he knew I'd need six days to prepare, five wouldn't have been enough. I looked at the dry, burnt garden with apprehension. By the time I made it to the pear tree, I had twisted my ankle in one of the many cracks in the ground. The pickaxe was dull, the dirt had hardened into rock, soon all of my bones ached. God, make it rain! I fired off a terse, ardent prayer. After an hour of digging I struck the wooden gate from our old fence. The fire must have jumped across the highway; I could hardly breathe because of the ash and smoke. Apricots were breaking their branches; pears were rotting on the apple trees. The wooden gate of our old fence was covering our old washtub. I felt diabolic vibrations. I opened the gate to hell. The man in the washtub reminded me of someone. My last thought before passing out belonged to my mother: 'Lord, protect her, who's been living in my father's bed?'

Grandpa Kohút was a trained tailor. He had three apprentices, but in 1948 he got 'nationalized'. Ever since then things went downhill, Grandma said. He worked at the beer brewery until retirement, he took up drinking, and after he had a few drinks he was ill tempered. He made money on the side by doing alterations, he shortened and took in trousers, but he no longer felt up to doing jackets. In the attic, beneath forty years of dust, there was a dress form and a tailor's dummy.

'For three years no one looked for him?'

'No.'

'What about your sons? Didn't they come over?'

'Once in a while. They took care of things around the house, loaded the coal into the shed, chopped wood for us.'

'Didn't they ask about their father?'

'Of course they did. I always let them see him. They got used to him sleeping all the time, they didn't want to disturb him, they're well-raised boys.'

'What about the neighbours?'

'They envied me. My neighbour would often yell across the fence, Katrena, you're living in paradise, you should be praying three hundred Hail Marys every day and thanking the Virgin for such blessings . . . If only my old man wanted to be in bed like that, what more do you need, you've got a husband, he doesn't go drinking, he doesn't have the strength to beat you, and on top of it all you get his pension. The postman gave me the most trouble. Delivering Grandpa's pension. He said Grandpa had to sign for it personally, he kept bugging me until I raised his tip by 10 crowns. After that he stopped bothering me.'

'Who was your accomplice?'

'Accomplice?'

'You can barely walk.'

'You're right . . . I can't even hold a glass of water any more.'

'Who helped you?'

'He died.'

'When?'

'A year ago. Leave him in peace.'

'Old Šándor?'

'He loved me. He was a good man.'

'Were you scared?'

'Not really. It was easier than I had imagined.'

'Why are you laughing?'

'I remembered Grandpa. When our hens stopped laying, he secretly kept giving money to our neighbour.'

'For what?'

'For eggs. She'd buy them, and then he'd bring them home to make it look like the hens were still laying. He was in love with the neighbour, and he thought that I didn't know.'

'Were you jealous?'

'The night before he died, he closed the chicken coop, locked the gate and brought two eggs into the kitchen. He set them on the table, stood at attention, saluted and gave a report, "General, mission accomplished, sir, I'm so hungry I could eat a horse."'

I fervently prayed in tongues because I didn't know what to pray for in my own words God heard my desperate prayers and that's why I survived Satan's latest and hardest counterattack Satan doesn't understand prayer in tongues and he's not able to cut the connection between us and the Holy Spirit Oh Lord thank you for the gift of tongues halleluiah I moved aside the washtub the body was intact the corpse showed no signs of decay the physical appearance was unchanged the face had turned a little brown but despite the cracked washtub the skin remained extraordinarily supple the facial expression was unbelievably mild my father looked like he was sleeping after a vacation by the Mediterranean an intoxicating smell of roses wafted from the washtub, the forest fire was approaching at rapid speed . . .

I was relieved when I realized he wouldn't be too much trouble; after a six-day fast and the strenuous digging I was quite exhausted, I didn't have energy to spare.

I placed my hand on my father's forehead.

The Engagement

> It is not a good idea to try to explain things that cannot be explained by reason. It is no less false to deny their existence only because they do not have a reasonable explanation. After all, they leave a trace and they have an effect, therefore they must be real.
>
> —Hans Erich Nossack

1

Finally, I had a room all to myself where I could continue writing my first book in peace and warmth. It was actually a full-blown flat—two rooms, a bathroom and a small kitchen, in short—a homeless man's opium-induced dream. The building was old, two-storey, located downtown, on Karadžičova Street. It had four sections around a central courtyard. The courtyard was paved with concrete, and in the middle, there was a metal stand for carpet dusting. Wastebins lined the walls, always full and always reeking. The second floor had an exterior hallway—shorts, underwear, shirts, bras and diapers drying in it—and old ladies always sitting around up there, enlivening their final days with incessant spying and gossiping about the other tenants.

I made up my mind to do nothing other than work on my book; that was also why I broke up with the woman I loved. It was one of my landlady's conditions: no female visitors, no drinking parties and no using *her things*. No women, no sex, no alcohol, strict asceticism—that was the promise I made myself, and I was sure that those malicious hallway biddies stood no chance: no amount of scheming would turn up anything.

It took me half a year to find the flat; cold autumn days had just set in, and this place had gas heating; it was nice and warm, and quiet—if you could ignore the constant din of cars and the loud shaking of the walls and floors when train carriages were being shunted; to this day Karadžičova is a particularly busy street—if it hasn't been renamed, that is. The landlady worked as a receptionist at a chalet in the Harmónia Resort, and she lived there as well, so we agreed she'd only come check on the place once a month. The flat actually belonged to her son, who was doing his mandatory military service, so it was a mutually benefi-cial arrangement: she didn't have to worry about paying the rent, and I finally had a roof over my head.

Previously, during my landlady's son's first year of military service, a friend of mine had lived here, a former colleague from the department; we used to call him Edgar. I actually found the flat thanks to him. One day we ran into each other at Café Krym, I told him about my unsuccessful flat hunt, I admitted I had been homeless and bouncing between dorms and friends' couches, and he kindly offered to help, 'You fool, I don't know why you left the university, but you can have my flat if you'd like. I can't stand it there any more.' Granted, he did warn me, but I didn't care. He said it was unbearable, but he seemed somehow overwrought, bordering on hysterical, and I thought he was greatly exaggerating. From his incoherent words I gathered that while the landlady visited only infrequently, she was *completely* in the know about everything. You couldn't hide from her; you couldn't escape her prying eyes . . . I interrupted him: 'I thought you said she lived in Harmónia.'

'She does.' He nodded. 'She lives way out of town, but she shows up when you least expect it, and when it's *completely* humiliating.' He cursed some toothless biddies, which as he put it, watched his every step; he said he was leaving, even though he was sorry to let go of such a flat, but his nerves, he said, his nerves couldn't take it any more. In short—a *complete* paranoiac, I thought spitefully, that's what you get for not having left that *completely* 'dumb' university; you could have been sane.

I bought myself a tin cup, two porcelain demitasses and two glasses—a service for coffee and wine. I was ready to face all intrigues; the fee for my recently aired TV-script will comfortably get me through at least half a year, I thought with glee, and I hoped to put in some good work and finish at least one book.

2

The first month went well. In two nights, I came up with the short story 'On a Tram', and over the course of the month I also wrote the ten-page piece 'Dog Days', which got published in the weekly *Cultural Life*.

On a Tram
The story takes place amid the greatest concentration of anonymous bodies—in a crowd on mass transportation.

An involuntary, anonymous, impersonal 'touch' in the crowd on a tram is transcoded into an erotic touch. The narrative situation itself implies the necessary conditions for this type of transcoding: physical contact in a crowd eliminates the requisite personal space and leads to the erosion of an individual's 'bubble'—this type of elimination of personal space is, however, permissible and indeed, imperative, for sexual intercourse. The narrator has rear-entry intercourse with a woman who is standing in front of him on the tram but, in the end, he is separated from her by the crowd. (This separation is foreshadowed in the text by the reference to the protagonist's waning attention after intercourse.)

> The tram began to move, leaving behind the woman, whose face I never saw, at the stop. I caught a glimpse of her profile, but that wasn't enough to be able to recognize her later amid the multitude of other women with similar hair, a similarly tan, supple, youthful skin. She had no distinctive features.

The moment of enchantment is nearly identical with the moment of parting. The woman is not individualized by any 'distinctive features'. And yet at the outset the protagonist asks the question: 'Wasn't it a real, genuine, once-in-a-lifetime union, which could be called an act of love?' This union really is 'once in a lifetime', given that the protagonist does not know, and will not get to know the woman with whom he has experienced it. It is possible to meet the all-important person in our lives purely by chance. The protagonist could meet his 'fellow passenger' the next day on another tram, but he would not be able to identify her because of her indistinctness—Tomáš Horváth, *Dušan Mitana*, p. 32.

The publisher told me I needed at least ten stories for a book; so far I had six; with any luck, I'd wrap it up in three months. Every day I wrote until 4 a.m., I got up at 11, had a cheap lunch and a beer at a nearby restaurant, from 2 to 6 p.m. I wrote, then I went out for a cheap dinner and a beer, I came back home and made myself some coffee, and put my nose to the grindstone from 8 until 4. The landlady hadn't shown up, and I felt safe, because I was living up to my promise: no women, no sex, no parties, no phone calls. Just to be completely in the clear, I hadn't used the landlady's things even once, but that wasn't much of a sacrifice, because other than making coffee, I only cooked a couple of hard-boiled eggs in my tin cup once in a while at night. But after a month of a hermit's life I hit a wall. The things I was working on were worthless, I'd write and tear up the pages, it was all gone: my inspiration, my enthusiasm and my desire to work.

Of course, I knew the cause: unsatisfied yearning. I yearned for the woman I had broken up with in order to write a book about our relationship: it had the promise of becoming a hundred-page novella. Finally, I couldn't take it any more. I called her, but her husband informed me that she no longer lived with him and he didn't know her new address, but even if he had, he'd certainly not let me have it. Nothing to be done about it, I said to myself, *c'est la vie*, we'll always be together—but only in the book I must write. I started on the novella, but I was not meant to finish it in my comfortable, warm flat on Karadžičova Street . . .

3

On 21 November at 9 p.m. the phone rang. I thought it was the landlady calling to check on me; I hadn't given the number to *anyone*.

I heard a woman's voice . . .

'Viera?' I asked with my throat closed up; my mouth had gone dry. I immediately realized my mistake because the voice on the other end of the line said: 'No, I'm sorry, it's just me.'

It was a woman's voice, but it didn't belong to the woman I yearned for, my one and only love.

'You have the wrong number,' I said, 'I don't have a telephone.'

'Did you write the short story "On a Tram"?'

'I did,' I admitted.

'Then I have the right number.'

'What's your name?'

'I don't have a distinctive name.'

Needless to say, I immediately knew who was hiding behind that tan, supple, youthful voice.

'I'll come over?' she asked, but it was more of a statement than a question.

I remembered my landlady, but my hesitation only lasted a split second; curiosity and desire got the better of me, I had been living like a hermit far too long. She was one of those women who could arouse you with just her voice.

'You may, but first I have to take certain precautions.'

'Thirty minutes, I'll be there in thirty minutes,' she said with an appallingly delightful impatience in her voice. Outside, a thick, moist, cold November darkness had set, but just to be on the safe side I tripped the breakers in the whole house—on account of the biddies—and I lit the candles in a nine-branched brass candelabra.

She came exactly thirty minutes later, she came as a shadow. She brought a bottle of champagne and some chestnuts, supposedly to celebrate our *engagement*.

4

I can't recall the exact details of the beginning of our encounter. Long years have since elapsed, and my memory is feeble through much suffering. Or, perhaps, I cannot now bring these points to mind, because, in truth, my protagonist from the tram had with her character, her rare learning, her singular yet placid cast of beauty, and the thrilling and enthralling eloquence of her low musical language, made her way into my heart, unobtrusively and imperceptibly, slowly but surely, like Lady Rowena in Edgar's short story 'Ligeia'.

I would in vain attempt to portray the majesty, the quiet ease of her demeanour, or the incomprehensible lightness and elasticity of her footfall. She came as a shadow. I only became aware of her presence when she placed her hand on my shoulder, and I heard her quiet, sweet voice say, 'Darling, change this one little word . . .' Clearly, she even wanted to do my writing for me.

In beauty of face no maiden ever equalled her. It was the radiance of an opium-dream—an airy and spirit-lifting vision, yet her features were not of that regular mould which we have been falsely taught to worship in the classical labours of the heathen. 'There is no exquisite beauty without some strangeness in the proportion,' Edgar said when I told him about my unpleasant little episode the next day, and he was right. Her features were not of a classic regularity, I perceived that her loveliness was indeed 'exquisite', and I felt that there was much of 'strangeness' pervading it, yet I have tried in vain to detect the irregularity and to trace home my own perception of the 'strange'.

What's the problem? I kept racking my brain to no avail. My guest was making me dinner, the delicious aroma of roasted chestnuts wafted from the oven. Despite her refined and graceful elegance, she turned out to be quite resourceful in the kitchen: when she didn't find a cookie sheet, she roasted the chestnuts in my landlady's springform pan.

We ate chestnuts, drank champagne and she was explaining to me why a complete union had not taken place on the tram, despite the fact that there had been penetration.

I seem to recall that her family had something to do with it. Yes, she talked about her family. And she said hers was an old Pressburg family, whom we upstarts from the country could never fully appreciate, and that's why we could *never satisfy* the daughters of the ancient lines on trams, trolleybuses or buses—basically on any mode of mass transit. Perhaps the champagne she had brought had Noxyron or some other sedative in it, because no matter how much I ponder questions suited to bringing back the impressions of my surroundings, all I can remember are her words: '*I love twilight, spiritual mysteries and the purest ivory.*'

As we were finishing the last of the chestnuts and there was no more than a glass of champagne left, as I was undressing her, there was loud banging on the door.

The banging kept getting scarier, and more and more voices joined in. It was a ground-floor flat, the windows had bars—there was no escape.

It was the landlady. Three hallway biddies rushed in with her.

I won't bore you with the embarrassing details of what followed. I watched the three biddies like a hawk, in hopes that by observing their behaviour, I could determine which one had reported me to the landlady, but I didn't succeed; they must have worked together, the old pros. I had no doubt that they called her; the timing fit. The thing that upset the landlady most was that we had used her springform pan. She put on quite a show. I was worried she'd have a heart attack. Thankfully, the rest of our champagne and the last two chestnuts pulled her through. The poor woman survived. What else is there to say? I wouldn't wish it on anyone. My anonymous reader was devastated, I could understand. But I also understood that she, the damn Pressburger, took it out on me. As I examined the contour of her lofty and pale forehead, she said, 'How awful! Where have I ended up? Oh, these country bumpkins!'

As if I hadn't done everything I could not to be seen. As if I could have fooled those hallway biddies. And just for the record, they took all my candles.

5

In the days that followed I went back to working with diligence and fervour. My *fiancée* had probably broken off our engagement, and the trauma of that night tormented her for two months.

Then she called.

It was the middle of January, so cold the frost crackled; it turned out that the only place we could meet was my flat. She didn't invite me to her house, she was careful not to—I expect she wanted to remain completely anonymous until the end of the game she had started. She only gave me her phone number and said, 'Call me Lady Rowena.' It was all I could do not to laugh, I didn't want to offend her, but that was going too far. Why, of all people, did I have to screw this ridiculous apparition? Were there not enough *normal,* hard-working women weaned on realist literature travelling on Bratislava trams? Naturally, I was afraid that our second get-together would also end prematurely; I kept trying to come up with ways to trick those damned prying hallway biddies. I found out exactly how long it takes to get from Harmónia to Bratislava and calculated that after a tip-off, the landlady could be in town in about an hour. Then I waited for a freezing cold night, 20 below, a snowstorm. I double-checked all the hallways and windows. After the last light went out, I was certain there wasn't a soul awake in the whole house. Well, the biddies would have been awake; that's just how it goes with old women, but they couldn't have seen us, because they would have frozen to death out in the hallways. Just to be on the safe side, I tripped the breakers again and lit the candles in the nine-branched candelabra.

I called her and at midnight I opened the door. Lady Rowena from the tram entered my living room, bundled up, in a snow-covered fur coat. While I was helping her out of her coat, I confided my worries to her and politely asked her for patience. We had to wait at least an hour to be absolutely certain that my landlady wouldn't surprise us again. After all, we'd have plenty of time until dawn for a more intimate introduction—she agreed. In order to kill time, I pulled a bottle of light wine my physician had prescribed out of the sink, and I hastened across the room to bring it. But as I stepped beneath the light of the nine-branched brass candelabra, two circumstances of a startling nature attracted my attention. I had felt that some palpable although invisible object had passed lightly by my person; and I saw that there lay upon the old, worn-out carpet, in the very middle of the rich lustre thrown from the candelabra, a shadow—a faint, indefinite shadow of angelic aspect—such as might be fancied for the shadow of a shade. I didn't say a word. I poured some wine into a glass and held it up to her lips. She took the glass, and I sank down onto the couch with my eyes fastened upon her person. She downed the wine in one gulp and said, 'I'm hungry.'

I found two eggs, farmers' cheese, sugar and a bottle of milk in the refrigerator. I withheld the fact that I had inherited these from the previous occupant of the castle. For a long time we couldn't figure out what to make of those ingredients, but then

Lady Rowena discovered flour and vanilla in the cupboard. She decided to bake cheese tarts. She kneaded the dough. I studied her forehead, the gentle prominence of the regions above the temples, and then the raven-black, the glossy, the luxuriant and naturally curling tresses; I studied the delicate outlines of her nose, with a scarcely perceptible tendency to the aquiline, and the harmoniously curved nostrils speaking the free spirit. At half past twelve she put the cakes into the gas oven, poured herself more wine, and sat down next to me on the ottoman. She pulled out a deck of cards from her décolletage and started to play solitaire. I regarded her sweet mouth: the magnificent turn of the short upper lip—the soft, voluptuous slumber of the under—the dimples which sported, and the colour which spoke—the teeth glancing back, with a brilliancy almost startling, every ray of the holy light which fell upon them in her serene and placid, yet most exultingly radiant of all smiles. At 1.20 we finished the cakes and the wine, she took off her high heels, and we lay down in bed. It was clear the landlady wouldn't be coming that night.

She held my hand, and I scrutinized the formation of her chin, and here too, I found gentleness of breadth, the softness, and the majesty, the fullness and the spirituality; she poured out before me the overflowing of a heart whose more than passionate devotion amounted to idolatry. How had I deserved to be so blessed by such confessions? I kept asking myself, all the while gazing into her large eyes. They were, I must believe, far larger that the ordinary eyes of our own race, and more perfect than the eyes of gazelles.

She placed my hand on her soft pelt; her moist clitoris jumped into my hand like a switchblade . . .

There was a banging on the door. Of course, it was the land-lady; she was beating down the door like mad. Getting dressed seemed superfluous. She knew what we were up to; there was no point in trying to tell her that we had been playing solitaire.

How had I deserved to be so cursed as to lose her every time she was ready to transform penetration into union?

I lost the flat. Yes, I gave my notice. I couldn't come to terms with the idea that those damned biddies knew my every thought. I came to understand why Edgar had a nervous breakdown.

It was a no-win situation. Stalemate. There was only one way out—I had to leave.

As my parting gift I did a grandiose gesture. As I was packing my things, it was ten in the morning, I noticed the springform pan and I recalled the landlady's rage when she found out I had once again used one of *her things*. I hurled the piece of metal to the ground, and in a rage I jumped up and down on that damned thing, I crushed it, I *demolished* it. Then I picked it up, that *pan*, threw it in the rubbish, and I bought a *new one*. Let the landlady see how people who have class behave.

6

The next day I threw all the papers with my half-written books into a backpack, and I was at peace even though I had no idea where I was going to live. I felt relieved when I realized I was leaving that flat, that house, those deadly hallway biddies, for ever.

I was just locking up, when a young man in military uniform came up to me and introduced himself as the landlady's son. To make conversation, I asked if he was on leave. He said he had come for the funeral. His mother had passed away unexpectedly the previous morning. She had had a seizure, fell unconscious, then mortal agony set in; she never came to.

Agony, stalemate and agony, confused fragments of words and images swirled around in my head, what was her name, stalemate and agony, we had met on a tram . . .

'She died? Yesterday morning? What time?' I asked.

'At ten.'

'At ten?'

'Yes, exactly at ten. Her watch stopped too.'

He looked at me quizzically and asked, 'Do you know the cause of her death?'

I remembered the springform pan, but I didn't say anything; he wouldn't have believed me anyway.

'Please accept my deepest sympathy,' I said.

7

She was waiting for me in front of the house.

Lady Rowena from the tram, from the short story that was yet to be published.

She had never said she read it.

Old man, I finally said to myself, that woman is the archetype and the spirit of evil. She doesn't want to be alone, but she wants to remain anonymous. She's a creature of the crowd. You'd follow her in vain; you wouldn't find out anything more about her or her exploits.

I waved good-bye to her and invited the soldier for a beer at a nearby pub.

She left like a shadow.

8

As I write these words, it occurs to me that I never learnt the name of that miraculous maiden who had been my lover, my friend, my fiancée. *But how do you figure out which being is real? Do we not meet people every day, who are nothing more than shadows to us?* Was she toying with me? Or was I trying to prove to her how much I loved her, and that was why I didn't ask her name? I remember her as tall and slender, even emaciated the last time we saw each other.

But that memory too is foggy, so it's no surprise that I have completely forgotten the other details!

Epilogue

Twenty-five years later, I had a book signing at Hotel Kiev. A young man in military uniform stopped by, handed me a copy of *Patagonia*, and said, 'Sign it, Dad.'

'Dad, what dad? I only have two daughters, if I'm not mistaken.'

'I'm the one from the tram.'

I embraced him warmly. 'How's your mother?'

'Good, she passed away a year ago . . . '

'What was her name? What was her name?'

'Don't worry, Dad, she didn't have a distinctive name. She was called Jezebel.'

I thanked him for the information and invited him to the bar for a glass of champagne.

Tank 73

I tried to do it differently, but it's not working. Their form must be correct. It has nothing to do with self-obsession or egoism. An artist has no I. Or only to a very small degree, which is why he invents an I and puts his own words into its mouth. The human being is a creature with a unique talent for conversing with itself.

—Hans Erich Nossack

Tuesday

At 10 p.m. I went to see Dominik. He wasn't home. I left him the latest issue of *Romboid* featuring 'The Needle'. I got home at 1 a.m. At 1.30, Elo called from Crystal Bar. He was thoroughly depressed: they wouldn't let him make any films, except maybe a micro-comedy . . . See you tomorrow at Café Krym . . .

'Wait,' he said, 'when's tomorrow?'

'Wait,' I said, looking at my watch.

'The day after tomorrow. Today I'll be sleeping.'

'Me too. The day after tomorrow. Bye.'

My father wanted to kill me with an axe, while I was naked. Because our brick wall fell down—it was my fault: I had mixed 'bad mortar'.

We didn't see eye to eye. Perhaps it really *was* my fault, but I couldn't come to terms with him giving in, I couldn't accept his adage: 'Do what everyone else does. Say what everyone else says. Think the way everyone else thinks. Otherwise you'll lose your mind, go blind or commit suicide.'

They had beaten him down, I know—he could barely see any more, he had cataracts in both eyes. My brother and I had arranged for him to have surgery in Olomouc, where they were supposed to have the best specialists, but I was more scared than he was. If the operation didn't go well, it would be my fault again.

'And then?' I asked.

'What then, why then?'

'What will I do, who will I be, who will I turn into if I follow your advice? A regular piece of shit. A nobody!'

He nodded sarcastically. 'But you'll be like everyone else, and you'll survive until death. And maybe you won't even go blind.'

Maybe that was why I instinctively liked people who weren't like everyone else.

At dawn water started to drip from the ceiling—the autumn rains were upon us.

Wednesday

In the afternoon my wife told me that the office called, and that if I didn't show up, there'd be no help for me. Then she ordered me to exchange our empty gas tank for a full one the next day and to report to the housing bureau that there was a leak in our flat again. We lived on the top floor, the eighth, and whenever it rained, we had to keep trading out buckets—the water dripped: drip, drip, drip, drip, drop, drop, drop, drop, it'll never stop . . .

My brother called: Our father had decided to go to Olomouc after all—I wasn't sure whether to be happy or prepare for the worst.

'And the wall? Did it fall?'

'What?'

'I had a bad dream. But it's not my fault; I'm not a bricklayer. The mortar was good, maybe the cement was old.'

'That's possible. I thought it looked a little lumpy too.'

A month ago I had gone home; we were building a brick wall to replace our old, rotten, wooden fence. Everyone was having fun at my expense, saying that instead of writing all that bullshit I should at least learn to make *good mortar*.

It rained until morning, then it cleared.

Thursday

In the morning, Viera loaded a large backpack for me with an empty gas tank: propane.

'And don't forget to go by the housing bureau so they come fix that ceiling.'

'But it's not raining,' I said. 'And it's the roof that needs fixing, the ceiling's not to blame.'

'It's not raining now, but it will. Ceiling or roof, it's all, pardon my language . . . crap. Tell them that!'

'Don't worry, I will!'

On my way to the office I completed my assignment: the tank was full, that is to say, operational. I'll go by the housing bureau in the afternoon, I reminded myself, but first I have to stop by the office.

On the pavement in front of the Luxorka Building I found an axe. To be exact, I didn't find it; I just spotted it. It was covered in dried mortar; some labourer must have lost it. Or he had just set it down, went into the former coffeehouse for a beer and a borovička, and then forgot about it. It was lying around on the asphalt pavement, downtown, crowds passed by, stepped over it, cars honked, trams rang, and the axe waited quietly . . . For me? What was the meaning of this? Finding an axe in the middle of Bratislava couldn't be a coincidence. Should I, or should I not? I felt self-conscious. I stepped over it, but after a couple of steps I stopped. I lit a cigarette and observed the axe. What if it's some kind of a trick? What if someone's watching? What if I pick it up and they charge me with a crime? After a brief hesitation, I found my fleeting courage. I quickly doubled back and poof—hid the axe in my large backpack, and slipped it next to the full tank. Damn. Now what? I'll walk into the office with a tank and an axe, that won't end with just a 'slap on the wrist'. Last time they gave me a 'slap on the wrist'—that's what the new editor-in-chief called it—he had come from some ideological division of the Central Committee of the Communist Party of Slovakia, and he sweated like a pig. 'You called us swine, communist whores, fucking normalizers, you really lit into us, but I'm a decent person, I get it, you had a lot to drink, you're young, you can still turn into a human being. The party is merciful, even to non-party members, you won't go to court, I've arranged a "slap on the wrist" for you.' His heart was in the right place, I almost felt sorry for him, but couldn't help him. I cared, but everything was crashing down on me at once: my father, the wall, the axe, military service, the slap on the wrist, the ceiling, the roof, blindness . . .

I think I should move into an insane asylum. I'll go talk to Elo.

We talked at Café Krym until 2.30 in the morning. Elo wanted to make a film based on *Patagonia*—I had a signed TV contract, and Elo had already come up with a title: *Indian Summer*, but they nixed that; they didn't let people do what they did best—they got rid of them elegantly, bloodlessly and mercifully. In the end, I promised to write him a micro-comedy, he said they'd let him make that. When I told him about my plan to move into an insane asylum, he warned me, 'Don't do it, they'll never let you out!' But I had two years of mandatory military service coming; in 1968, during the Dubček-era euphoria, we lost our minds—our entire class—we refused to do our reduced military service alongside school, and then the Russians came, and now we were looking at two years of full service.

As I was explaining my reasoning and rationalizing my preliminary decision, my friend and classmate Dežo showed up at our table. He took an interest in my plan, which scared me. 'Old man, if you try it, I'll come join you.' He started to hug me. I was afraid he'd fuck up everything again because had no sense of when to quit. I'll let them give me sedatives, but he'll ask for electroshock therapy just to get a new experience—the adventurer. 'Dežo, stop fooling around,' I pleaded. 'I may not end up going.' I kissed his sweaty forehead to calm him down.

'You'll go, I'm sure you will,' he said. 'And if you survive, I'll come join you.'

'Thanks, Dad.' I laid him under the table; we were all pretty hammered by then. 'An insane asylum is not the solution. The thing to do would be to leave this world,' said Elo and fell asleep with his face on the marble coffee table. In that state I set out for my native office. With a tank and an axe.

Luckily, the only person at the editorial office was a pleasant older secretary, who gave me a sincere warning: 'Dušanko, don't ruin your life, you're still young.'

'What do you mean?' I asked.

'Dominik came by.'

'When?'

'Yesterday. Why do you keep seeing him?'

'Because I like him.'

'Dušanko, you have no idea how much harm it's doing to you. Take my advice, I experienced the fifties. Firsthand.'

'I don't give a damn about them.'

'You're terribly irresponsible. Aren't you expecting?'

'Expecting what?'

'A baby. Aren't you?'

'No, don't worry. My wife's having the baby.'

'Dušanko, you're a real nutcase.'

'Thank you. I hope you won't retract that when the time comes.'

'What new antics did you come up with?'

'I'm prepared. For everything,' I said and opened my large backpack.

When she saw the tank and the axe, she gave me a sad smile, 'You're out of luck. The boss won't be back today. Too bad.'

'Where is he?'

'Out partying somewhere. He came in this morning, totally wasted, announced that normalization was complete and we're finally living in real socialism, and then he left. Maybe he's at a sobering centre.'

'That's OK. Tomorrow's another day. And Dominik?'

'He wanted to see you, but he must have known you'd be sleeping. He left you a letter.'

I sobered up instantly.

'Was he angry?' I asked.

'I don't think so. What are you afraid of, Dušanko? No one cares about what he says any more.'

'Some people do,' I said and took the letter with trepidation.

I was afraid to read it. I was hoping that my story hadn't disappointed Dominik, but I couldn't be sure. In short—I was as anxious as a teenager before a first date.

'Thank you,' I said, and slipped Dominik's letter into my backpack, next to the tank and the axe. I felt that I needed to have something to pluck up my courage before reading it . . .

I woke up at the Two Lions, the police headquarters.

Policemen were asking me why I carried a tank and an axe in my backpack. They must not have given any importance to the letter—in many ways, they were right. It was only important to me.

'As conversation pieces,' I said. They whacked me across the back with a nightstick a few times—to perk me up. I asked them for President Husák's phone number and a glass of water. They filled a glass jar with tap water, 'Drink up,' they said, and then they walloped me, 'Comrade Husák is the general secretary, don't you know that, fuckhead?'

'I demand that you address me in the formal!'

'Really?' They laughed and struck me again.

I didn't give up. 'I warn you, you'll be in trouble,' I said. 'He's my uncle. And I dreamt that one day he'll be president.'

They looked at my ID; they weren't convinced, but at least they started addressing me in the formal: 'Your last name's Mitana, not Husák!'

'He's an uncle on my mother's side. Her maiden name was Husáková.' I affably caressed one's hair, and on a whim, I poured out the jar of water over his head with the words: *'I baptize you with water for repentance. But after me comes one who is more powerful than I . . . He will baptize you with the Holy Spirit and fire. Do not suppose that I have come to bring peace to the earth. I did not come to bring peace, but a sword.'*

They whacked me again. I was starting to get tired of it. I hate monotony, if they want to beat me, fine, but they don't have to keep beating me the same way each time.

'Besides, Uncle Husák is also my colleague. Not just my uncle.' I gave them a second warning.

'Really? You're also a president, fuckhead?'

'I'm a writer, and Uncle has also written a book. About the Slovak National Uprising. It's an autobiography. He thought he was always organizing something.'

They may have busted me up completely, but the angels were with me, as always. One from the legion showed up, in a captain's uniform, and dismissed the whole thing with a wave of his hand: 'Forget about him, it'th that crazy writer. Thomeone mutht be protecting him . . . '

'You're right.' I nodded. 'I'm under the protection of the blood of Jesus Christ.'

They whirled their tomahawks, but they didn't dare strike.

'Thanks, Indians, you're merciful. You'll get points for that in the next world. And don't be afraid, of anything. Someday, every other Slovak will be president.' I thanked them with a sincere, encouraging smile. It was a mistake, one of them decided to wallop me anyway—right on the head. He turned towards the captain and said, 'I'm sorry, but I hate rabble-rousers.'

'Hate kills the hated as well as the hater,' I warned them for the third and final time. Then I lost consciousness.

I dreamt that I was wandering around in front of the Luxorka Building, naked, everyone was pointing fingers at me, and I flew up to get away from them, to the top of the Manderla Building, but then my wings fell off, and I was being chased by the police, they shot at me from slingshots, and I was terrified when I looked down at the ground, and then bricks started to fall on me from the wall we had been building in my native village, and my father was chasing me with a sharpened axe, yelling, 'You won't be embarrassing me any more, I'd rather kill you, your mother and I won't be ashamed any more in front of the whole village because of your revolting book, I'd rather kill you, you can't even mix some stupid mortar, my wall fell down and everyone's laughing at me,' and then he sicked our German shepherd on me—Chico barked at me in a human voice: 'Dog days are here, save your souls,' and I was holding the tank and looking sadly at the city beneath my feet . . .

I woke up on the last night bus. Confused, I stared at the open backpack which had *a tank and an axe* and Dominik's letter . . . I hadn't read it yet, but for some reason it was of great importance to me; I had the feeling that my fate depended on Dominik's reply. I moved the envelope to the back pocket of my jeans, but a moment later I got worried that I'd lose it, or that someone would *steal* it. To be safe, I folded it and hid it in the pocket of my undershorts. All in all, paranoia.

'Excuse me, am I going the right way?' I asked the only other passenger.

'I don't know,' he snapped.

'Is it raining?'

'It is.'

'Then I'm going the right way. Thanks. Good night.'

He looked at his watch. 'Good morning,' he said, and peeked into my backpack. He saw the tank and the axe, and ran towards the driver. He kept explaining something to the driver, the bus stopped.

The accordion doors opened with an angry hiss. The driver and the passenger ran out, into the darkness and rain, and I didn't know how to drive.

I zipped up the backpack and got off the bus. It wasn't raining, it was pouring!

I looked for our building. It was a new, monumental residential complex, all of the buildings looked exactly the same. I felt like I was in a maze. Then again, if one wanders around a maze long enough, it gradually turns into his residence, almost his home, therefore, even I, as navigationally challenged as I was, was finding more and more often not only the right building but also the right street, the right entrance and the right floor.

Half an hour later, I was in front of our building—I had found it! Who knows whether it was instinct, habit or simply luck; truth be told, I didn't care. I was happy to be home at last. It was quarter to three, an hour when my wife is in her deepest sleep, an hour most suitable for coming home. I think that every husband who cares about living in harmony should know the time of his wife's deepest sleep. Only boors don't know to come home at the right moment. I didn't take the lift, I didn't want to risk it falling down and waking up the whole building. I walked up the stairs to the top floor, took off my muddy shoes in front of the flat, and discreetly unlocked the door. The flat was quiet, dark and rainy. I heard water dripping in the living room, and based on the sound I estimated that the bucket wasn't full—only quarter full. It wouldn't overflow by morning. I undressed to my underwear in the dark and tactfully crawled into the warm lair. My wife fidgeted restlessly, but she remained asleep. Instinctively she stuck out her charming tooshie—ever since she got pregnant, we only made love from behind.

Thursday

I was awakened by a woman. She looked surprised, but not shocked. A twenty-five-year-old blonde, thin, busty, I had often turned to look at her.

'Would you like some coffee, neighbour?' she asked.

'No,' I groaned.

'Why not?'

'I'm sorry, ma'am. I was drunk,' I said, feeling guilty. 'Well, it was nothing special,' she said in a hurt tone, as if I had *offended* her. 'Almost like with my old man. Does your flat have a leak too?'

'It does.' I nodded.

I got dressed in a hurry. 'I'm sorry, ma'am,' I apologized a second time. 'It was a mistake.' When I saw that she was about to take offense again, I added, 'But a pleasant one.'

She nodded graciously, 'There are worse things.'

With a polite bow I thanked her for the compliment. One building over on the right, a ninety-year-old retiree was hanging out on the top floor—no wonder the old timer got lost now and then.

When I finally made it home, my wife was singing a popular tune: 'What a waste, the love I gave you, what a waste, the tears I shed for you . . . ' she sang, hugging my achy head, 'Everything's going to be OK, don't worry. Tomorrow you can check in at the asylum.'

'Which one?'

'On Mickiewicz Street. The university hospital.'

I started to kiss her dearly, 'Thank you, my darling, Pezinok is far away. But don't tell Dežo where I've gone, because they'll kick us out of there too . . . '

'Don't worry. Elo called. He said you promised him a micro-comedy.'

'That's fine. I'll come up with something. I'll have plenty of time.'

'Oh, I've arranged a stipend for you.'

'You're my angel, I've always known it . . . '

'And your brother called too. About your father. He said you should call him.'

I called my brother. 'How's Dad?' I asked, 'Can he see?'

'The operation was successful. He can already see out of one eye. Next year they'll fix the other.'

'And the wall? Did it fall down?'

'Are you insane? The wall's fine, Dad can see, only you've rounded the bend.'

'Thank God. Are there mushrooms?'

'There are. So many boletes you could mow them. That's why I'm calling. Everything's fine. Will you come?'

'I will,' I said and hung up.

'Viera, my darling, I've got one more piece of news for you: I reached into the back pocket of my jeans, but Dominik's letter wasn't there. I panicked. I started to curse like a sailor: 'Those fuckers stole it from me.'

'Who? What? Have you really gone round the bend?'

'Dominik's letter,' I said. 'Vitally important, you know what I mean?'

Water started to drip from the ceiling: drip, drip, drip, drip, drop, drop, drop, drop, it'll never stop, there's nothing left to do, but have them cut off your pecker, his glory days are through, no one loves him, he's a flop—I improvised on a song from the repertoire of Pavol Hammel . . .

'Did you take care of the housing bureau?' my wife asked, and then she answered herself, 'You forgot, I knew it. Our flat will flood, but you don't care. And I—the stupid cow that I am—carry your child around Bratislava.'

The doorbell rang.

Had they come for me? Finally. Let's get it over with.

It was a neighbour from the next building.

'Neighbour, you forgot your backpack and undershorts at our house,' he said apologetically.

He astutely threw my large backpack with a tank and an axe into our hallway, stuck my blue-and-white striped undershorts into my hand, and darted down the steps towards the lift landing.

I pulled out Dominik's letter from the pocket of the undershorts, opened the envelope, and finally read my verdict:

28 September 1973

Dear Dušan Mitana,

I delight in your name. Today I came by your office to give
you a heartfelt embrace (with a tear of joy in my eye), and
to thank you your story 'The Needle' that you brought
me yesterday. I embrace it like I embrace you. It is bril-
liant, very important. It's the philosophical core of your

future *oeuvre*. (A tiny thing: I suggest changing the tense of one verb 'I didn't understand' to 'I don't understand.')

I kiss you like a treasure, and long for you not to stop shining like a star.

Yours,

Dominik Tatarka

In my mind I made an editorial note: insert *for* before 'your story "The Needle"', I sobbed from joy and from yesterday's alcohol, full of hope, almost pregnant, I hugged my wife who was looking at the backpack with the tank and the axe and asked, 'Who was that?'

'A neighbour. From the next building.'

'Oh dear,' she sighed. 'If they at least didn't make all the keys the same.'

I took a shower, lay down in our bed, and opened a book on dreams: *to be naked* = guaranteed success, *an axe* = you'll lose property, but it'll be the lesser of two evils, *to find something* = maybe you'll win something.

I breathed a sigh of relief: Thank God, nothing's lost . . .

Before noon I got a call from the TV studio. It was the producer. 'Comrade Mitana, I am sorry to inform you that your contract for *Patagonia* is invalid.'

'Why?'

'Because you're insane, and Comrade Husák isn't your Uncle. Not even on your mother's side.'

'I understand,' I said. 'You've been informed, then?'

'I'm in a lot of trouble because of you. I hope they don't fire me.'

'I'm sorry. It was a mistake.'

'A fatal one,' she said and hung up.

The phone rang again; it was Elo's landlady. 'He has locked himself in his room, and won't open the door.'

I was standing at the top of Bratislava's skyscraper and terrified, I watched the city beneath my feet . . .

I felt as though the abyss below was bottomless, yet there was nowhere to fall.

I whirled the axe above my head and jumped.

With a tank in my arms.

Tuesday

I just got back from Elo's funeral. I started to write the micro-comedy: *A Waste of Love* . . .

With Knife and Axe

He didn't hear her strumming and singing to herself the melody of 'Non ti scordar di me' with the strange sentence that was impossible to forget: 'My husband is a billy goat?'

—André Pieyre de Mandiargues, *The Blood of the Lamb*

1

The beginning of August is often unbearably hot.

For the third week in a row, forest fires blazed in southern Europe and here at home—not even a dog deserved to be sent outside.

Between 12 and 3 in the afternoon, even the liveliest person couldn't hunt, and the most faithful dog would drag behind its master with slow steps, eyes squinting in pain, and a drooping tongue.

And that was exactly when Fido's wife decided to go visit the House on the Hill—that was how they referred to a relative's house in Koliba, a ritzy neighbourhood. Diplomats occupied most of the nearby villas; they were the private residences of West European ambassadors.

First, they hauled themselves up to Kramáre on a trolleybus, from there they had to go on foot. Fido thought it was more strenuous than a hike to Téry's chalet in the High Tatras, where he had lost his virginity many years ago. With his own wife. With whom he hadn't made love for three years now, because she hadn't been in the mood for three years. But he kept hoping that one day . . . maybe . . . still—a miracle would happen and she'd open her arms, and his would get up even at home, and everything would go back to the way it was in the beginning . . .

Along the way his wife kept promising him a pleasant surprise, practically a *gift*, but even the promise of a *bonus* couldn't placate him; when they reached their destination, his eyes squinting in pain and his tongue sticking out longingly, he collapsed in the shade of the beautifully neglected garden and for a good ten minutes he cursed like a heathen.

The purpose of their visit was to feed the poultry and to clean.

Fido's mother-in-law, who hated him with all her being despite his gratitude and love—he loved her for having borne his wife, though he hadn't been able to persuade her of his affection in thirty years—had died in the middle of winter. Buses and trolley-buses ended their routes at Kramáre, it was snowing and windy —a typical winter, in short—a total calamity. By the time they waded through the snowdrifts to the crematorium in Lamače, his mother-in-law had already flown up the chimney; the funeral service was over.

All they could do was take their places at the end of receiving line of the surviving family and accept condolences from the participants of that morbid ritual. He was resting under the wilted grapevines, and with respect and admiration he observed the changes that had taken place in the garden since his mother-in-law's passing. Like every other gardener, she too dreamt of cultivating roses. And she didn't stop at dreaming. She approached the selection and combination of species, varieties, hybrids, types and colours with care, in order to achieve the most striking effect: crimson as well as pastel roses, roses for everyday occasions and the last roses of summer, full moon roses and roses with the most tender names that bloom in poetry, blushing roses and proud roses, roses that were lovers and roses that were queens, all in all, a rose romance. That's what she called it, that's how it was.

Fido's brother-in-law, a ripe forty-something, a bachelor on principle, had different tastes; the rugged vitality of fauna excited him much more than the ethereal nobility of flora. In place of his mother's roses he started to raise goats, geese, chickens—which was why they were there: to feed the fauna and to clean the barn.

He asked them to do it over the phone—from Greece. He had gone on a beach vacation to have peace and quiet to think about his next steps in shaping his future. His mother's last will had put him face to face with a cruel dilemma: if he got married and had a child, he'd inherit everything—if he didn't get married and remained without a successor to the throne, half of the inheritance, thus half of the house and the garden, would go to his sister. Naturally, Fido would become a co-heir and co-owner.

His brother-in-law wasn't into women, but he wasn't stupid either. He'd certainly try to fulfil the terms of the last will. He was, in a nutshell, a visionary. For thirty years he had been repeating a single prophetic sentence: 'Forty more days, and Nineveh will be destroyed.'

2

The house was a pigsty. The meat he had left out for his seven cats in the August heat had rotten and stank, the cats were doing their business in the kitchen, Fido's wife was cleaning, washing the dishes, scrubbing the house, and Fido was trying to help her, even though his stomach was turning.

'Look at this.' His wife opened the door to the bathroom.

On the tarnished mirror there was writing in lipstick: ERICA, MY LOVE, DON'T MISCARRY! I'LL BE BACK IN FORTY DAYS!

'So he does have a girlfriend,' his wife said, surprised, irritated.

'Tough luck.' He nodded. 'There'll be trouble with the inheritance yet.'

That upset her, she seemed downright *offended*.

'I despise your morbid statements,' she lashed out at him. Her irritation surprised him.

'Erik's no spring chicken.' He laughed. 'Are you jealous of his girlfriend?'

'Moron!'

'I'm sorry,' he said apologetically. 'You've been quite irritable lately. Can't you take a joke?'

'I may be late . . . ' she said.

'Menopause, I understand, Grandma.'

He embraced her tenderly around her shoulders.

They had been grandparents for three years, and she was a year away from retirement. Fido had no idea it was taking such a *toll* on her.

'Don't touch me,' she screamed hysterically. 'Everything's a joke to you, but I feel a sense of responsibility.'

'So far I've been sleeping with a grandmother, but in a year I'll also be sleeping with a retiree,' he said, attempting to give an exact definition of the situation. She gave him a quiet, questioning look, then shook her head and said: 'We don't sleep *together*, but *next to each other*.'

That reminded Fido of a short story he had read some thirty years ago, when their first daughter was born: the author described watching his wife after their son had been born: 'They looked like conspirators, and Rudolf didn't know the password. I have a son now, but I've lost my wife . . . ' Fido felt as though the same thing had happened to him when his daughter gave birth to their grandson three years ago—they hadn't made love since then.

'Whose fault is that?' he asked, and when no answer came, he went on the offensive and continued in an accusatory tone, 'Soon you'll make an impotent of me!'

'You don't know the things you're capable of when you're drunk.' She finally smiled and kissed him on the lips.

Before he could be fazed, she went back to the matter of the inheritance: 'If he gets married and has a child, he'll inherit the whole house. And we won't have a roof over our heads.'

And then she *explained* the subtle terms of the will to him again: his mother-in-law was taking her revenge on them from beyond the grave.

'But we own a flat!'

'Yes, but our children need it!'

'Let them take care of themselves. No one gave us anything.'

'Oh, you're so egotistical! It's what I hate about you. That's the problem!'

'The problem is that you're just a mother and a grandmother any more, and you don't even remember the fact that you're my wife,' he growled.

'Someone has to take care of the children and the grand-children,' she said with her gaze glued *at* the mirror.

From the depths of the mirror, from beneath the writing in crimson lipstick emerged her careworn face.

'You look like an old mother hen.' Once more he resorted to sarcasm to dull the sharp edges of her terrible premonition, and she relaxed unexpectedly, 'More like an old goose,' she said, laughing. 'You're right, half a loaf is better than none. Let's roast a goose,' she said, came up to him, and kissed him on the lips *again*. 'To celebrate,' she said.

And she slaughtered the fattest goose.

And she brought out a bottle of his brother-in-law's home-made wine from the pantry . . .

At that point he got tired of cleaning the barn, he walked out, into God's light.

Roasted goose . . . he was salivating . . .

3

The fattest goose was roasting on the spit . . .

'Eric won't be too happy about that,' a neighbour yelled from the other side of the fence, and when Fido's ears perked up in confusion, she explained, 'That's Erica.'

'Who?'

'The goose you're roasting, her name's Erica.'

'Erica?'

'Erica! Eric likes Ericas,' she laughed, lifted her skirt, and jumped over the fence. 'Let me help you,' she said. 'I'm the ambassador's housekeeper,' she introduced herself.

'I see,' he nodded. 'You're a servant to an ambassador. Which one?'

'The German one. The masters are in Greece right now. On vacation.'

'You're very kind, because, to be frank, I'm not enjoying this.' He handed her the grill crank.

In all honesty, no one would enjoy such a thing—sitting by a fire in Turgenev-like heat and roasting Erica.

He sipped his brother-in-law's wine in the front yard, the neighbour kept turning the crank on the spit, Erica was starting to give off a pleasant aroma, and he watched the bedlam in the yard with disdain: cats, chickens, guinea hens, goats, geese, all in all—livestock. Just like at home, in his native village, he spat with disgust; he hated his childhood.

The best-looking goat was, as could be expected, cheeky as a monkey. Pushing and shoving, she kept trying to make her way inside, as if she were the lady of the house. It was all he could do trying to keep her out of the kitchen; she literally started to bump him. He raised his hand and commanded, 'Goat, I order you to get away from this door! You've got no business here!'

The goat bleated sarcastically, but obeyed—she went into the garden, grazed and gnawed the bark off the apple trees; his mother-in-law's roses had already been consumed.

His wife yelled from the house, 'Come see this! Now!'

He obediently went inside, following his wife's voice.

He found her in the bedroom.

She pulled aside the thick bedcovers and pointed to the sheet.

'Do you see this?' she asked him an almost insulting question.

'I do.' He nodded, insulted. 'I may need thick glasses, but I'm not blind yet.'

'What's this?' she asked *as if it were his fault.*

He saw tiny, hard, black pellets.

'Eric owns a gun?' he asked cautiously.

'He has a pellet gun and a rifle,' she said. 'He shoots swallows and ambassadors.'

'In that case, I see ammunition,' he said with a sense of relief, but he failed the test, because his wife grabbed her hair and cried out in despair, 'Ammunition? You think this is ammunition?'

'Does he happen to have a machine gun?' He took another guess, because by then he also had the sense that the bullets on the sheet would be used with a larger weapon.

In order to prove his mistake, she picked up one of the pieces with disgust and gave it a hard squeeze between her thumb and her forefinger; both fingers grew out of the palm of her right hand.

The bullet crumbled into black dust, she literally crushed it between her fingers.

'Impressive.' He nodded appreciatively.

'Not impressive,' she said. 'It's a different kind of ammo!'

He carefully examined the remains, compared them to the pellets on the sheet, and pronounced his verdict: 'Droppings!'

'Droppings? In Eric's bed?'

'Don't blame me.' He scrunched his muzzle in apology.

'You shouldn't drink so much. Dumbass. Cats don't produce droppings.'

She was practically correct: no animal larger than a cat could have got into the house through the barred windows, and cats don't normally produce droppings.

'Who knows? Our cats have normal shit, but we don't know Eric's cats . . . '

'That's true, Eric's always been extravagant . . . What did this?' His wife kept agonizing. 'Cats don't produce droppings!'

'What about goats?' He offered an alternative.

'Do you think it's goat droppings?' His wife thought about it, but three seconds later she dismissed the notion with a wave of her hand: 'Goats can't get in here,' she said, and there was *blame* in her voice again.

He had to admit she was right; no goat could get into the house through those barred windows, but *why is she blaming me?*

After all, a goat doesn't go into a house through the window; it goes in through the door.

He needed to take a leak.

4

The garden gate creaked, and a buxom young woman cheerily waving around the weekly ad paper *Bratislavsko* shouted with excitement: 'Hey, brother-in-law, you pissing?'

Damn, he does have a girlfriend after all, he thought with a pang of nostalgia.

'Yeah, I'm pissing.' He nodded and pulled up the zipper on his jeans.

'Take your time,' she said with a friendly wave. 'By the way, did you take good care of our animals?'

'We did,' he answered truthfully.

'Would you like a goose leg, *postwoman*?' his wife asked.

With snide generosity.

'A leg? Gladly. Which one are you roasting?'

'Erica.'

'Erica? Thank goodness!' the postwoman exclaimed. 'At least I don't have to kill her. You can't imagine how much she was getting on my nerves. She acted like the lady of the house, that godless slut!'

'Postwoman, how far along are you?' his wife asked with distrust, her gaze glued to their future sister-in-law's big belly.

'Seven months,' the postwoman said.

'Have a seat. You must be tired. At seven months.'

'Thank you, brother-in-law. You don't know how relieved I am.' Then she clarified: 'I'm pregnant, but don't worry, we won't bring disgrace to the family.'

'What disgrace?' his wife asked. Sternly. 'We call it a scandal.'

'Don't worry, we won't cause a scandal,' the guilty party corrected herself.

'We'll get married as soon as Eric gets back from Greece. I'm sure the baby won't come before the wedding. I know what's proper.'

'Imagine that.' His wife shook her head. In amazement. 'You can't even rely on your own brother any more. You blink, and he brings a bastard into the family.'

'Let me tell you, ever since the Berlin Wall fell, the world has been going to pot. But thanks to our patroness saint, our nation will survive!' The mischievous neighbour nodded her head significantly, then out of nowhere she squealed and yelled at the top of her lungs: 'For money a Slovak won't even spare a goat.' And she added in German: '*Guten Appetit!*'

'Allow me to introduce myself,' the postwoman said and actually curtsied. 'Erica be my name . . .'

And then, ignoring diplomatic protocol, she suggested: 'We could be on informal terms, since we're family.'

'We'll see about that,' Fido's wife said with a hint of sarcasm.

'What do you mean? We'll see about what?' There was an aggressive undertone in the postwoman's voice.

'Whether we're going to be family.' His wife didn't let herself be derailed.

'I'm Fido,' he introduced himself and barked politely.

'And I'm Erica.' His wife bowed gracefully.

'I'm also Erica,' the neighbour said. *'Mein Name ist Erica. Verstehen Sie?'*

Fido's heart leapt for joy, a German, she's one of my kind: he sniffed her longingly, even though he thought her accent sounded fake.

'I'm Erich,' he said. *'Mein Name sei Gantenbein. Erich von Gantenbein,'* he introduced himself, and his wife translated: 'He thinks he's Swiss, and his name is Gantenbein, the poor dear.' She patted his head soothingly: 'Come on, Styopa.'

He sniffed the air, on alert: 'There are too many Erica's per square foot around here.'

His wife must have come to the same conclusion, because she scratched behind her right ear, which made him sick to his stomach. And afraid. He was intimately familiar with that gesture: year after year, before killing the Christmas carp, she'd scratch behind her right ear, spit into her hands, and cross herself in three swift motions, saying: 'Forgive me, Lord, but someone has to kill him . . .'

And there she went: 'Bring the knife!'

His wife studied all the Ericas, carefully, malevolently; the neighbour couldn't take it any more, she peed her panties: 'I lied. My name is Gertrude,' she confessed, and left the battlefield in shame.

'Spy,' Erica said. With contempt. 'She has no whatchamacallit
... national pride. Slovaks are the Slovaks' worst enemy. Stupid
cow.' Erica expectorated with pleasure.

'Bring the knife! Or an axe!' his wife yelled.

'I don't know where it is. I don't know where the axe is. I don't
know my way around here.' He tried to put up some resistance,
acting like a coward, making up excuses, but the postwoman
didn't let him get away with it: 'In the woodshed,' she said. 'The
axe is in the woodshed. Stuck in the chopping block.'

'Sister-in-law, you poor thing, please keep your mouth shut,'
he warned his potential relative, but she took offense. 'Brother-in-
law, don't insult me, I know what I'm talking about, even though
I'm just an ordinary postwoman. The axe is in the woodshed.
Stuck in the chopping block.'

'You can lead a horse to water, but you can't make it drink.'
He sighed and went to get the axe. The entrance to the woodshed
(for some unknown reason) was in the bathroom, so he was forced
to read Eric's message written on the mirror in crimson lipstick
again.

ERICA, MY LOVE, DON'T MISCARRY! I'LL BE BACK IN
FORTY DAYS.

When he came back with the axe, Erica's head was in his
wife's lap and she was crying her heart out. From happiness.
Because they had accepted her into the family so readily, even
though she was just an ordinary postwoman.

'Erica, please don't cry. I'll catch cold, you've completely
soaked my skirt,' said his wife, gently caressing Erica's rust-
coloured hair. 'Put your head here, on this block.'

Erica obediently put her head on the block, and his wife tenderly moved aside her long hair, exposing her neck, and the sun was setting over the Danube, westward, and the best-looking goat was jumping around in a funny way, as if it were trying to jump over its own shadow.

'Erica, did you say you were seven months pregnant?' his wife asked. With hesitation in her voice. Perhaps her better self was coming out. After all, one blow with the axe, and two lives would be gone—it was a heinous task.

'Relax, relatives,' Erica said, laughing. 'I'm not pregnant, I'm a prankster.'

'Stop!' he yelled at his wife.

'Why?'

'Think! Logically! If Erica isn't pregnant, she can't miscarry, right?'

His wife guffawed. 'Not pregnant? With such a huge belly?'

In her excitement Erica lifted her skirt, and out of her belly she pulled a backpack full of ad papers: Bratislavsko, Avízo, Titan . . .

'See, I don't have a belly. I'm just a prankster,' she said.

'Pranksters are the first to die,' he said. 'By mistake.'

Then Erica the prankster confided in them ruefully, 'I love lovemaking, but, sadly, I'm not able to have children.' Followed by a plea: 'But please don't tell Eric. He'd kill me.'

'In that case . . . ' His wife put away the axe and with a sense of largesse she finished the sentence: '. . . Erica, live as you like.' Erica looked at her left wrist, slapped her forehead to kill a mosquito. 'My God, I still have to deliver the ad papers,' she exclaimed, then slung the backpack over her left shoulder and sprung towards the gate.

'The inheritance won't be as complicated as you thought,' his wife said in an unpleasant, almost triumphant tone.

It made him feel like taking a piss.

5

He went under the apple tree—the trunk had been chewed bare—whipped out his cock, and at that moment the best-looking goat came up to him and respectably sprinkled the cracked soil with a series of black pellets.

His wife was puzzled. 'Is it out of its mind?'

The neighbour chimed in from behind the fence: 'It's got used to living well, the stupid goat.'

He was looking—with his two near-sighted eyes—at the sun, and with his third eye he was seeing those hard, black pellets in Eric's bed.

The arrogant beast's huge green eyes were filled with desire and glued to his wilted firebird. Long-necked, indeed—that goat had an unbelievably long neck—because of which it was able to have its back to him and at the same time gaze into his eyes.

'Erica, that's not the master,' said the neighbour, laughing. 'The master went on vacation, to the beach. Maybe he'll bring you a Guinea pig or a ram.'

Erica uttered a disgusted 'baa', waddled away towards the grapevines, aggressively started to poke the smallest goat with her horns, and Fido puked.

Erica was munching on the grapevines looking dignified and proud, he almost envied her.

She had something to be proud of: she was pretty wide in the hips already.

Erica had noticed it too.

Aghast, she stared at Erica, and kept shaking her head in disbelief.

'Is this possible?'

'You've got a problem,' he said with a snide grin. 'The inheritance won't be as easy as you thought.'

'Poor thing, here chickie-chick, here,' Fido's wife called to Erica, inviting her to a feast as she threw handfuls of grain on the ground; her inheritance was disappearing like the sun setting behind the Danube, yonder, in Austria.

'Erica's not a hen,' he said to her.

'That's just it! She's an ordinary goat.' A happy smile came across Erica's face and then she ordered, 'Hand me the axe!'

'Come on, Erica,' he said, looking at his wife pleadingly. 'Quit your nagging. You've nagged me for thirty years—that's enough. You can't eliminate everyone for our children's sake.'

She scratched behind her right ear, resolutely spat into her hands, and crossed herself in three swift motions. The sun was disappearing behind the Danube, somewhere in Austria, the wind picked up behind the peak of Devínska Kobyla, and Erica didn't jump over her own shadow.

6

As they were feasting on Erica, the phone rang.

'There must be a fire,' the neighbour said laughing, and spat into the fire.

'Neighbour, don't spit into the fire, or you'll piss yourself . . . pardon my language,' Fido warned her and went on to answer the phone.

Gertrude stopped spitting into the fire, Fido enjoyed his brother-in-law's wine with bites of fragrant, crispy, roasted-to-perfection steak, and Eric was calling from Greece: 'How are things at home? Everything's on fire here, the mountains, the forests, the sea, everything. And back there, at home? Is everything OK? How are you? Have you been taking care of my geese and goats?'

'Oukay, howareyou.' Fido allayed his fears with a soothing bark. 'We fed them, don't worry, relax.'

'And Erica? How do you like her?'

'Really well. She's delectable . . . '

'Isn't she? I'm glad. I was worried you'd be, whatchamacallit, prejudiced against her . . . '

'Why? She really is quite delectable.'

'Be nice to her. So she won't miscarry. We're going to get married.'

'Congratulations. She really is quite delectable. And juicy. She's roasting on the spit as we speak.'

'Erica? On the spit? Put her on the phone. I want to speak to her! She was in a delicate condition . . . '

'Too late, Eric, now she's in the fifth dimension. Enjoy your vacation.'

'Vacation? Me? Don't you read the papers? Don't you at least watch CNN? It's total hell here. Everything's on fire. I can't breathe, the smoke is suffocating . . . baptism by fire . . . we're waiting for a helicopter or for Armageddon . . . Forty more days, and Nineveh will be destroyed!'

And Eric fell silent, although he had not hung up; Fido heard some indistinct voices speaking in a foreign language, frightened screams, muffled car horns and sirens—Eric had always been extravagant.

He hung up, and asked Erica, 'You promised me some kind of a surprise. What is it?'

His wife looked like she didn't know what he was talking about, but he thought she feigned forgetfulness.

Finally, she confessed, 'I'm two months pregnant. You'll be a father again.' He gave her a sympathetic smile.

'You're a visionary, I love you, but don't scare me!'

'I'm not scaring you. It's true!'

Everything went dark, as if she had whacked him over the head with an axe. Crimson dark. He, a two-time grandfather, was to be a father again? Waking up in the middle of the night, changing wet diapers, cleaning up his shit-covered offspring . . . ?

'Quit messing with me,' he howled miserably. 'I haven't been able to get it up around you for three years now.'

His wife gently caressed the back of his neck: 'You're not completely impotent yet, it's just your memory that's going. Don't forget about your amnesia.'

Perhaps she was right: once-in-a-blue-moon things could have happened; miracles can happen even after thirty years of marriage.

'Impossible! I'm not Abraham and you're not Sarah.'

'I hope you don't mistrust me. You don't think that some other man impregnated me?'

After thinking about it for a moment he said, 'Let's come to an agreement. If I can't remember it, nothing happened . . . '

'I hope you're not asking me to have an abortion,' she said in a threatening tone, like a good catholic.

'Lord, why are you punishing me?' He looked up to the heavens with reproach.

'You're just lazy, because you have no motivation,' she said. 'But from now it's going to be nose to the grindstone for you!'

Then it all became clear: Eric's Erica was infertile, she didn't fulfil the requirements of the mother-in-law's will; they'd leave their flat to the children, and he and his wife would share the barn with his brother-in-law—as co-owners. And he, Fido, would till the soil, muck manure and guard the property. And howl at the moon on long winter nights. The way he had a long time ago, at the native cemetery in his native village, east of Eden.

'Styopka, Styopushka, don't worry, we'll like it here,' his wife said, handing him a half-eaten bone.

He knew where she was coming from; maybe a change of scenery would be good for them; if we can't trade our partner, at least we can move, any change can be exciting. Either you change your roommate or your flat—there were no other options. That's how they used to think together, back in the day, until they had given up completely, until they had got used to each other.

'Cut it out! I'm not Styopka any more, and I never was Styopushka.' He growled menacingly. 'I'm your loyal Fido.'

And he had a terrifying thought: Life is hopelessly long.

Start over, everything all over again? My God, I'm *awfully* tired.

And he needed to piss again—from his brother-in-law's wine.

Or was it his prostate?

'Whenever there's a sunset and the wind's blowing, and I'm able to watch it, I think about my friend Rudo from Devínska Nová Ves with whom I did my military service, and it makes me want to cry . . . Do you know what happened to him? He had had enough, he was awfully tired . . . ' he was saying as he took a piss, his wife wasn't listening.

The inheritance was exacting its tax: Erica walked around the house with a dazed smile and her tongue hanging out, like an old guard dog tied by a chain to its doghouse, and Fido kept pissing, and his urine was eagerly, aggressively soaking into the hard cracked ground: towards the roots of the former roses.

'Take it from me, neighbour,' the housekeeper to the German ambassador said with a sad smile: 'A Slovak has no luck. We're all victims of our heritage . . . '

Her words took him by surprise: it was as if she had popped out of her role, as if she had stepped out of a painting and the framed white canvas stayed on the wall, but when he asked her why she had been hiding her true identity, she snapped back with some nonsense: 'WHY is not important. When we figure out HOW, we'll know WHO.'

Then she jumped over the fence and went back to her own yard.

Fido looked with pity at Erica tied by a chain to her inheritance. Her collar was digging deep into her sparse fur, she couldn't break the chain, she couldn't pull the brick doghouse with her, so she just circled it in despair, drawing fast circles with the radius of the length of the chain, and Fido thought: *I must free her, I must finally free us from our hereditary curse.*

7

A fiery glow blazed in the southern sky.

He gripped the axe tightly in his right hand, and began to howl miserably at the rising moon.

8

Ever since then, Bratislava natives as well as visitors who walk up to Koliba or Kamzík can see a large house with two towers, derelict, with a caved-in roof and shuttered windows, jutting out almost to the road.

At noon, when it's bright and sunny, there's nothing gloomier than this ruin, from which a single sentence can be heard, repeated endlessly: 'My husband is a dog.'

The Needle

I didn't know my father. He left when I was two; he left and I never saw him again. I don't remember my mother. She died less than a year after my father left, and since I didn't know her, I always imagined her as beautiful and perfect, because to me she was a mystery, which is at the core of all beauty.

After my mother's death I went from one house to another. Her relatives always treated me well and didn't even expect gratitude in return; they were perfectly content knowing that they were kindling a hatred for my father in me. I realized very quickly what they were after, and indulged them out of politeness; I feigned hatred for my father with such sincerity that in their gratitude they paid for my university studies. However, their efforts had the opposite effect—had they not made my father out to be the worst criminal the world had ever seen, he would have remained a stranger to me, and though I may not have hated him (I don't know how one could hate someone they don't know), I would have been completely indifferent towards him. As it was, they had managed to pique my interest in my father, an interest which over time grew into sympathy.

My mother's relatives didn't realize their mistake until I was a freshman at university, or more precisely, until they found out that I had started to write short stories. That ended our relationship, because in essence I had declared my allegiance to my father, thus confirming what they had secretly feared—that I had inherited his crazy genes.

My father was a priest, but at the age of thirty he took up drinking and writing poetry. When he wanted to recite his verses from the pulpit, the faithful got so indignant that the church was forced to forgo his services. One of his poems survived; my relatives often read it to me as a cautionary tale. It was titled 'A Researcher's Hope', and went like this:

If you live long enough,
You'll reach the interior,
You'll swim through the deepest of groundwater.
You'll discover the secret of the interior,
And you'll realize that it's simple:
It is the source of boats for others.
Don't worry, you'll live long enough.

I'm not surprised that the church let him go—he didn't offer the faithful much hope for rich rewards in the afterlife. One night he went to the pub and never came back. He was out of touch for the next seventeen years, but we had news of him anyway. Some men from our village had seen him in Ostrava; he worked in a mine and had no desire to change jobs. When I was nineteen, I got a letter from him, which I will cite here.

My boy, you probably think I've no right to write to you— unless we consider the fact that I sired you as giving me that right. But just because I didn't take care of you all your life doesn't mean that I didn't think about you or that I don't love you. Perhaps the best proof of my love and care is precisely the fact that I didn't take care of you. If you knew me, you'd realize that, sadly, the previous sentence is no paradox. But let's set that aside; I don't want you thinking that I feel the need to apologize. I chose what I chose, and I want to see it through to the end, because steadfastness is the last refuge of those who erred.

I'm writing to you because I read your story in a magazine, and I want to warn you. I sense that the same thing that destroyed me is destroying you—a messiah complex. It led me to theology, to the pulpit, it took away my faith in God, brought me to writing poetry, made me an alcoholic, which brought me here, to the mines, where my soul finally found peace. Yes, my boy, I became an alcoholic because of my messiah complex. I didn't take up drinking out of helplessness; I took it up to save mankind. One thing bothered me: Why did God make everything so perfect but botched man? Why? How's that possible? Have you ever thought about it? I have. Often and hard, very hard. And I came to a conclusion: God created man in a delirium. Totally wasted. Don't you see? It also explains the seventh day, the day of rest. Why would God, who is perfect, require rest? The need for rest—that's definitely not a divine attribute. But he had to rest—he was sleeping off a hangover. Now do you see why I took up drinking and writing? I wanted to bring myself into the Creator's state, into a delirium, because that's the only way to figure out where he made a mistake. To figure it out and correct it. In essence. Those were my motivations, but I had miscalculated. I think I should have studied maths, physics, chemistry or biology instead. That's right, my boy. Take this, for example: mathematics is capable of producing a mathematically exact proof of its nonexistence. You see? That's poetry. The theory of relativity, the theory of anti-matter. My boy, that is poetry! The most exact theories are the most irrational. The most exact science is magic. The most exact formula can appear in a dream. That's poetry, my boy, that's poetry. Science is amazing, but it speeds up the end. When it solves everything, that'll be the end. People won't have a reason to live, because a world without mystery is inhumane. I'm scared of that moment, but I'd like to live until the discovery of the supreme, final formula. Some impassioned curiosity drives people forward, even though they know there's danger ahead, which could turn out to be deadly. Curiosity and the desire for perfection. (Perhaps perfection is a measure of freedom.) If nothing else, perfection is satisfying. Consider my life: I wondered around in it as in a labyrinth, but it never felt hopeless to me. On the contrary, I always felt perfect in some way—there was no exit. So then, curiosity, the desire for perfection, and courage. Courage filled with fear. A brave man knows about the abyss, he's afraid of it, but he still walks towards it— he yearns to explore and to surmount it. I bet it's mostly curiosity. The greatest obsession is the obsession with curiosity: when it takes hold of a man, he'll jump off a roof just to see if he could fly.

I've known a man like that.

My grandfather, your great grandfather, was a bricklayer. He built our house with his own hands, with love, from the foundation to the roof, so that he'd have something to fall off of when he was raising the topping tree. 'He fell like an old bird with its wings paralysed,' my mother said as she was covering my grandfather with the small cloth I had brought clover in. Since then I've often dreamt that I'm flying—sometimes I feel that man didn't come from apes but from birds. Do you think that he just fell off that roof? Certainly not! He jumped in order to find out whether he'd grow wings. Yes, my boy, your great grand-father was very curious, and we inherited that from him.

My father, your grandfather, was a tailor. He made clothes the way people write poetry—in ecstasy. He put his whole heart into every prick of the needle, he pondered every stitch like a poet looking for the right word; he made very little money, but the clothes he made were perfect. When he was sixty years old, he sat on a needle. I will always remember the words with which Doctor Krištofík, my father's admirer and long-time customer, stated the cause of death: 'He died as a result of a puncture to his heart by his own needle which had stuck into his buttocks, made it into his circulatory system, and travelled with his blood all the way to his heart.' Doctor Krištofík wrote those words and shook his head in disbelief. At the time I thought it was unjust mockery, bad and malicious irony. Back then I didn't know that it was inevitable, I didn't know that my father's buttocks and the needle were following ancient laws of our lineage. Yes, my boy, the men in our family have always died of the things they loved most.

I feel that the needle, which gets stuck into everyone's buttocks at birth, is nearing my heart. Maybe that's why

I'm writing to you. I don't want to die, but what is to be done, a needle's a needle.

I actually wanted to write to you about trivial things. Perhaps everything I've said so far was just stalling because I'm afraid of your reaction to what I'm about to say. It's a purely practical matter, and if you can, take it as such, and try to set aside any moral considerations. Over the years I've saved up some money for you, which I've now transferred into an account in your name at a bank in Bratislava. Legally and formally everything is fine, I'm just worried that you'll get angry and refuse the money. I can understand how you feel, but I tried to explain to you why I acted the way I did in the earlier part of my first and last letter to you. If you don't accept the money, I've arranged for it to go to the people who raised you.

Mining coal in the dark, dust and heat—that's going to be your lot if you're serious about writing. And there's only one reward: the hope that someone will turn your coal into ashes and be a little warmer on long, freezing nights.

Live the way you like and must—that is my only message.

—*Your father*

PS. It just occurred to me that the supreme, final formula doesn't have to be discovered by a scientist. Maybe it's long been hidden in an ordinary replica of Shakespeare.

My father's letter stirred up chaos within me. Right after I read it, I wanted to put it back in the envelope and return it to sender, but I thought about it some more that night, many words I should write to him popped into my head, and then I realized that I wouldn't be able to say them in an ordinary letter, even if it had hundreds of pages. I had an irresistible urge to meet him. Even though we had never said a word to each other, I had the feeling that all along we had been having a perpetual, silent dialogue. I had to meet him, to see his face, to touch his hand, just to believe that he was real.

In the morning, I looked for the return address, but there wasn't one. Neither in the letter nor on the envelope.

Two weeks later, I received a telegram: 'Your father died in a mining accident.'

Nothing else, once again no return address.

●

The Earth Is Round

When I came home one evening, my wife introduced me to her friend from college; she had arrived in Bratislava from Košice only to find that her hotel lost her reservation. Even though we had a studio flat and two small children, my wife invited her to spend the night on our only pull-out sofa; she was probably counting on me sleeping on the floor or spending the night at a friend's house. But I had about half a gallon of wine in me, I was tired, and on top of it all—my wife's friend was attractive. I feigned being a lot more tired than I really was, I undressed down to my shorts, and in spite of both women's objections, I lay down in the middle of the couch.

I woke up in the middle of the night. I was lying between two women; they must have trusted me. The room spun strangely with me from the evening's wine, I felt nauseous. My wife's friend was lying on her right side, with her back to me, her naked shoulder glowed dimly in the darkness; only the diffuse light of a streetlamp streamed in from the outside. I got curious. How would she react? Would she scream? Would she cause a scene? Or would she pull away quietly?

My curiosity and desire to sin were stronger than my morals and principles. My lips touched the warm shoulder; the woman didn't budge. I listened for a moment—everyone's breathing was calm, deep and regular. I knew that people would be in the deepest sleep at that hour; there was no danger.

I carefully slid my hand under the covers and lightly passed my fingers over a silky female thigh. I didn't know whether she was really asleep or just pretending. Maybe she was scared; I thought she stopped breathing. Then she shifted a little, as if by chance, in her sleep, and that was it—everything happened as if in a dream; I even had my eyes closed. I admired her sensitivity— or was that part of her plan?—in the morning she could look as though she didn't know a thing, as if nothing had happened. When it was over—I had never experienced such ecstasy with my wife—I felt as innocent as a new-born. My wife was asleep. I caressed her hair and gently kissed her ear. I was thrilled to realize that I still loved her; over the last few months I had started to have my doubts. I couldn't figure it out—the first time I cheated on her I realized that I loved her. I quietly slipped out of bed; all of a sudden the thought of lying next to a strange woman seemed revolting. I pulled my wife's fur coat out of the hall closet and lay down on the kitchen floor. My wife's pleasant scent wafted from the fur coat, and that was when I felt the first pangs of remorse for my adultery. The idea that she'd never find out calmed me down; I wasn't going to confess, and I was hoping that her best friend wouldn't go bragging about it either. Soon I fell asleep.

I had a dream in which I was killed just outside of Bratislava, at a spot I knew well. I had passed by there on a bus many times when I was going to see a friend in Záluhy, or when I went on business trips to Prague or Brno. It was a turnoff from Prague

Street, the place was familiar, but I couldn't remember how I died. I didn't know whether I had been on a bus or in a car, or whether I had been riding a bike or a motorcycle. It was an accident; I knew that much. And there was something else I knew: the date and the time—20 February at 10:30. Those were the first words I said aloud as I woke up. It caught me off guard. It seemed unfair that the warning would come so late. It was 3.30 a.m., and I had seven hours to decide what to do. The ominous threat in my dream seemed like punishment for my adultery. But wasn't it too harsh—death for adultery?

Perhaps everyone gets the chance to find out the truth once in a lifetime, and I had just got mine. But what if the moment of truth is coincident with death? It should be put to a test. I felt as though my dream had hidden meaning, and I was the only one who could decipher it. It seemed like there was a point of departure, and it got me all confused, because I was becoming convinced that I was the one who had to discover where it was and how it worked. It was as though at a given place, of which of course, there were many, death rays would land at a particular time, and whoever was in that place at that time would have to die, and I had been chosen to test this hypothesis because of my prophetic dream. I had to go there in the morning, at 10.30, I had to be at that intersection, and if I died, then it was true. The question, however, was whether it was a personal or an impersonal point. If I didn't go, and someone else died at that spot, then the point would be impersonal. But that would mean that death didn't lie in wait for a person in time, but in space. These thoughts possessed me, but that was nothing new; I had had strange inclinations since childhood. For example, there was a time when I was convinced that the further I went from a particular place, the deeper my memories could reach into the past. Had I gone *as far as possible* from my native village, perhaps I could have remembered myself all the way to a prenatal state. But the roundness of the Earth was a problem, because it made it impossible to go away as far as possible from anything.

The roundness of the Earth was responsible for the fact that to go as far as possible from anything meant to be coming back to it.

I arrived at the office at 9.30; they were already looking for me. 'Go see the boss, right now,' said a young red-headed secretary.

'Finally,' the editor-in-chief said when I walked into his office.

'What's going on? Is there a fire?' I asked and lit a cigarette.

'You're going to Prague. Immediately. The car should be here any minute.'

'Prague?' I wanted to ask why, but I didn't manage to. The road to Prague surfaced in my mind, and all of a sudden, my blood drained down to my calves; I had to sit down. I got a stomach cramp, and it moved up, towards my heart. I felt nauseous and put out the cigarette. I pressed it into the butts in the ashtray until it fell apart, leaving the residue of tobacco and ashes on my fingertips; I squeamishly wiped my fingers on my trousers.

'What's wrong with you? Did something happen?' my boss asked. 'You're quite pale.'

I unbuttoned my top shirt button and wiped my sweaty forehead with my hand.

'Heart trouble,' I said. 'I was supposed to see a doctor today.'

'Nonsense. Heart trouble at your age. You shouldn't smoke so much.'

'I can't. Not today,' I pleaded.

The boss gave me a quizzical look. 'How come? It's an order.'

An order, I thought. It's an order! Last night I didn't actually believe it, I was just toying with the idea. I still had a choice—to go, or not to go. Now it was an order.

'I can't,' I said again. 'I don't feel well at all. The trip would be too much for me.'

The boss looked at me silently and then said angrily: 'A thirty-year-old man with heart trouble. What kind of a generation are you people?' Then he added: 'Find Jožo Berka. He'll go in your place.'

The blood from my calves started to flow to my head.

'I'm on it,' I said. 'Thank you.' I got up and was already at the door when I heard my boss say, 'Take some time off and go on a vacation.'

How simple it was. Make up some heart trouble and cheat fate. Once more I had that liberating feeling that comes with hearing the ringing of the first morning tram. I don't believe in that stuff anyway, of course I don't. Or I'm a coward, I thought, but I didn't get that demeaning sense of shame; I was surprised to learn that even cowards can enjoy life.

I walked Jožo Berka to the car, but something else started to bother me on the way. What if something really happened to him; I'd feel guilty for the rest of my life. As Jožo was getting into the car, I felt as though I was knowingly sending him to his death. I'm a coward, I said to myself, and by then I felt the full weight of the word.

'Drive carefully, the roads are icy,' I said and shook Jožo's hand. Taken aback, he asked, 'What's with you? Are you expecting us not to come back?'

'I had a strange dream. A car accident and such. It's foolish,' I said, and with satisfaction I thought: that's the ticket, I warned him without making a fool of myself. The driver swore, 'For Christ's sakes. I love morbid talk before a trip.' Jožo burst out laughing. I was leaving, I could hear Jožo's laughter behind me. Idiot, let him get killed, if he doesn't believe. I looked back; the car was going out the gate.

They stopped briefly, waiting for an opening to pull out into traffic, and I felt like running after them, pulling Jožo out of the car, sitting in his place, and going to face my fate. I stood in the middle of the courtyard and looked after them long after they were gone, and then I felt the extreme tension dissipate and my whole body relax in an unexpected, liberating sense of relief.

I woke up—this time for real—fresh and well-rested; my wife had come to the kitchen to heat up milk for the children.

'It was crowded, so I moved,' I explained quickly. She didn't say anything, she just kept looking at me silently, and I thought I saw a smirk flash across her face. I got tense. Does she know? I got up, put the fur coat back in the closet, and washed up. Then I walked into the room. My older daughter was standing in her crib, eating an orange. The younger one was sleeping in a large basket, sucking her thumb. My wife's friend was wearing a yellow bath-robe, her short blonde hair was dishevelled, but it suited her. I had the gratifying thought that she was worth the sin. She was talking with my daughter, peeling an orange, and putting the pink segments into her mouth. My wife came out of the bathroom brushing her hair. When I saw them side by side, my wife and her friend, I couldn't help comparing them; my wife was the clear winner. She was much prettier and had a better figure. She had only one flaw—I had known her merits too well and too long.

'How'd you sleep?' I asked cheerfully. Then I yawned and added: 'I slept like a log.'

Her friend sneered at me. 'I had a terrible time. Someone kept disturbing me.' She chuckled and went to the bathroom. A moment later I could hear the shower running.

I was stunned, that wasn't the reaction I had expected. The woman practically insulted me. I was quite offended. To say that she had a terrible time! Unbelievable! I felt like walking into the bathroom and slapping her a couple of times.

My wife caressed my face tenderly and said: 'Last night you were wonderful. It's never been that amazing. Eva must not have got much sleep next to us.' And she gratefully mussed my hair.

I felt as though I had a crate of wet dynamite in my head instead of a brain.

'I have to go.' I stepped away from her.

'This early?'

'You know I'm going on a business trip.'

'Oh, right. Prague. Sorry, I completely forgot about it.'

'No wonder. With all this commotion. Next time, please don't invite strange women into our bed.'

'I couldn't let her sleep outside,' she said quietly, apologetically.

'OK, forget about it,' I said graciously.

'I'll go pack your things.'

'There's no need. I'll be back this evening. What should I wear? An overcoat or a fur coat?'

She gave me a concerned look, then she walked up to me and put her hand on my forehead.

'You caught cold in that kitchen. You're running a fever!' she said and led me to the window.

It was a clear, hot August morning, and when I saw it, a familiar cramp gripped my stomach and rose up to my heart. I lit a cigarette and started to count in my head: August, September, October, November, December, January, February. Seven months. It seemed unfair that the warning would come so early. Seven months of waiting and decision-making when I already knew the outcome seemed like too harsh a punishment for something that happened completely differently than it was supposed to.

●

A Walk Through a Winter Landscape

'We should go to the rock quarry this afternoon,' Jana said, and we both laughed at my words: 'Today we will for sure.'

Every day we set out to go to the rock quarry, but we never made it, and we both knew that we wouldn't make it today either. Jana was just finishing her eighth month of pregnancy, and it was too far for her, but in spite of that every day she said: 'We should go to the rock quarry this afternoon.'

'Good day and bon appétit,' we heard from behind, and then an older gentleman appeared in a dark, stylish suit, and just as he did every day, he bowed politely and kissed Jana's hand. He had sat down at our table on the first day of our vacation because there were no other available seats, and from then on we all considered his presence completely natural. His name was Jozef Klimo, he was almost seventy, and a retired doctor—a heart surgeon. He had interesting stories to tell; the one that stuck with me most—it was actually just a situation—I labelled it in my own mind 'When I Was Dead'. It seemed like a suitable name for a short story. It happened when he was performing heart surgery. During surgery the patient was clinically dead, and when he woke up, he said: 'When I was dead, I dreamt that I was sledding across a wide snow-covered plane.' I envied the older gentleman that he had had a job which allowed him to learn the dreams of the dead.

The older gentleman pulled out his glasses and looked over the menu, meanwhile, the waitress brought us our chicken soup. 'I'll have chicken soup as well,' he said to her, then he took off his glasses, and added, 'And trout. I feel like having trout.'

'We'll wait for you, the soup's hot,' Jana said, pushing aside the plate of steaming soup. I was about to start eating, but after what she said it seemed impolite, so I also set down my spoon, slightly vexed, and I nodded, 'Yes, it's hot.'

'While we're on the subject of the trout,' the older gentleman said, 'I recall an incident I'll never forget. Actually, I shouldn't say I recall, because you can only recall something you've forgotten, and I've never forgotten about that trout. Yes, a trout was the main character. The more I think about it, the more convinced I am of that. Indeed, he was in charge.' He shook his head, deep in thought, and stopped talking for a moment. My stomach rumbled from hunger; I thought that everyone could hear it, but Jana and the older gentleman looked as though nothing had happened. I blushed anyway, and felt so embarrassed that I got up, stammered out an 'excuse me', and went to the bathroom. For a moment I stood behind the closed door, and when I calmed down a bit, I went back to the table. The older gentleman was just saying, '—that trout was literally taunting me. It was a beautiful fish, and the villagers were afraid of it. They really treated him like a patron of the village, they didn't believe that it could be caught and, in all seriousness, they claimed that whoever caught it would certainly die, but that was before the war, in a very remote area, you couldn't find such boondocks any more.'

The waitress brought the soup and the older gentleman had to interrupt his story.

'I won't hold you up, bon appétit,' he said after the waitress left. 'In the end, I did catch it. Here, with this'—he reached under his shirt and pulled out a heart-shaped silver locket that was dangling from a silver chain. He pressed an invisible spring, and the case popped open with a low click. Inside was a lock of black hair. 'My wife's hair,' he said. 'I braided several strands of it, and the trout couldn't break them, the patron. He broke my line, but not the hair. My wife was waiting for me at the blacksmith's—where we were staying. At first, the villagers were hostile towards me, they didn't want to let me try to catch it, but afterwards they got very excited, you should have seen it, I didn't realize until then that they had really thought of that trout as something special, untouchable, you see, that's why they were so happy after I caught it, as if I had freed them from a curse or something like that. It was the boondocks, and I had the feeling that some secret pagan rituals were still being practiced there, you won't find such boondocks any more, but we enjoyed vacationing there. It goes without saying that they dragged me to the tavern, and as you can imagine, I have no idea how I made it home.' Then he fell silent and quickly started to cram the lock of black hair back into the silver locket swaying back and forth on his chest.

'Pardon me,' he said embarrassed, looking at Jana. 'So distasteful, I don't know what came over me, here at the lunch table, I apologize.' He blushed. It really was distasteful, one of the hairs fell into his soup. Jana turned pale. I was afraid that she was getting nauseous, but the older gentleman's embarrassment was so great that one couldn't take offense. Jana smiled, overcame her nausea, and asked, 'How much did it weigh?' She probably wanted to help him out of his embarrassment, but his thoughts had already shifted. 'Excuse me?' he asked after a while. 'Sorry, did you say something?'

'No, not at all,' Jana said. 'Would you excuse me, I have to go lie down, I don't feel well.'

'How far along are you?'

'I just started the ninth month. My due date is in three weeks.'

'Hmm, ninth.' He nodded. 'Just like her. And I was busy catching a trout.'

'How much did it weigh?' Jana repeated her question; her perseverance made me smile.

'That one? I didn't weigh it. I didn't even taste it. The villagers ate it. They ate it, the patron. Perhaps even with the bones.'

He smiled and pushed aside his soup plate.

'I don't feel like eating either,' he said and got up from the table.

That afternoon we went for a walk, as we did every day. A few snow-covered cars were parked in front of the hotel, and a bus with a roof-rack full of skis was coming up the icy road dusted with ashes. The whooping of skiers and the indistinct creaking of a ski lift were coming from a nearby slope. Frozen snow crystals glistened a light-blue colour in the afternoon sun; it was as though the clear, transparently frosty sky was being reflected in the snow. Jana was wearing a fur coat made of some brown animal that may have once been a marmot. It reached halfway down her calves, and the fur around the buttonholes had been worn out long before we had bought it in a tucked away consignment store. She had on grey-felt boots, and a white cashmere shawl was draped over her head; despite the fact that she was nine months pregnant, she was still attractive. Medical books had warned us against lovemaking in the last two months of pregnancy, and we heeded their warnings and calmly waited for the approaching big day.

We walked towards the forest. I wanted to light a cigarette, but I realized that I had forgotten the pack in our room.

'Wait a minute, I'll go get my cigarettes,' I said and went back. I didn't feel like going all the way up to the third floor, so I went to the hotel bar. Our lunchtime companion was sitting at the bar, sipping cognac, and looking out through the front window.

'Out for a walk?' he asked in a well-meaning tone. 'Be careful, anything can happen at this stage.' He looked outside again, and I realized that he was watching Jana who was waiting for me. Irritated, I snapped, 'Mind your own business.' He turned around in dismay, and looked at me with such a bewildered and guilty expression, that I felt ashamed about my irritable tone.

'A pack of Marice, please,' I said to the bartender and set money on the bar.

'I know that my behaviour at lunch was inappropriate, please don't be upset,' he said, and before I had a chance to respond, he quickly continued, as if he were afraid that I wouldn't let him get to what he really wanted to say. 'You see, your missus reminds of my wife, I can't even say in what way, but they have something in common, I'm not just talking about the fact that she was at the same stage of pregnancy, it's something else, something in her expression . . . don't you ever feel that you don't deserve her?'

God damn it, I thought.

'Please don't take it the wrong way, I don't mean it badly,' he was quick to add, 'I'm just trying to recall exactly how I felt back then . . . you see, that's what I felt with my wife . . .'

'I don't feel that way,' I snapped, grabbed the cigarettes, and turned to leave.

He grabbed my arm, insistent, almost pleading, and even though I tried to free myself and shout at him to leave me alone, I stayed on.

'You see, earlier, at lunch . . . I didn't tell you that she died. Had I been with her, it may not have happened, after all, I am a doctor, pre-term labour isn't such a big deal . . . but those villagers . . . and I was at the tavern, drunk, all because of that accursed trout.'

He let go of my arm and took a sip of his cognac.

'The hair is all I have left,' he said, but it sounded as if he weren't saying it to me, as if he were somewhere else again, and so I slipped away quietly, feeling angry and irritable, but he didn't notice.

'That took you long enough,' Jana said when I returned to her. She took my hand and we walked towards the forest. 'That old fool was sitting there again,' I said. 'I've had enough of him.'

'Oh please, he's quite nice. If only he didn't drop hair into his soup.' She laughed.

A light-blue minibus appeared from around a bend in the road; it didn't have skis on the roof. 'They made it,' Jana said. The minibus stopped in front of the hotel, and several young men with long hair got out; I noticed that all of them were smoking cigars. Then I remembered that a beat band was supposed to be playing at the bar that night. Up until the last moment it wasn't certain that they'd make it, and the guests were on edge. While the band was unloading their drums, guitars, microphones and other strange equipment, a bunch of admirers flocked around, shoving hands with scraps of paper towards them, quickly engulfing them. I remembered their thick cigars, and just as we reached the first trees, I lit a beaten up Marica.

It was a lot colder under the trees, but the slight uphill climb warmed us up. Soon we turned off the beaten path and walked north directly through the forest towards the open hilltop, which looked like a skull that had been cracked vertically with one brusque, precise blow of an axe—the rock quarry. The rocks were reddish, covered with an icy glaze. I went first, the thin frozen layer made a dry cracking sound as it broke, my boots were sinking into the ice. I took short steps, and Jana walked in my footprints. A couple of times we had to make our way around fallen trees. I was sweating, clouds of white steam condensed in front of my mouth; I completely forgot about Jana. I turned around. She tried hard to keep up with me, her fur coat was unbuttoned, her scarf in her pocket, her face was burning, her hair was falling into her eyes and sticking to her sweaty forehead. When she lifted her head, our eyes met and we smiled at each other apologetically; she too had probably got so absorbed in the rhythm of her own steps that she forgot about her fatigue as well as about me. A tiny scar on her forehead right at the hairline had turned white and stood out in sharp contrast to the red of her face.

Perhaps it was this detail that released my long-suppressed arousal; I felt unspeakable tenderness towards her, which I hadn't felt in a long time. There was something animalistic in our mutual arousal—perhaps the sight of her nostrils had awakened that feeling; they flared as if she were picking up the scent of blood in the air, and the cloudlets of white steam she was breathing out looked like animals which reproduce by splitting. We forgot all about the warnings from the books.

In the spot where we had been lying down the snow melted, leaving nothing but frost-seared grass.

I buttoned up Jana's fur coat.

'Do you want to head back?' I asked.

'Not yet.'

'Are you tired?'

'Not yet.'

I held her hand and we started walking towards the reddish rocks in the north. We were silent. The thought occurred to me that it would never be the same, and my throat closed up with sadness.

'I wish the baby would come soon!' Jana said.

'You really don't want to head back? Are you sure?'

'What time is it?'

'Three thirty.'

'Let's go to the rock quarry. It's not far any more.'

'OK. But if you get tired, you'll tell me, right?'

'Uh-huh.'

It got colder. The sun was going down, and low, dirty clouds started to cover the sky in the north. From somewhere up ahead we heard the bubbling of water, and soon a deep ravine cut our path; a small stream that had not frozen wound its way at the bottom of it. I was trying to decide whether we should go down the steep slope when a horse-drawn sled appeared. It was down in the ravine, going alongside the stream, and the horses looked tired.

The ravine was too narrow for them, the horse on the left had to wade through the shallow stream, which made it look like it had a limp. The splashing of the water and the creaking of the snow were getting more and more distant until the sled disappeared from view. For a moment longer, I looked at the empty turn and listened to the fading sounds. Something made me feel uneasy. 'There was no driver,' Jana said. I hadn't realized it until she said it. The horses went by themselves, no one was driving, no one was sitting in the sled, no one was walking alongside them.

'Maybe he went to take a leak,' I said.

We waited to see if someone would appear, we stood up there in silence for good ten minutes. No one showed up. Only the smooth, distinct tracks of the sled runners cut sharply into the deep snow.

'You know what, let's go back,' Jana said.

'OK,' I said, relieved. 'Let's go back.'

'Through the ravine, OK? I'm a bit tired, and this looks like an easier path.'

'I just don't want us to get lost.'

'That's the stream that runs by the hotel.'

'I hope it's the same stream.'

'I'm sure it is.'

I would have preferred to go back along our tracks, it would have been safer. But Jana seemed tired, and the path through the ravine did look more comfortable. Slowly, cautiously, we made our way down the steep slope. Then we walked along the ravine following the sled tracks. We couldn't have been far from the hotel, twenty minutes at most. I was beginning to calm down.

'Too bad we didn't make it to the rock quarry,' Jana said, and a moment later she added, 'I wish we were at the hotel already.' As if she felt the need to hide something, she immediately followed it up with, 'We could go to the bar this evening. It's a good band.'

I shot her a surprised glance.

'You know them?'

'A few of their recordings.'

'If it won't exhaust you too much . . .'

After about ten minutes the ravine widened and we came out into a small clearing. In the middle of it stood a green trailer covered in snow. It may have housed workers from the rock quarry, or perhaps it had been left there from the time when the hotel was being built. The door was closed. A narrow path led up to it, and there were old tracks in the snow, they looked like doe or fox tracks. But the trailer looked as though it was still in use; the green shutters with cracked paint were wide open, latched to the outside with little hooks, and there was no padlock on the door. The glass in the barred windows was unbroken, clean, a flowery curtain was clearly visible in the dim light inside; I thought I saw it move, as if someone had touched it lightly or passed by it. I walked around the trailer; the snow had not been disturbed. Only the tracks left by the sled that had passed by recently and continued down the ravine. Behind the trailer stood a ramshackle woodshed; the workers must have used it to store their tools. I wanted to peek into the trailer; I paused by the door. A wooden step (one of three) made a dry cracking sound, which made me realize that the stairs had been swept, and just then I heard Jana's scream. Frightened, I quickly turned around. She was ten paces from me, her face was white to the point of being transparent, distorted in a spasm, and she was holding her belly.

When I finally made a move towards her, the door of the wood shed flew open, and three angry dogs darted out. The dogs were large, with scant fur; they looked like German shepherds. They didn't bark, they just fumed, and they had long dirty grey threads of saliva dripping from their mouths. Jana screamed. The dogs paid no attention to her, they focused on me. They stood in front of me, as if I were trying to block their path to Jana. I heard her groans of pain, and I tried to recall what I had read about pre-term labour. I couldn't remember a thing. The dogs growled, bared their teeth, but they didn't attack. I was aware of the fact that we could end up there until nightfall; a motionless, absurd sculpture. Jana took off her fur coat, she was calling me. I ran towards her, but the dogs jumped on me. I kept kicking, and I could feel that I was hitting them; their constant whining confirmed it as well. Jana kept yelling, I swore loudly, but no one showed up. I realized that the stream we were following was not the right one; otherwise we would have been near the hotel and someone would have heard us. Even though my boots had clumps of bloody fur on them and several dogteeth were lying around, it was no use. The dogs were in a rage. I could feel one of them biting my calf; my sock got damp. I kept covering my throat, and hoping they were not wolves. I couldn't see Jana, I could only hear her. It's 11 February today, I thought. I should remember the date, so that we'd know when to celebrate this birthday. I felt like laughing. I looked at my watch, at the second-hand moving in even intervals. I remember being very surprised by the regularity of the movement. 4.35. That was when it hit me: they were protecting her from me. The possibility of such a misunderstanding frightened me.

It started to snow soundlessly. The snowflakes floated in the still, frosty air and landing gently on the ground, as if they were afraid to hurt it.

At a quarter of five, I heard a baby's crying. I had never imagined that children came into the world with such terrible yelling. Almost at the same time the door of the trailer opened, and a young man with long blond hair stood at the entrance. I could see he had just finished shaving; he was using a towel to wipe off remnants of shaving cream by his left ear. He whistled some kind of a signal, and the dogs obediently came to him. He lovingly scratched all three of them behind their ears, and they devoutly cuddled up to his legs. Then he motioned towards the woodshed, and the dogs obediently went in.

'What's going on here?' he said, looked at us briefly, and then he went in and closed the door.

I got up. Jana was lying on her fur coat about thirty feet from me, her face was waxy pale, she had dark circles under her eyes, large beads of sweat rolled down her face. There was blood all around her, and the blood reflected off the snow with an unprecedented, grimly scarlet colour.

I set out towards her. She shook her head and tried to smile, as if trying to apologize for the rejection. I nodded and I wasn't that surprised: it was an unmistakable sign of what I had suspected all along. Then the trailer door opened again, and the man asked, 'Are you staying at the hotel?'

I nodded.

'Do you know, did the big beat guys show up?'

'They did.'

'Great,' he said and rubbed his hands together, pleased.

'Can we get back to the hotel this way?' I asked him and pointed down the ravine.

'Sure. It'll take you five minutes.' After a moment, he added, 'You might make it faster if you run.'

He closed the door.

I took off running towards the hotel along the stream, following the tracks of the unattended sled.

I spotted the doctor from afar. He was standing in front of the hotel, dressed lightly, wearing a dark, stylish suit, smoking, and watching the skiers on the nearby slope.

●

Evening News

In the evening I went to the cinema; they were showing Luis Buñuel's *The Exterminating Angel*. It was my second time seeing it, but certainly not my last. I'm fascinated by the idea of the impossibility of crossing the threshold of a wide-open door.

Right before the end of the film, I got worried that I didn't have the keys to my flat. I started to rifle through my pockets in haste and confusion as if my fate rested on the keys. Meanwhile the film ended, the lights came on, and people pushed their way towards the exit with unusual insistence, but I kept turning out my pockets, pulling out forgotten coins hidden under the torn liner (they could have been long obsolete), crumpled tram and bus tickets, empty pen refills, old lottery tickets and used matches, I scattered tobacco shaken out of broken cigarettes all around me, but there were no keys. 'The film really got to him,' I heard a sarcastic remark, and finally got a hold of myself. I looked around. There was a pile of rubbish by my seat and the people who were leaving looked on with dismay. I felt hot, blood was rushing to my face. My whole body started to itch unbearably. A flea as usual, I thought. I always bring home a flea from the cinema; they like the sweet taste of my blood. I pushed my way towards the exit, intending to hide in the bathroom, catch the flea, and get rid of it before it could suck me dry.

A long line of people stood in the foyer waiting for the coat check. My coat, I completely forgot about my coat. I felt a sense of relief because I clearly remembered the keys—they were in my right coat pocket. I got in line; the itch was slowly subsiding. It only persisted in one place—my left calf. I pulled up my trousers inconspicuously, bent over pretending to have dropped something, and quickly scratched. Then I stood up briskly, and felt another rush of heat. With a dull headache I started to search my pockets. I found a ticket to the National Museum and Galleries of the Bratislava Castle, which reminded me that I had visited them the day before with my older daughter, but there was no coat-check ticket. I must have thrown it out when I was looking for the keys, I thought, so I went back to the empty theatre.

Noisy fans were pushing out the moist, stale air; an old, seventy-something cleaning lady was bent over a dustpan, her thin, grey, permed hair was falling onto her forehead, she muttered angry, incomprehensible sounds as she swept the contents of my pockets onto the dustpan. 'Pardon me, ma'am,' I exclaimed and leapt towards her. 'My coat-check ticket is in there.' 'What?' she asked. 'I lost my coat-check ticket.' 'So?' she scoffed as she emptied my rubbish into the bin with everyone else's. It was overflowing; from her smirk I gathered that it would be best to leave. I walked towards the exit.

'Asshole,' she yelled in a high-pitched voice that was breaking.

I turned around, shocked.

She looked at me with hatred.

'You asshole,' she repeated and spat from between her sparse teeth. I ran away.

The line in front of the coat check was quickly getting shorter. Calm down, just stay calm, I told myself. I'll wait for everyone to leave, my coat will be the only one left, she'll have to give it to me without the ticket. I spotted it. It was hanging on the long bar of the second coat rack from the left. ID, I'm sure she'll ask for my ID, I thought. It wasn't in my back pocket, maybe it was in my coat, but I couldn't be sure. If I told her it was there and it happened not to be, she wouldn't give me the coat, I couldn't risk that.

I was the last person in the foyer.

The coat-check attendant looked at me quizzically, her hand was on the counter, waiting for the ticket.

'Please hurry up, ma'am, I've got things to do,' I said and drummed my fingers on the counter impatiently.

She looked at me with surprise that turned to uncertainty, and I knew I had her. She asked, 'Did you give me your ticket?'

'For heaven's sakes, I gave it to you before the other man did,' I said indignantly, and I pointed to the door behind me where an older gentleman with a greying pointy beard had just vanished. 'People keep jumping the line, and I can't keep up,' she mumbled and handed me my coat. I handed her a crown, and when she tried to give me my change, I waved her off like a person who couldn't lose another second. I could feel her stare piercing my back, and I briefly turned around at the door. Her expression said that she no longer trusted me and regretted her momentary weakness; I had made another enemy.

When I walked out of the theatre, it was 8 p.m. Wet snow was falling. A wooden stage was being built on Hviezdoslav Square in front of the theatre; soon Bratislava children would get to delight in the arrival of Santa Claus. For a moment, I stood under a tall fir tree decorated with multicoloured lights and packages with wide ribbons. A cold wind was blowing from the Danube, and the light, empty boxes swayed on the branches.

The anxiety that had come over me in the theatre was slowly waning. I bought a pack of Spartas at the coat check of the Carlton Café and headed home. At the entrance to my building, I panicked again; I didn't have the keys to my flat. I had been so convinced that they were in my coat pocket that I didn't check. Either I had really lost them, or the children had misplaced them. I had to ring the doorbell, and when my wife opened the door, I smiled apologetically: 'I forgot my keys.' 'Forgot? I'm sure you lost them again,' she said and shook her head. 'That's your fourth set this year,' she added and went to the bathroom.

The children were still awake. They were chasing each other around the room on all fours, squealing, and my older daughter was pointing at the eight-month-old, saying, 'You see that naughty child? She has a cold but she won't let me check her temperature. Hold her still so I can pull out the thermometer.'

'You gave her a thermometer? She'll break it and cut herself,' I said. I quickly pulled out the little one from under the bed, stuck my hand under her shirt, but there was no thermometer.

'Don't worry, it's not breakable,' the older one said to allay my fear. 'It must have fallen into her pants.' She started to search the little one, and soon she pulled out a plastic straw: 'Look, here it is. What did I tell you? It was in her pants.' She looked at the straw and shook her head in dismay: 'See? She has 106 pounds of fever, but all she wants to do is run around.'

'OK, that's enough! Off to bed with you, or we won't go see Santa tomorrow.'

I tucked them into their cribs and turned out the lights. The older one didn't object, but the younger one, who couldn't have cared less about Santa, started to grumble in disapproval.

My wife was in the bathroom, washing diapers. 'Here you go, you exterminating angel,' she said and stuck a wrung-out diaper in my hands. 'Hang them up while I make you dinner.'

'Later,' I said. 'I'm not hungry yet.'

'As you like. But you can still hang up the diapers, I'll fix something in the meantime.'

'You know I have a tonne of work. My article's due tomorrow, and I haven't written a line yet.'

'But you did have time to go to the cinema, didn't you?' She ripped the diaper out of my hands. 'I wonder when I'll get to go to the cinema. I think the last time I went was three years ago.'

'Oh, I remember. They were playing *The Magnificent Seven*.'

She slammed the door.

I regretted provoking her, but I couldn't help myself. Whenever she reproached me, I felt the need to taunt her. Despite the fact that her reproaches were well deserved!

I closed myself in my study and started to write an article about the housing crisis facing young married couples. I thought it would be an easy topic, because we had also spent five years renting rooms hither and yon before they assigned us our flat, but it turned out not to be so. The topic wasn't that relevant to me any more, the article wasn't shaping up well. Truth be told, I was no longer interested in the topic at all.

At 9.30 I went to eat dinner. I ate scrambled eggs, my wife ironed children's clothes, she was tired, underslept, and watching me angrily. 'Leave it and come eat something,' I said in a conciliatory tone and touched her arm. 'You won't take care of it,' she snapped and pulled back her arm. She was right, as usual, and that irritated me, as usual. But I wanted to avoid a fight, so I didn't say anything, but turned on the radio instead.

'Please turn it off, I'd like to have a little peace and quiet at least in the evening,' she blurted out in a shrill, jumpy voice. I pushed my plate aside and turned up the volume—the news was on.

'I guess the food's not to your liking. Maybe you should do your own cooking.' She was choking with anger.

I turned my attention to the news.

'A Chilean military junta continues its brutal murders . . . '

'The least you could do is take out the garbage,' she said and kicked the overflowing bin.

'In the Middle East, Israel continues its military provocations and refuses to pull back its army from the occupied Arab territories . . . '

'The toilet's not flushing. Call a repairman,' my wife said, and threw my fork into the sink.

'Fighting continues in South Vietnam in spite of the Paris Peace Accords . . . '

'When will you install the coat rack? The coats are all over the floor,' my wife said and yanked the power cord from the outlet.

The announcer's calm, unemotional, slightly bored voice suddenly faded out.

'Bitch,' I said.

'Jerk,' she said.

'Stupid cow,' I carried on.

'Get out,' my wife raised her voice.

'I'm sorry.' I sighed.

'Me too.' My wife calmed down.

'Forgive me. You know how much work I've got,' I said.

'Why don't you ever help me out? At least you could talk to me in the evenings,' my wife said.

'I know. You've got your hands full. I'll do better, you'll see. Right after tomorrow's deadline,' I said.

She waved her hand in resignation and kissed me on the cheek.

'Thanks for dinner.' I kissed her forehead.

After we made up, I went back to writing the article; I finished at 3 a.m.

I felt it almost immediately. Its patience was admirable. It had waited this whole time while it was at the source. I turned on a light, took off my pyjamas, checked my whole body as well as the sheets inch-by-inch, but it wasn't there. Then I took the pyjamas and the sheets to the bathroom, immersed them in the bathtub, and took clean things out of the closet. I lay down, but couldn't fall sleep. The flea made me think about *The Exterminating Angel*. I tossed and turned, and Buñuel's images kept flashing in front of my closed eyes.

Finally, I dozed off. I dreamt that I was dreaming about being asleep, but in the middle of sleeping inside the dream I was aware of the fact that it was just a dream.

A buzz woke me up. Had I slept at all? I couldn't say. The only evidence of me having slept was that I woke up. What if I don't wake up one day, I thought, but I calmed myself: It would mean that I've reached a state of permanent wakefulness. It wasn't much of a consolation. My musings were interrupted by a sharp, insistent buzz of the doorbell—I wasn't dreaming. My wife and children hadn't woken up.

I threw a bathrobe over my pyjamas, picked up my wife's keys, and walked downstairs from the fourth floor; the lift hadn't been working for three days. I expected to see a group of my drunk friends, but when I opened the gate, it wasn't my friends, but two men from the secret police and a car.

'I'm sorry, you've made a mistake,' I said, sounding guilty for some odd reason, as if I should have been apologizing for their error.

'You think we can't read?' one of them said in an irritated tone. 'Are you Štefan Kráľ?'

'I am, but I don't understand what you want from me at 3 a.m.'

'You're coming with us.'

'It's a mistake. It must be some kind of a mistake,' I kept insisting, but they were silent. When I was sitting in the car between them, one of them asked me attentively: 'That's a summer bathrobe, isn't it? We wouldn't want you to catch cold.'

We barrelled down empty night-time streets into the unknown, and what bothered me most was the unfortunate bathrobe. Had I been wearing a winter coat, I would have felt much more confident; but what weight do the words of a man who's wearing a summer bathrobe on a chilly December night carry? At best they can elicit a smirk.

Soon we arrived. The officer on duty smirked at my outfit. I decided I'd take off the bathrobe and only wear the striped pyjamas that resembled a prison uniform. I preferred to be thought of as a prisoner rather than a laughing stock.

We went up to the first floor, and they left me waiting in a cold corridor on a hard, wooden bench. I took off my bathrobe and folded it under myself—it felt more comfortable that way, but I was cold. I waited. I kept getting colder, my teeth chattered. I put on the bathrobe; I was warmer, but my rear end felt a lot less comfortable. I must have looked quite unappealing in a wrinkled bathrobe, but the uniformed people who walked by me once in a while paid no attention to me. They must be used to worse, I thought, perhaps it won't be so bad after all.

Then someone walked out of the office in front of which I had been sitting—the coat-check attendant from the cinema. 'Good evening,' I said, but she didn't respond, even though it was clear that she recognized me. She remained silent and smirked at me; then she headed for the exit. 'Ma'am, excuse me, ma'am . . .' I shouted, yearning for an explanation, but I didn't get one from the coat-check attendant; they called me in.

An older, grey-haired lieutenant colonel was sitting behind the desk, looking kind and worried, as if he felt sincerely sorry for me. At first, he just looked me over in silence, shaking his head, then he stood up and sighed: 'Oh man, oh man.' He placed his hand on my arm in a fatherly gesture, and shook his head again, baffled. 'Man, oh man,' he repeated, '—so young, oh my.' He went back to his desk, and looking tired, he sank heavily into his chair. He sat with his face in his hands for about a minute, leaning on his elbows, and watched me quietly, intently. I tried to come up with something to confess to make his job easier, but nothing occurred to me. Wait a minute! The coat-check attendant, the coat-check ticket, my God, what had I got myself into? My whole body started to itch, but I was afraid to move, so as not to disturb the gravity of the moment. There was obvious pity on the lieutenant colonel's face, and I felt it too. It was such a sudden and acute sense of pity that tears welled up in my eyes. I gathered it was supposed to be that way, because the lieutenant colonel nodded appreciatively.

'Well, there's nothing to be done,' he said and opened a drawer. I huddled down into the chair and covertly scratched my thigh. He pulled his hand out of the drawer. It was a firm, strong hand with blocky, almost square outlines. The meaty, tough skin had a greyish brown, earthen colour. He opened his hand and placed a set of keys on the desk. I recognized them immediately; they were my keys, tied with a string.

'Take him away,' the lieutenant colonel said, but this time he sounded relieved, as if he had managed to get rid of an unbearable burden, which had been crushing him like a nightmare.

Once more they loaded me into the car, once more we barrelled down night-time streets in an unfamiliar direction. I didn't know where they were taking me, but this time I didn't feel the need to ask. On the contrary—I was calm and collected, like a person who's fulfilling his duty.

They stopped in front of the entrance to my building. They unloaded me, said good night, and left. I didn't even have time to

229 • EVENING NEWS

thank them. I stood there in the freezing night, in a summer bath-robe, holding two sets of keys: my wife's and mine. I used my keys, and they fit, it wasn't a trick.

I walked up the stairs, took off my shoes outside our flat, and quietly walked into the room; no one woke up. I lay down next to my wife and pressed up against her hot body. Soon she warmed me up, and in the pleasant warmth I had no trouble falling asleep.

Itchiness all over my body woke me up. In the darkness I felt the large welts on my legs; the flea had feasted. I waited. I knew from experience that there was only one way to get rid of it—catching it in the act. It was waiting too. It's hoping for me to fall back asleep, or it's had its fill, I thought, and then I felt it. On my right calf. In an instant I pressed my index finger on the spot, and manoeuvred the flea under my nail. I wasn't sure that I got it, but a strange, victorious thrill of the hunt was convincing me that I did. Holding it tightly under my nail, I turned on the lights and walked to the tiled, sterile, white bathroom. I stoppered the sink, turned on the faucet, and immersed my index finger. The flea swam. A tiny, barely visible dot. It was unbelievable; such a nothing, and it had caused me so much suffering. I pushed it towards the edge of the sink and squashed it with my thumbnail.

There wasn't just a pop, there was an explosion!

The water in the sink turned red and welled up quickly. I pulled out the stopper. The draining slowed the filling, but it felt like the opening was too small.

I washed my hands and went into the room. My wife was resting calmly, the little one had one nostril plugged, her breathing was laboured, it made a faint whistling sound. My older daughter was lying on top of her covers, her feet were cold, she rolled over in her sleep. Who knows what dreams were running through her head. Maybe she was dreaming about Santa Claus. I placed her head on her pillow and covered her. Her tender pink little face was smiling.

Before lying down I went to urinate. As I was walking back to the room, I noticed a narrow, dark strip snaking its way out from under the bathroom door.

I watched my sweet blood and felt my body get weaker and weaker.

On the Threshold

A MYSTERIOUS DISAPPEARANCE *Bratislava*—an unusual occurrence disturbed the owners of garden cottages in Koliba. On Friday night going into Saturday, a father and daughter disappeared without a trace. According to the testimony of neighbours who had spoken with them late Friday evening, nothing suggested that they intended to go anywhere. They seemed calm, and there didn't appear to be disagreements between them. The neighbours' concerns and those of the ex-wife and mother are exacerbated by the fact that the man in question had spent some time as an inpatient at a psychiatric clinic. Several years ago, he gained public notoriety for publishing certain very idiosyncratic 'theories'. The police is searching for both missing persons. The man's name is Vít Nehoda, he's of medium height, with short chestnut hair, brown eyes and symmetrical facial features. No special identifying marks. The little girl is four years old, her name is Dana. A letter has been found in the empty cottage, probably written by the missing man. The letter, entitled 'A Useless Person's Message', is reproduced here:

I've been asked to rework my theory about light that dampens sound. I have ascertained that for most people night means silence, as if light were louder than darkness. What surprises me most, is that even people whom I've respected for a long time are subject to this deception.

When I submitted my proposal to study the inside of air, they sent me for treatment. I proposed that the research be conducted by leading world philosophers, painters, musicians, poets and me. The project should be sponsored by the United Nations or UNESCO. My inspiration for this project was the word 'inland'. Everyone told me that it was useless nonsense, because science had already analysed the individual components of air a long time ago. Based on this I gathered that they had completely misunderstood my proposal, and I thought it was superfluous to try to persuade anyone of its usefulness, given that I had proposed the project specifically because of its apparent uselessness.

Naturally, I wasn't insane, but I was happy to go to the insane asylum—I had always wanted to experience it. After I got tired of the constant electroshock therapy, I retracted all of my theories, even though I was convinced they were true. Besides, I concluded that it made no sense to try to persuade people of the truth of my theories by force; they'd have to get there on their own.

At the insane asylum I learnt many things from my new friends, and I knew I'd miss them a lot. For that reason alone, I suggested a mass breakout, but they explained to me that it would be an irreversible mistake, because sooner or later we'd get caught, and the work that had already been done would go in vain. They considered the insane asylum an ideal environment in which they could work on the doctors and nurses without interruptions or worries. I can affirm that this method is delivering its first modest results. It is an effective method, even though its success depends on many generations. But my friends are convinced that in every generation there'll be several people to carry the torch.

After being released from the insane asylum, I spent some time with my family, but living with them didn't work out well. Neither I nor the family enjoyed it. The thing everyone feared most was my influence on our three-year-old daughter. Over time I gained her unconditional affection, which was probably love. I've never been stubborn, so I agreed to my relatives' proposed solution, which seemed ideal to me: they bought me a wooden cottage with a small garden on the outskirts of town, in the so-called summer district. As soon as I arrived at the cottage, I knew it was the one thing I had always wanted. I'm surrounded by many similar cottages (some of them made of bricks), and by similar and larger gardens. But I'm the only person who lives here all year. The owners of the other cottages come only on the weekends starting in the spring. Around the beginning of autumn, they usually come for the last time. A few impassioned fruit-growers come a little later too, but during the winter I'm here all by myself.

At first, I had a neighbour who lived here year-round too. He was very old, though I never knew his actual age. Come to think of it, I never asked him about it. He didn't have any friends, but for some reason he took a liking to me. Initially I thought he liked me out of solidarity, because it turned out that he also pondered the inside of air. He had made it a lot further than I had, but he didn't share any of his knowledge; I'm sure he sensed that I couldn't shake my doubts about the purpose of our thinking. As a result, he didn't consider me qualified, perhaps he even believed that I wanted to insinuate my way into his good graces. Now I know that we were friends because of my daughter, who still visits me. But the old gentleman left without so much as a good-bye. He raised various kinds of poultry, birds and livestock. He also had a dilapidated old bus in his garden and claimed it was a spaceship. Once in a while he'd go to town and bring back a pile of old metal parts that he found at the dump or bought at scrapyards. Using drawings that were completely incomprehensible to me, he worked on the internal outfitting of the bus. He never let me in, but my daughter had free access. Whenever I asked her what she had seen there, she just said that it was beautiful. One morning when she came to see me as usual and we wanted to go visit the old gentleman, his cottage was empty, as were the chicken coops, the cages and the barns. I wasn't that surprised because I had always allowed for the possibility that one day he'd be taken to an asylum. Then my daughter pointed to the spot where the old bus used to be. The bus was gone; all that was left was a rectangle of yellowed grass, which was unlike the surrounding vibrant greenery. 'He flew away,' my daughter said, shaded her eyes with her hand, and looked into the sun. I also looked up: the sky was clear, blue, but dark, heavy clouds were starting to gather in the distance. It didn't look like an ordinary thunderstorm, more like a long rain. Then it really rained for two days, but it didn't cause any flooding. I was relieved to conclude that the old gentleman wasn't a real Noah.

I've not had a permanent neighbour since. My wife divorced me. Understandably. But she hasn't stopped our daughter from visiting me. Now that I don't live with my wife, I like her a lot more than before. True, she got on my nerves for some time, and when she complimented my pearly white teeth one day in an effort to cheer me up, I was so overcome with anger that I grabbed a pair of pliers and immediately pulled one out. I still regret that.

At first, I was worried that she'd try to turn our daughter against me, to raise her full of hatred and contempt. Thankfully, I had been mistaken.

Besides my daughter, a certain thirty-year-old woman visits me and we make love every Monday. It's natural, and we both take it as such. She probably has several lovers, but I couldn't care less about that, and I'm not jealous at all.

In order not to burden my relatives' finances, I started to raise chickens, rabbits and two pigs. I also have three beehives. It doesn't cost me much, because the chickens find enough worms and other food in the garden, and the rabbits graze on grass, which I improved for them by planting clover. The pigs get kitchen scraps from a nearby pub, which are free, because the woman I make love with every Monday is the manager there. And the bees are the easiest of all. They fly from one flower to another, and another, and another . . . I can't remember how I wanted to finish that sentence. That happens to me once in a while—a memento of electroshock therapy. But I believe that even a person who had been through treatment has a chance of recovery. Whatever cash I need, I get by playing cards.

Thanks to the countless tricks I learnt at the insane asylum, I regularly win small sums.

I remember that when I was a child, I couldn't stand the thought of killing chickens and rabbits. Nowadays I lop off their heads and break their necks as if I had been doing it all my life. And I'm confident that they're not angry with me, because they, like me, know that it's natural, and I'm helping them fulfil their purpose. Each winter I kill two fattened pigs, make yards of sausages, bacon, and I either smoke or can the meat, which lasts me until the following winter.

At first, I thought about death a lot, and sometimes I had the feeling that life was telling me: 'Nehoda Vít—eat my shit.' One morning when it was raining and it looked like it wouldn't stop all day, I decided to kill myself. But I felt that doing it on an empty stomach was in poor taste, so I got out of bed. I saw an egg. I sucked it down. Raw. In the meantime, it stopped raining, and I didn't kill myself. I thought about that experience for a long time. Had it stopped raining later, I'd had been dead now. An ordinary raw egg saved my life.

Since that day I've been convinced that the world isn't chaos, on the contrary, it has its immutable laws. Yes, the laws exist, we just don't know them all; and therein lies our hope. I realized that life is dangerous and unpredictable, but at the same time there's no point in being afraid of it. So I stopped thinking about death, for good, I hope. It was then that I also came to understand Spinoza's sentence, which had caused me so many sleepless nights: 'A free man thinks of nothing less than of death, and his wisdom is a meditation, not on death, but on life.'

And so I spend summer afternoons sitting on the threshold of my cottage, in the quiet sunshine, and I ponder my theories. Chickens and rabbits wander around the garden, pigs wallow by the barn, and the bees fly around, making a low, calming buzzing sound. The cottage has two rooms and a kitchen. My daughter's room has a couch and a chair. My room is empty. I sleep in a sleeping bag on the floor. But I'm afraid that one day I won't resist; I'll buy furniture, fill the empty room, and take away my options for ever. That's probably my most natural desire.

I've ascertained that my old theory about light that dampens sound was correct. Previously I had reached my conclusion more or less by speculation, but now I can prove it through experience.

The day is quiet, but the night is filled with unbearable noise. The rustling of trees and grass, the panting of a hedgehog, the singing of cicadas, the creaking of wood in the walls of the cottage, the barking of dogs, the whistling of trains, the vibrations of train tracks, and the swish of falling stars. Yes, darkness magnifies sound.

I'm thinking about the inside of air and I regret not having gained the trust of the old gentleman who had already solved it. How much time it would have saved me! But back then I had doubts about the purpose of such thinking, so I don't blame him at all for not trusting me. Now I believe that there's a purpose to it all, and I know that even he would find me worthy of his trust. But the solution was lost with him and there's nothing for me to do but discover it for myself. It's very important that I solve it, because after much effort I've finally managed to acquire a dilapidated old bus. Actually, I only got it thanks to my daughter, who's a great help to me . . .

•